Horace Rumbold

The Great Silver River

Notes of a Residence in Buenos Ayres

Horace Rumbold

The Great Silver River
Notes of a Residence in Buenos Ayres

ISBN/EAN: 9783742811936

Manufactured in Europe, USA, Canada, Australia, Japa

Cover: Foto ©Andreas Hilbeck / pixelio.de

Manufactured and distributed by brebook publishing software
(www.brebook.com)

Horace Rumbold

The Great Silver River

·THE
GREAT SILVER RIVER ·

NOTES OF A RESIDENCE IN BUENOS AYRES
IN 1880 AND 1881

By SIR HORACE RUMBOLD, Bart., K.C.M.G.

WITH ILLUSTRATIONS
PARTLY FROM SKETCHES BY R. S. WILKINSON, C.E.

LONDON
JOHN MURRAY, ALBEMARLE STREET
1887

TO

ROBERT EARL OF LYTTON

THESE PAGES ARE INSCRIBED

BY AN OLD FRIEND AND COLLEAGUE

PREFACE.

In these days of universal travel great would be
the presumption of the writer who should aim at
recording something absolutely new about any of
the accessible regions of the earth. These recollections of a few months' residence in so well-known
a region as the River Plate cannot, therefore, in
any way pretend to novelty.

For the convenience, however, of those who
may be tempted to look through the pages of this
book, I may state that if it contain anything approaching the '*adhuc indictum ore alio*' with which
Horace prayed to Bacchus to inspire him, it will
be found in some account of a journey to the
little-frequented upper reaches of the Uruguay,
where I had occasion to visit the sites of several
of the strange, mysterious Jesuit settlements that
flourished up to the middle of the last century
on the banks of that majestic river.   Here,

I venture to think, I have struck on a partially unworked vein. Possibly, too, what I have said of Argentinia in general as a field for the European, and more particularly for the British, settler—especially since such large tracts of its most fertile soil have been wrested from the Indian tribes—may not be very generally known. I may also justly claim that my sojourn at Buenos Ayres coincided with events which could not but exercise a decisive influence on the fortunes of the country, and of which I was bound to be a close and attentive watcher.

Nearly six years have elapsed since I left Buenos Ayres, and in that interval the Republic has passed through the trying ordeal of a change in the Presidency without any disturbance of the public peace. The evil spell seems to be broken, and the prospects of the country have notably improved in every way, while its material development has made immense strides.

The predictions I ventured upon as to its progress have, in fact, been more than borne out. The number of immigrants pouring in every year has fully trebled, and such has been the addition to the population of the city of Buenos Ayres alone that, in the course of four years, it has risen from 300,000 to 400,000 souls. The mileage of the railroads open to traffic has more than doubled. Already the locomotive reaches the very foot of the Andes, and the day is fast approaching when it will be possible for the traveller to pass uninterruptedly by rail from the shores of the Atlantic to those of the Pacific. The capitals of the Chilean and Argentine States will thus be placed within three days' journey of each other. A new and much shorter mode of access to Australia being thereby thrown open, the entire country will be brought more and more within civilising influences.

That a highly prosperous future is assured to the Argentines can no longer be doubted. The pacified and consolidated Republic is happily launched on its career among the nations, and of its well-wishers none can be more sincere than the writer of this slender record of a too brief, but in every way pleasant and interesting, sojourn on its hospitable soil.

H. R.

March 1887.

CONTENTS.

CONTENTS

CHAPTER V.

PAGE

CONTENTS [13]

CONTENTS

CHAPTER XIX.

PAGE

CHAPTER XX.

CHAPTER XXI.

LIST OF ILLUSTRATIONS.

THE

GREAT SILVER RIVER.

CHAPTER I.

JOURNEY OUT—ARRIVAL AND FIRST IMPRESSIONS.

So FAR we had had the fairest, but hottest, of weather. We had gone on board at Pauillac on a cloudless August day, and every mile we steamed had placed us more hopelessly at the mercy of a pitiless sun. We had been broiled at Vigo and Lisbon, stewed at that most unenviable of French possessions, Dakar, baked brown at Bahia, and, but for one cool night up in the clouds at Petropolis, had had no respite from the insupportable heat which radiated from every part of our steamer, roomy though she was, and fast though she sped through the oily waste of waters on her way to the southern hemisphere. Now, however, we had reached that hemisphere, and it was mid-September of a tempestuous spring. From overpowering light

B

and heat we rushed suddenly into gloom and
drizzle and broken cross seas. At night we came
in for a tremendous tossing, and by morning lay
labouring in the very trough of it. Our hitherto
cheery, though somewhat noisy, fellow-passengers
—mostly French or Italian—all knocked under at
once; the crowded saloon became a perfect desert,
and with every port closed below, and the deck
above untenable, we passed two as cheerless days
as I have ever experienced at sea.

These magnificent Messageries boats, be it said
en passant, carry a great top weight in their hur-
ricane-decks, and the lurches our steamer gave
from time to time were positively alarming. It
might have been a comfort to know that we were
somewhere off the mouth of the River Plate, and
thus near our journey's end, had not that comfort
dwindled down to nothingness on a confidential
whisper from the friendly *agent des postes*—our
neighbour at breakfast-time—that the *commandant*
had been unable to take a good observation for two
whole days, and, except by dead reckoning, knew
practically nothing of our exact whereabouts. So
we slowed down, and sounded the fog-whistle, and
bumped and rolled all day long—the second day
—and tried to derive some satisfaction from the
commandant's complete change of demeanour. A
terrible *rouge* this *commandant*, who hitherto has

shown exquisite good taste and gallantry in airing
his mostly unsavoury views, political and religious,
for the special delectation apparently of a bonny
little French Legitimist bride who sits next to him
at meals, and who—brave little woman—is going
out with her husband on a sheep-farming venture
somewhere on the Uruguay River. Very quiet and
silent now, the *commandant*, and clearly much
exercised, and though the victim of his delicate
pleasantries cannot benefit by the contrast—the
poor soul is curled up in her berth somewhere
below—it is quite a relief to see him so subdued.
But the poor man has, in truth, had a bad time of
it on the bridge for the last twenty-four hours,
feeling his way along this treacherous coast.

Towards dusk it gets smoother; there is a
slight break in the clouds, and, through the murky
atmosphere around us, one of the men on the look-
out is believed to have espied a light, which should
be that on Cape Santa Maria marking the entrance
to the River Plate. And so, a couple of hours
later, it turns out to be, much to the general satisfaction. One by one the passengers emerge from
their cabins, and a more cheerful tone once more
pervades the lighted saloon. For a number of us,
too, it is the last evening on board ; and even to the
most enthusiastic lover of the ocean there must
come, I suspect, some sense of deliverance after a

long three weeks of ship life and its many discomforts.

Early in the morning we bring to at the outer anchorage of Monte Video, the town itself remaining shrouded from sight in a chilly fog not unworthy of Gravesend. It is still blowing very hard, and the shallow, peasoup-coloured water has fretted itself into such a condition as makes it no easy matter for the tugs and steam-launches to come alongside to take off those who, like myself, are going on shore. There is no more abominable roadstead than that of Monte Video in a *pampero*, and it is fortunate for me, therefore, that I am expected here, and am fetched away, and comfortably landed, by a powerful little steamer belonging to the Captain of the Port.

Monte Video, which I had already visited some years before in lovely weather, certainly did not look its best on this occasion. Its long, straight streets, swept by a pitiless blast and driving showers, were perfectly empty ; and I was thankful for refuge at the house of a most hospitable friend, who kindly entertained me till late the following afternoon, and, in exchange for my budget of home news, gave me alarming accounts of the ravages said to have been already made by the storm, which had been raging now for a couple of days. It was only on my arrival at Buenos Ayres that I was to hear of its full effects. The weather moderated a good deal during the night, so the 'Cosmos' being advertised to sail at six the following evening up the river to Buenos Ayres, I took my passage in her, and after a comparatively smooth voyage was at my destination shortly after daybreak.

The morning was raw and gloomy, a low, leaden sky making but a dismal background to the long line of buildings, broken here and there by towers and cupolas, which, with more favouring accompaniments of light and atmosphere, give the city so deceptively imposing and alluring an aspect. No time, however, was allowed me for more than a hasty glance at it, for here again kind friends were on the look-out for me, and I was speedily put on shore, by British oars and under British colours, at the end of one of the two long black piers that crawl out, like a crab's claws, over a quarter of a mile of ooze and slush, and are easily accessible only at high water. Fortunately the tide was full at the time, and I was thus spared the graduated ignominy of removal from boat to cart, and from cart to men's shoulders, which not so long ago constituted the only mode of landing. Even now, at very low water, a string of red carts on very high wheels can be seen meandering out to the boats and lighters.

A short drive over very rough pavement, past a big square of considerable pretensions, and along a couple of narrow, and for the early hour sufficiently bustling, streets, brought me to the hotel, where rooms had been engaged for me. Immense rooms, with vulgar, tawdry decorations and would-be luxurious furniture, but looking on to a dull yard, and so utterly sunless and cheerless that I was driven out of them by sheer cold. The next day, after paying a most exorbitant bill (I breakfasted and dined out, and was charged some seven pounds simply for a night's lodging and my servant's food), I was glad to remove to another inn and more modest apartments, which at least had a tiny fireplace, where, towards evening, I just managed to make a semblance of a blaze, and could do without my great-coat. The temperature, fortunately, soon became milder; nor could the cold, as long as it lasted, be really termed severe, since it hardly exceeded freezing-point at night-time; but nowhere had it seemed to me more penetrating— the fact being that nowhere, as I knew by past experience, is less provision made for meeting it than in these South American cities.

What were my first impressions of the place in which for an uncertain period—possibly some years—my lot was now cast? Very mixed and ill-defined, and not altogether favourable, I fear.

Certainly at first sight it appeared by no means dull. All around the Bolsa, or Exchange—the heart, as it were, which sends the life-blood coursing through the big money-making city— there was plenty of stir and bustle; throngs of eager, keen-eyed men elbowed their way along the pavement, or stood in knots at the street-corners, talking loud and volubly with much gesticulation. The full throbs of life and business were every- where so audible, that clearly the town could not be charged with dulness or torpor.

Nor did these brisk crowds of men of many tongues and tribes—Italians and French, Basques and Spaniards, and Germans and Irish and English —seem by any means indifferent to the amenities of existence. They swarmed in the numerous coffee-houses and restaurants—pale, but tolerably faithful copies of Parisian cafés, with Gascon waiters and *dames de comptoir*; the many places of entertainment—circuses and skating-rinks, public gardens and theatres and music-halls—all throve with their custom. Absorbed as they all appeared to be, and were, in trade and speculation, and well girded up in the race for wealth, they were all equally lovers of pleasure, spending their money fully as freely as they made it, and living high and well.

For much of this I was of course prepared; but

one or two traits soon struck me as standing out from the rest. These sharp, bustling men of business never seemed in any particular hurry, as men do in the wear and tear of great commercial centres elsewhere, but appeared always to have plenty of leisure on their hands. They all seemed to take things easily, and there was none of that high pressure visible about them which with us makes time synonymous with money.

Another thing! Cosmopolitan as they were—a perfect *macédoine* of races—it struck one at once that they mingled but little, and formed very distinct and separate communities, living side by side in perfect harmony, but with relatively little fusion, in the city in which so many of them had settled for good. Most of them too, as one soon learned, were still dwelling as strangers among the Argentines, and showed themselves, as a rule, singularly indifferent (excepting as regards criticising them) to the public concerns of the country of their adoption. This indifference, or rather, perhaps, lack of sympathy, was the most remarkable feature of all, and was attended with important, and indeed very unfortunate, results, as events had quite recently shown.

The inhabitants, however, I could not, of course, presume to judge of in any degree at first sight. Their buildings and houses, private and public, the outward traits and lineaments of their city, I might with less temerity attempt roughly to take stock of at once, subject to future correction.

Here my first impressions were, I fear, disappointing, and, unfortunately, I had to a great extent to abide by them. I had, it is true, heard much of the sumptuous dwelling-houses, and even of the public edifices, erected here of late years, and was thus possibly led to expect more than I found. The Exchange, the Banco Ipotecario or Mortgage Bank, the Cabildo (Town Hall)—then in course of restoration and improvement—the Post Office, are all very creditable and fairly handsome buildings—especially the last-named—though more striking, perhaps, than perfect in taste. As to private houses, the Florida and the streets adjoining are graced with the *façades* of a good number of what, in auctioneer jargon, may be termed 'desirable mansions'—marble-fronted and with several stories. Both style and materials of these have for the most part been imported from Italy, and, unlike wine, have not improved with the long sea voyage. Showy and effective enough some of them are, but they somehow convey the impression of mere frontages run up with nothing behind them —like the sham villages raised on the progress of Catherine to the Crimea—and are certainly not to be compared with half a dozen houses I could mention in another South American capital. The shops, too, on the ground-floor of some of these magnificent private abodes, are real blots, showing that their owners were not solely guided by considerations of art and comfort in their erection. Indeed, one is almost tempted to ask oneself whether, like the converse of the skeleton at Egyptian banquets, they may not be kept on the premises to remind their luxurious masters not of whither they are going, but of whence they came. Nevertheless, Buenos Ayres is, on the whole, to be congratulated on the dwellings of her wealthier citizens, and on a blazing summer's day the eye is charmed, as well as relieved from the trying glare, by a passing glance into one of their cool marble *patios* (inner courts), redolent of the most fragrant of flowers, and bright with groups of graceful girls.

At the same time, the plan on which the city is laid out, and which is common to most South American towns, deprives it of nearly all character, and is to my mind exceedingly wearisome. The town is a huge chess-board, with almost mathematically even squares, formed by one set of interminable narrow streets which run north and south from the riverside far into the boundless plain, crossed at regular intervals by another set of exactly similar streets which stretch east and west a long way into the open country and

abruptly lose themselves there. The houses seem
somehow to come to a sudden ending, without the
toning-off or preparation which in other places is
to be found in outskirts or suburbs. Towards
Flores and Belgrano a zone of *quintas* and gardens
marks the approach to the city, but in most other
directions it rises up all at once and takes you
unawares, and you pass, without transition, from
the original wilderness superficially tamed into
acres of flimsy bricks and stucco piled up only
yesterday. These, however, are familiar aspects
throughout the Western Hemisphere, where most
things look painfully crude and sudden and
shoddy by the side of nature, hushed, as it still
seems, with the unbroken solitude of centuries.
Nowhere do man and his handiwork appear so
restless and so immature, or mother earth so
crowned with the majesty of ages and so perfect
in her repose.

Commandingly placed on a kind of natural
embankment above the mighty stream, and with
illimitable level space for extension behind it, never
perhaps had a great maritime capital grander or
healthier site assigned to it than Buenos Ayres. It
is aggravating, therefore, to find it such a city of
wasted opportunities. For the primitive design
of the town and the narrowness of its streets its
Spanish founders are of course answerable; but

these mistakes have been so perpetuated as it expanded to its present large area,[1] that it now appears as if, like Hamburg or Chicago, it could attain transfiguration through nothing short of the stern ordeal of fire.

Far more serious, however, than cramped thoroughfares, with side pavements barely four feet wide, past which a stream of tramway cars sweeps dangerously near, are the total absence of any port, and the almost total neglect of drainage and water supply. The want of a port has been most justly described as a ' national calamity and disgrace,' and it is dreadful to reflect on the tax it entails on a trade which probably now amounts to little less than twenty millions sterling a year. Several schemes have been devised and loans contracted for the purpose ; but the money raised has been squandered or diverted to other uses, and still the city is harbourless, and inaccessible within ten miles to any ocean-going steamer.[2]

So is it, too, with the draining of the town. Although the fall of ground to the river is, for so flat a country, providentially ample, no attempt

---

[1] Some seven or eight years ago this was put at 1,200 hectares, or about three thousand acres. It must have increased considerably since then.

[2] The charges for lighterage have been reckoned as equal to one-third, and sometimes even to one-half, of the total freight from Europe.

was ever made to turn it to account till a few years ago. Elaborate drainage-works and water-works in connection with them were then commenced, but were soon suspended, owing to some dispute with the contractors, and are left unfinished to the present day. It is devoutly to be hoped that they may speedily be taken up again, for, meanwhile, the soil remains saturated with the accumulated sewage of centuries, and every year, as the hot season sets in, Buenos Ayres lies invitingly open to some such scourge as the cholera, or the yellow fever, which swooped down upon it in 1867 and 1871, and wrought such havoc as had hardly been known anywhere since the Great Plague of London. Indeed, the strong winds and violent storms which periodically sweep the vast plain around the city, and the powerful draught of air produced by the immense body of water that rolls past it, alone preserve it from an annual recurrence of plague and pestilence, and render it habitable under conditions of insalubrity too frightful to dwell upon. For even the water, beyond that which is daily fetched in carts from the turbid river, comes from old surface wells sunk here and there in all directions, and, however carefully filtered, is utterly unfit for anything but cooking, so that in the thirstiest of weather one has to take refuge in Seltzer and other aërated drinks—with or without accompaniments—and dare not risk indulging in a cool draught of the pure element.

Such, roughly stated, are the principal counts of the indictment which the most impartial of new comers cannot but lay to the charge of Buenos Ayres, and they are serious enough in all conscience. It is a relief to dispose of them at once, and, having done so, to feel free to record one's many pleasant and interesting reminiscences of the aspiring Argentine metropolis ; for aspiring it is in most senses, and decidedly so in the best. Day by day it is mending its ways and treading with firmer steps in the path of rational progress.

It so happened that the turning-point in its existence, and in that of the country of which it then became the recognised head, almost coincided with the writer's visit. These fugitive notes, written in all friendliness, in some measure bear, therefore, the impress of what he then witnessed. Through bitter strife, and even bloodshed, the young nation had at last reached a unity till then denied to it ; the golden portals of peace and concord lay wide open before it, and beyond them a domain such as has seldom fallen to the lot of any race of men. How would the thrice fortunate inheritors use the gifts lavishly bestowed upon them ? Time alone would show this ; the friendly observer could only note what means and resources they had of turning their inheritance to good account.

CHAPTER II.

A DESTRUCTIVE HURRICANE—CAUSES OF THE LATE CIVIL WAR, AND REMINISCENCES OF THE SIEGE—PALERMO—ROSAS AND SOME OF HIS ATROCITIES.

THE wild *pampero* had finally wasted its fury, leaving behind it a tale of inland wreck and damage almost unparalleled in the records of tempests in even these storm-swept regions. The papers were full of its ravages, and a piteous tale they told of the hecatombs of poor dumb creatures it had immolated in its destructive course.

A heavy fall of snow, such as had not been known so far north for years, had accompanied the hurricane. Following upon an unusually prolonged drought, it had found the shelterless flocks and herds in a weakened condition from insufficient pasturage, and had absolutely overwhelmed them. The story told was everywhere the same. Horses and cows and sheep had feebly fled before the bitter blast with its frozen arrows, and sought refuge in the infrequent hollows and dips which occur here and there in the endless level expanse, instinctively huddling together for mutual warmth and protection. Every ditch was filled with them; up against the fences, or on the verge of the plantations which rise above the country at rare intervals (and are hence picturesquely termed *montes*), they had gathered in dense masses of hundreds, till there they had fallen at last and been buried in the icy drift. In many places the poor beasts were found closely packed by the edge of some watercourse or some *laguna*, whither they had staggered in their agony and terror, and where they had finally lain down in the attempt to reach a last drink. I had, myself, ghastly evidence of the accuracy of these accounts a short time later, though at first the computations made of the loss of animal life found me incredulous, I confess, swelling daily as they did by thousands, till it was reckoned that over a million of beasts of all kinds had perished in a few brief hours. In that short space of time the province of Buenos Ayres had been turned into an open-air shambles, and ruin sown broadcast far and wide.

Soon there arose the question of what should be done with the innumerable carcases strewn all over the country—and with the near approach of the hot season a very serious question it was. The evil, however, was on so gigantic a scale that before long it was felt that there was no dealing with it radically. These mountains of flesh could not be buried, and still less burned; so, after considerable discussion, it ended in their being left to the winged scavengers and to the purifying currents of the air. For a time the market was glutted with hides and horns, but to this day the myriad skeletons of the victims lie in many places bleaching where they fell on those terrible September days. But even the severest calamities have their uses—'ill blows the wind that profits nobody'—and this disastrous storm did important service by turning attention to the necessity of planting more freely all over the *estancias*, so as to provide places of refuge for the stock in wild weather. If this plan should be systematically carried out, it will before long in every way beneficially transform the aspect of the country and improve the climate, besides greatly increasing the value of the property invested in land.

There is a peculiar edge and freshness in the air after these furious but cleansing tempests, and with them comes a buoyant sense of renewed life and spirits surpassing anything I had ever experienced elsewhere. In so brilliant and exhilarating an atmosphere as that which succeeded the chilly rain and vapours of the first few days, Buenos Ayres seemed to me, for the time, fully to deserve the somewhat deceptive abbreviation which alone

has survived out of the pious designation[1] originally bestowed on it by its founders. On the
earliest of a series of absolutely perfect spring
days, I sallied forth under the guidance of a much
esteemed friend on my first ramble through the
city. From the extreme upper end of the Florida,
where he had his lodgings, a few yards brought us
to the Retiro, which of late years has been trans-
formed into a kind of public garden. A few
shrubberies and clumps of trees affording but
scanty shade, half a dozen benches, and an eques-
trian statue of General San Martin—the counterpart of that which decorates the Alameda of
Santiago de Chile—here occupy the site of the
bull-ring of Spanish days.

The spot brings unwelcome recollections to the
ordinary Englishman still wedded to old-fashioned
notions of national honour and *prestige*. Here
Whitelock's regiments made their last stand, and
here, full of fight and well intrenched in the precincts they had stormed, they received the news of
their chief's disgraceful capitulation, and with it
the order to withdraw. Often have I sat on one
of those benches and pictured to myself the sullen
retreat of the victorious and unbroken battalions,
and have dreamed of what might have been, had
they only been allowed to hold what they had taken.

---

[1] La Santísima Trinidad de Buenos Aires.

Within easy distance of the beach and of the light-draught vessels of the expedition, and commanding the city from their almost impregnable lines, they might well have maintained themselves till the first shock of the repulse of their comrades, almost defencelessly massacred in that deadly parade march[2] through the murderous streets—the most insane operation to which British troops were ever, perhaps, committed—had been overcome, and their commanders were able calmly to face a position which was anything but irretrievable, since not more than one half of the force had been engaged. Consider only what might have been the results. The treasures of these vast regions wrested for good from the blighting influences of Spanish misrule; the quick, impulsive colonial race steadied and energised by the infusion of English blood, trained from its infancy to English habits of thought and action, and nurtured in rational English notions of freedom; the grateful soil enriched and fertilised by British wealth and industry; in short, a second, and fully as bounteously endowed, Australia started on her

---

[2] The general order given for the entry of the troops into the city expressly enjoins that the men should march in without any flints to their firelocks. It is impossible to read this and other statements in the proceedings of the court-martial on General Whitelock without feeling that that commander's imbecility well deserves to be called by another name.

career within three weeks' sail of the British shores. And if, in the course of that career, independence should have become the final lot of the young nation fostered by our care—that crowning consummation achieved without any of those hideous interludes through which it had to pass under Rosas and others before attaining its present liberties and comparative prosperity. So might this ill-planned, and most shamefully mismanaged, expedition have brought, instead of disgrace to our arms, manifold blessings to both invaders and invaded. But it was not to be, and the gallant colonists were to be left to exult in their triumph. One great good they at least derived from it, in the proud consciousness of strength which shortly after nerved them to cast off a debasing servitude. And with this final reflection, even the Englishman of ridiculously obsolete patriotic sentiments may calmly pass along streets christened in memory of the crushing defeat of his countrymen, and, if so minded, gaze with equanimity on the captured standards that droop mournfully from the arches of Santo Domingo.

But it is high time I should leave my bench, and, with it, the digressive train of thought into which I have allowed it to entice me. From the Retiro several roughly paved inclines lead down to the level of the river. Passing in front of the old

Cuartel de Patricios, of repulsive associations,[3] now an infantry barracks facing the public walk, and skirting the Hotel de los Inmigrantes—a long low building where, under the excellent arrangements recently introduced, the poorer immigrants are housed on first landing, and where they are given the necessary directions as to their future movements and chances of employment—we follow one of these slopes, and soon find ourselves opposite one of the stations of the Northern Railway, which runs to Belgrano and San Isidro, and on an avenue running parallel with that. line.   Commanding, as it does, charming views of the town and river, this road might, with a little care and outlay, be made into a magnificent marine parade.   At present, it is but a thoroughly neglected country road, full of deep ruts and holes, flanked here and there by low drinking-shops and ship-chandlers' stores, and forming altogether a very mean approach to the Park, a couple of miles further on, which is the favourite resort of Argentine society.

As we were trudging along this very uninviting thoroughfare, my attention was called by my companion to a row of workshops and sheds on the right-hand side, belonging to the gas company, if I

---

[3] The original building was erected in 1702 by an English company to whom the Spanish Crown had granted a monopoly for the importation of slaves into the colony.

remember right. I was wondering what his object could be in making me cross over to look at them, when he led me up to an ordinary wooden paling, between three and four feet high, which stood a little way back off the road and barred the entrance to the works beyond. The top rail of this paling, originally straight, had, for a distance of some yards, been roughly hacked into the jagged shape of a saw, the task having apparently been attempted with some very clumsy instrument. 'You see that,' said my friend ; 'but I am sure you will never guess how it was done.' I admitted that I was at a loss, when he pointed out to me marks of erosion all over the deep notches of this kind of wooden fringe, and explained that it was the work of the horses that had been tethered there during the recent siege. The wretched brutes were in such a starving condition that with their strong teeth they had almost gnawed through this stout piece of timber fully six inches thick. No sight could more forcibly convey an idea of the straits to which, for a short time, the beleaguered city had been reduced. Not that, in a country where animal life is relatively of such small account, the famishing state of cavalry horses and beasts of burden could by any means be taken as a proof that equal privations had been undergone by their masters. Still, the Buenos-Ayreans had

no doubt been sorely put to it themselves ; and as
for their horses, kept pent up in the town lest they
should be turned to account by the enemy outside,
my friend told me he had himself frequently seen
the poor brutes staggering along the streets till
they dropped down never to rise again.

A little further on, we came upon another re-
minder of the siege in the stumps of a considerable
willow plantation, stretching from the road down
to the river, which had been cut down as interfer-
ing with the practice of a battery posted there to
shell the vessels of the attacking force.   Little
real damage comparatively was done by the big
guns of these ships, with the exception, oddly
enough, of the day on which—mainly by the exertions of the foreign representatives—an armistice
had been agreed to by the contending parties. On
that day the commander of one of the gunboats,
noticing signs of an infraction of the truce, in work
carried on by the townspeople in the earthworks
raised on the Retiro, fired several shells in that
direction which did terrible execution, killing two
and wounding seventeen harmless passers-by—
much to the terror and indignation of the numerous foreign residents.

My friend had had special opportunities of
noting the incidents of this curious siege—or, more
accurately speaking, blockade—and had much

that was interesting to relate about it. That month of June 1880 will long be remembered in the annals of Buenos Ayres, and a heavy responsibility must ever rest with those of its leading men who, in the rash venture to break away from the Union, brought such defeat and humiliation upon the city. It would be entirely out of place here to attempt to enter into the origin and history of this brief but sharp bit of civil warfare. Its character and bearings were only imperfectly understood abroad at the time, and, like the rest of South American politics, they have little interest for the world at large. It is sufficient to say that the struggle bore a distant resemblance to the gigantic contest which, twenty years before, had convulsed the great republic of the North. Leaving aside the purely North American question of slavery, the proximate causes of both were indeed identical. Like the states of the Southern Confederacy, the province of Buenos Ayres seceded and fought for hegemony. Either it would continue to lead the Union, or it would live alone. On their side, the National Government, representing the bulk of the confederated provinces, fought to prevent a disruption of the Union, and to put an end for good and all to the pretensions of the metropolitan province, and of those who ruled it.

The Provincial Government, in throwing down

the glove, seem to have singularly miscalculated both their own forces and those brought to bear against them. They had above all counted on the defection of the National navy, and in this they were altogether deceived. The power of the purse, successfully used on former occasions, this time proved utterly unavailing. The naval commanders of the Republic were, to their honour, proof against all temptation, and their vessels pitilessly faced the contumacious city, effectually cutting it off from all contact with the outer world. On the land side, too, the National leaders collected, with remarkable speed, forces sufficient to complete the rigid circle of investment, and were ready by the end of June to storm the lines of the besieged. The position of the Provincial Government soon became desperate. Not only were their means of defence very limited, but they were maintaining themselves in a city, one half of the population of which were foreigners practically indifferent to the contest (though some of the better class may have had Provincial leanings), and all, at any rate, impatient of its disastrous results to their trade and occupations. It may, with almost absolute certainty, be said that any future outbreak of internal discord in these regions would be sternly checked at once by the foreign element. In this, as in most other respects, the controlling power of the foreigner must make itself felt more and more, and it is only matter of surprise and regret that the wholesome forces he represents should not have asserted themselves sooner, and spared the Republic its most recent and, it is to be hoped, final civil war.

After some sharp fighting on the road to Flores, where the Remington rifles of the Nationals did considerable execution, the beleaguered Executive yielded to the voice of reason and the friendly pressure of foreign diplomacy, and the bases of a capitulation were soon arranged.[4] Matters might have gone far worse than they did for the citizens who had been kept during those few weeks 'stewing in their own juice.' The greatest perils they escaped were indeed internal ones, for, with the withdrawal of the local police force—a fine and very efficient body of men, who were at once drafted into the city battalions—the town lay very much at the mercy of bands of rough Gauchos brought in by the 'secesh' land-owners from their estates, not to speak of the scum of the foreign population — low Neapolitan and Gascon and Basque.

Credit is specially due to the thousands of poor Italians who swarmed in the town for their orderly

---

[4] The veteran General Mitre took a leading and very honourable part in these negotiations.

conduct in times of great temptation. A certain proportion of them were induced to join the Provincial forces, and, being placed in the first line at the outposts towards Flores, were the principal victims of the engagement there; but the great bulk continued quietly to follow their avocations, and gave no trouble whatever. Much of this was owing to the internal organisation of the vast Italian colony, which is in some respects very complete, and was turned to excellent account by the consul-general, a man of admirable judgment and great influence with his countrymen. The foreign men-of-war collected in the river for the protection of the several communities were, for the most part, anchored at too great a distance to afford any real succour, though measures had been concerted for landing a combined force from them in case of emergency. Their commanders, however, worked very harmoniously together, and did their best not only for their own countrymen, but also for the natives. Among others the first lieutenant of one of H.M.'s gunboats volunteered to do a chivalrous bit of service one night. He undertook to convey the wife of the admiral in command of the National besieging squadron from the town, where she no longer felt in safety, to her husband's ship. The trip proved a venturesome one, for by some mistake the boat was not recognised, and was fired at several times—fortunately without effect—before reaching her destination, the admiral little knowing that his guns were directed at his own wife.

Beguiling the time with this and other anecdotes of the siege, my friend soon brought me to the park at Palermo, or, as it is formally desig-

THE PARK AT PALERMO.

nated, the *Parque 3 de Febrero*. Here, as in other South American capitals, there is a curious propensity to name streets and squares and public walks after certain dates in the national history. Thus at Buenos Ayres we have 25th of May Street, and 11th of September and 16th of November Squares, and July Promenade, all commemorative of notable incidents in the brief Argentine annals. But these infant nations have so short a record of independent existence—unfortunately for the most part made up of ugly pages of civil strife and tyranny and sedition—that there is every excuse for their making the most of their anniversaries. Besides, has not the *grande nation* itself set them the example in its Rue du 29 Juillet (such a mean little street, by the way) and its Rue du 4 Septembre? Historical dates are at any rate more picturesque, and reveal a more fertile imagination than the bald, matter-of-fact ordinals by which our North American cousins have chosen to distinguish their streets and avenues.

This Palermo, replete with sinister memories of the ruffian reign of Rosas, is now the Bois de Boulogne or Hyde Park of the Argentine metropolis, and in the glare of its shadeless main avenue—lined with stiff, half-grown, stagy palm-trees, planted by President Sarmiento in emulation of the groves of the Botanical Gardens at Rio de Janeiro—the gay world of Buenos Ayres congregate on Sundays and *fiestas* to display their last Parisian finery and feed on dust and gossip. The walks beyond have been turned into a feeble, though meritorious, attempt at a zoological garden, and elsewhere within the precincts of the park there is a race-course and a *tir aux pigeons*. Here, too, the British residents have made a very fair cricket-ground, on which they have periodical matches. The Porteños[5] are not a little proud of their Park, and on the whole the place is neat and pretty enough, and is laid out with considerable taste. It is, however, of such recent creation that as yet it lacks depth and umbrage, and *lucus a non lucendo* can certainly not be applied to its meagre groves and sparsely shaded alleys. Nor can I quite forgive President Sarmiento for his palm-trees. It seems to me that by their association with torrid wastes and rocky sun-baked heights they intensify, as it were, the already painfully arid aspect of all things in a region where the eye longs, above all, for the rest and relief of foliage.

The old *quinta* of Rosas—now utilised as a cadet-school—looks as if it had undergone but little change, and with a slight effort of imagination one can picture to oneself a barbaric cavalcade of armed men—decked out with the flaming crimson he fancied so much and imposed, under severe penalties, on both sexes as a kind of livery —sweeping up to the approach, and in their midst, drawn by mules, the bullet-proof, closely shut chariot of the Dictator. From this plain, low, un-

---

[5] 'Inhabitants of the Port.' The appellation commonly given to the Buenos-Ayreans.

PALERMO.—OLD QUINTA OF ROSAS.

pretentious building, half villa and half farm-house, issued forth the sanguinary decrees which, in the words of an eloquent Chilean writer,[6] turned the whole Republic into a huge slaughter-shed. Here the capricious and cynical tyrant feasted and intrigued; here the comely Manuelita flirted and held her court; and here, too, she pleaded for, and saved, many a poor wretch doomed to destruction. These insignificant, harmless-looking walls could vie in tales of cruelty and perfidy with the most blood-stained of mediæval fortresses. There is, no doubt, much exaggerated legend about Rosas and his deeds, but his worst and most undeniable crimes have fastened on the local imagination in a singular manner. I was present one day at a discussion between husband and wife as to the exact age of the latter—a most charming woman, who, rightly assured of her good looks, could indulge in the confession of more years than she showed. 'There is no use in contesting the point,' she finally said; 'I was born on the day on which the Caciques were hanged.' And then she explained how her birth had been accelerated by the shock and thrill of horror of the news, brought to her father's house, of the traitorous

* Benjamin Vicuña Mackenna: 'Bajo Rosas y sus capataces, la República Argentina fué toda entera una inmensa ramada de matanza.'

execution of some Indian chiefs whom the Dictator had invited to a solemn palaver at Buenos Ayres, and whom, after parading them with mock honours through the city, he had caused without any warning to be run up *séance tenante* on gibbets suddenly revealed to their terrified gaze under the portico of the cathedral. Surely a hideous tale, rivalling the worst traditions of an Almagro or a Carbajal.

We leave this *maison de malheur* behind us, gladly shaking its dust off our feet, as it were, and soon come in view of the penitentiary. This is a very massive and altogether creditable building, due, like most else of what is excellent here, to the enlightened rule of Sarmiento, and it has the reputation of being extremely well managed, which is more than can be said of other Argentine gaols. Even here the memory of Rosas and his misdeeds pursues us, for the governor of the prison happens to bear the same name as the victim of the blackest of all his crimes—the unfortunate girl whom the tyrant mercilessly caused to be shot under the most hypocritical pretence of morality and with attending circumstances of absolutely fiendish atrocity,[7] and whose death, like that of

---

[7] The lady in question, who was of very respectable birth, and, I believe, of English extraction, had been seduced by an unprincipled priest, her confessor. The erring couple were, under some barbarous

Virginia, filled the cup of popular wrath to over-flowing, and is said to have greatly hastened his downfall.

It was getting quite dark when we reached the Belgrano road, and re-entered the city that way. The gas-lamps were being lighted, and, as we walked along, the open windows on the ground-floor of the houses, which reach almost down to the pavement, afforded us, behind their bars, indiscreet views of the inhabitants gathered at the evening meal. In the shadow of the entrances girls and men stood laughing and talking; the millinery shops in the busier thoroughfares were full of female custom; the whole town had entered on its evening spell of gossip and jest, of music and shopping and aimless *flânerie*. We turned into the Café de Paris, and, over a late dinner, talked of many things far away and far behind us —of anything but Buenos Ayres.

ecclesiastical law, condemned to death, and the sentence ruthlessly carried out, the Dictator refusing to grant a reprieve to the wretched woman although she was *enceinte*.

CHAPTER III.

SUNDAY AT BUENOS AYRES—CHURCH PARADE—CHARM AND
MERITS OF THE PORTEÑAS—THE YOUNG GENERATION AND
THE OLD—THE GAY WORLD ABROAD.

SUNDAY—the harsh clang of the bells at the church
of the Merced hard by has been dinning the fact
into my ears at painfully short intervals ever since
early morning. Even on week-days the ringing
in the churches seems almost continuous, but just
now my neighbour round the corner is calling to
high mass with unusual vigour and persistence.
From the balcony of my rooms at the inn I have
a good side-view of the edifice, which bears evident
signs of having been recently done up, and albeit
of respectable age—it was the church of the
ancient nunnery of the Merced up to the suppression of the monastic orders by Rivadavia in 1826
—has an essentially modern air that somewhat
detracts from its dignity, but agrees with its character as the fashionable place of worship. A
scaffolding is still erected against one of its flanks,
and here only the other day the ancient walls

yielded up, it is said, an ugly secret. The workmen engaged on the repairs unexpectedly came
upon a walled-up recess, containing human bones
and a skull with long flowing hair, which only too
clearly revealed the sex of the wretched victim,
who, in the bad old colonial days, must have been
consigned there to the horrors of a living tomb.
As I survey the building now, its spick-and-span
look utterly belies so sombre a past, the metal on
its cupola and the fresh white of its frontage and
turrets gaily standing out, in full glare and glitter,
against the deep blue sky overhead and the hot
street below.

Hackney-coaches and private carriages come
clattering past the corner, and deposit their freight
of bright silks and lace, and airy bonnets and
flowers, at the gate of the railed enclosure, or *parvis*,
in front of the main entrance, in passing quickly
up to which the fair wearers have to run the
gauntlet of a double row of their admiring countrymen, faultlessly attired in tightly fitting garments
of the last Parisian cut. One by one the vivid
patches of colour vanish into the shadow of the
porch, many of the men following them in, but a
large proportion preferring to lounge on outside in
the company of their *papelitos* till the function
within is over.

The subdued drone of the organ and a faint

odour of incense presently stray forth and mingle with the pungent tobacco and the languid chatter of the idlers. After about half an hour the women begin to stream out again—walking more leisurely now, and with no attempt at demureness—preening their gay plumage in the sunshine, and in no way shrinking from persistent stares and comments uttered indiscreetly loud. They have come well prepared to be scanned and surveyed, and are intent on getting as full value as they can in return for their milliner's bills ; they look very smart, many of them are. extremely pretty, and all feel that they ' are fair to see ' and can well face the closest inspection.

To ordinary English ideas there is, of course, something utterly opposed to good taste in this crowd of well-dressed men blocking up the passage to a house of prayer, let alone the levity of their attitude and the coolness of the remarks that freely pass between them. One of the local British papers (innocently ignorant of certain London places of worship that might be named) periodically lashes itself into honest John-Bullish fury over these scenes at the doors of the churches ; in reality, however, it is but a very harmless matter, and has at any rate the merit of a complete absence of hypocrisy. The women, of course, do not object to the custom, or they would not put up

with it. The truth is that, in spite of the apparent
excess of familiarity or absence of respect which
might be inferred from such over-plainly expressed
admiration, they are rightly assured of the perfect
esteem in which they are held by their admirers.
On the showing of these same gallants—simple,
honest fellows many of them, for all their Don
Juanesque posturings—they are to be credited
with the very best of characters, make capital
housewives, and are devoted, though perhaps all
too indulgent, mothers.

In many ways the Porteñas are certainly most
attractive, and bear out the well-established reputation for good looks which they enjoy all over
South America. They are, as a rule, above the
average height, and have remarkably good figures,
with pearly skins and such naturally fine com-
plexions that there is absolutely no excuse for the
adventitious self-adornment in which they too frequently indulge. Not a few of them have fair
hair and blue eyes, and altogether depart from the
commonly received type of Spanish beauty. Unfortunately they often become prematurely stout,
and all too soon lose the supple grace of motion
which is one of their greatest charms. There are
few daintier sights than a young married woman
or girl, belonging to the best class of society here,
passing along the pavement with light elastic tread

and just a *soupçon* of undulation in her trim waist and neatly gathered petticoats, walking erect with well-poised head and with a full consciousness of the supremacy—in these countries most unquestionable and unquestioned—of her sex. Perfect assurance without boldness, and an engaging air of coquetry devoid of all *minauderie* or affectation, show her to be not only at her ease, but well able to take good care of herself, though quite ready to welcome the homage which is her due. *Incessu patet non dea sed pulcherrima nympha.* There is little of the goddess about the lady, but she suggests at first sight much of what is most captivating in woman. It is a passing impression in every sense of the word, but none the less pleasing for all that.

The women of the higher classes here certainly strike one at once as decidedly superior to the men. The fact is that in communities such as these woman is as the salt of the earth, and that whatever aristocratic sentiment has survived in these democracies has taken refuge with the fair sex, and there fortunately asserts itself with many of its refining influences. It is thus no doubt in a varying degree throughout the Western world. The sincere, although somewhat exaggerated, *culte* of womanhood which is so striking a feature in North American life, was doubtless at its origin

but a willing tribute paid by the men to something
which, in their ordinarily rough, hard, unbeau-
teous lives, they liked to feel was higher and
better than themselves. What, indeed, might not
society with our sturdy cousins in the North have
become but for their charming, highly cultivated
women? There is a good deal of the same feeling
towards their womankind among the Argentines
of the better class, though a native jealousy, in-
herited from Spanish, or more properly Moorish,
sources, denies the married ladies here some of the
absolute freedom enjoyed by their sisters in the
United States. The influence of the *éternel féminin*
is, however, none the less very considerable, and
the pretty ladies of Buenos Ayres have even been
credited with a leading part in the recent political
events of their country.

I think it may almost be said that the women
of the upper orders have benefited more largely
than any other class by the immense progress
made here of late years in all educational matters.
Not that the average course of studies they now
go through is by any means as complete, or as
judiciously directed, as it might be, but that their
early training is so different from that of their
mothers and grandmothers. Above all, young
girls of good family are no longer left, as was the
evil old creole custom, almost exclusively to the

debasing care of dependents — frequently half-castes, if not pure Africans—and are, at the most critical period of their lives, surrounded and guided by salutary home influences which were relatively unknown to their parents. Many of the young ladies, too, have been partly educated in Europe, or at schools conducted on European principles, and have acquired a degree of information and accomplishments far surpassing anything to which the more primitive generations that preceded them could pretend. As a result of this, an almost painful contrast may be noticed in the manners and conversation of ladies of the same family; the maturer generation appearing in every way inferior, not only in general knowledge, but also in refinement and habits of the world. One of the most charming and valuable elements of society is thus to a great extent missing here (although its absence is, of course, only transitory) in the controlling example and influence of older women of experience and cultivation; and this, no doubt, contributes to give to social intercourse an outward aspect of frivolity and exclusive pleasure-seeking.

The elder ladies seldom mix in society, or, if they do, keep well in the background—treated by their belongings with invariable kindness and respect, but content to remain in timid self-efface-

ment. In looks and dress many of them belong
to an entirely different age, and unconsciously
make admirable foils to the brilliant modernism of
their progeny. To the observant stranger there is
something pathetic in one of these poor old dames
huddled up with antiquated finery on a sofa in
some corner of the room, where the talk and
clatter and music around leave her all unheeded;
dreaming, she may be, all the while of bright and
simpler days when she sat surrounded by doughty
heroes of Oribe's or Urquiza's levies, proud to receive the circling *maté* at her hands or to listen to
the thin tinkle of her guitar. It is, indeed, a far
cry from those artless melodies to the latest difficulties by Prudent or Gottschalk; in the interval
a brand-new world has sprung into life, and been
civilised, as it were, by steam. The placid old
head may well shake over it, and feel unable to
take it all in.

With this perfect holiday weather all Buenos
Ayres is afoot, and most of it thronging to the
public Park; and in the course of an afternoon
stroll up and down the Florida and Calle San
Martin, and along the Avenue of the Recoleta to
the church and cemetery of that name, one has an
excellent opportunity of surveying the gay world
as it whirls past, on its way to Palermo, in private
carriages or crowded, open tramways. All classes

here sensibly avail themselves of the latter mode of conveyance, and the cars are at all times full of well-dressed ladies. The system is worked on the whole with much precision, both as to speed and regularity. On account of the narrowness of the thoroughfares, the trams are laid in single lines up one street and down another, and there being thus but few points of junction or intersection at which the cars have to wait, considerable distances are performed at a round pace, with only just sufficient slackening to take in female passengers and children, or infirm people. There is no halting for the male sex. The cars are mostly drawn by active little mules, which trot along gaily at a great rate, the men stepping in and out so nimbly, even when the carriages are in full swing, that accidents are of rare occurrence. Altogether these tramways are an excellent institution, besides having proved a very paying concern. For its size, Buenos Ayres is said to be the best trammed city in the world, and on such a day as this the cars go past in an almost continuous stream, the dull heavy rumble of the wheels and the ringing of the bell—with now and then a sharp discordant bray from a kind of cow-horn blown in warning at the principal crossings and street-corners—forming a kind of running accompaniment to existence from early morning till far beyond dewy eve. There is no getting away from the sound, except in some of the side streets, and it is not a little trying to one's nerves till they become inured to it.

It is a singular fact that, although so numerous and generally used, the trams have by no means decreased other vehicular traffic. At the same time they have certainly succeeded in making it well-nigh excruciating. To be mercilessly jolted along an endless street, when late for dinner, with one wheel in the middle of the ill-paved track and the other outside it, and at every hundred yards to have to make room for the cars by charging the rails, as one would a hurdle (only at an obtuse angle), is an experience not easily to be forgotten. So vivid are my recollections of it, that I for one am for resisting to the utmost the attempts of the tramway companies to spoil the best part of London. Carriages and trams can hardly to my mind coexist in harmony and comfort, and here, where they no doubt manage to rub on together, they do so on conditions with which our public at home would never put up. This, however, only makes it the more surprising that so many private carriages of various kinds should still be kept at Buenos Ayres. Statistics published some four years ago put them at 800, and to these must be added at least 200 hackney-coaches. Reckoning at an average of five the members of each family using a private carriage, this, in a population of 300,000 souls, would give one out of every seventy-five persons as in a position to indulge in this luxury, and would convey some idea of the length to which it is carried. Some two generations back every Buenos Ayrean of good standing was content to ride, while now he takes good care to be driven, leaving horse exercise to the inferior classes, from the Basque milkman down to that proverbial being—in this country a *proverbe en action*—the beggar on horseback.

Down they rattle along the slope of the Recoleta, all bound to the Park with the soft Sicilian name. Roomy French barouches, *de chez Binder*, with full complements of pretty people leaning back in the shade of brightly tinted parasols, the soft folds of their gay dresses overlapping the carriage sides and bulging up in the centre, so as to give the whole conveyance the effect of one of those huge Genoese nosegays put on wheels, the neat little heads and tidy bonnets nodding above like flowers on taller stems; big mail-phaetons, with under-sized horses driven by the gilded youth of the place, sitting bolt upright like men in buckram; dapper little broughams, with more effete occupants of the same class; and a good sprinkling of high-wheeled tilburies, much affected by the

brokers who live down Flores way, and used by
them on week-days when they come into town ' to
go on 'Change.'   A very few equestrians—one or
two on ambling horses, or *caballos de paso* ; these,
however, are fast going out of fashion—as, indeed, is
all riding, except in the ' camp,'[1] where the centaur
traditions of the race are still fully kept up.

The whole *défilé* conveys an impression of
lavish wealth and display guided by imperfect
canons of taste, and in this respect the remoter
Chileans seem to me to outstrip these more accessible Argentines.   There are, or there were some
years ago, at Santiago a few turn-outs that could
well have passed muster in Hyde Park or the
Bois de Boulogne.   Here there is nothing of the
kind.   Either the horses are badly harnessed or
ill-matched, or the liveries are ill-made, or the
carriages are painted the wrong colour ; there is
always something wrong somewhere.   Then the
coachmen and footmen all wear beards, or at least
a moustache, a clean-shaven face being looked
upon in the domestic class here as a degrading
badge of slavery.

The show to-day, however, is, I am assured,
relatively a poor one.   The *élite* of Buenos Ayres,
its more exclusive class, still smarting under a

---

[1] I protest against this barbarous Anglo-Spanish term, but in
writing of this country it is difficult altogether to avoid it.

sense of defeat, have withdrawn to their tents and for the present do not show in public. Just now they are in the full winter of their discontent, for the transfer of the Presidential powers is close at hand, and in a few days more the man whose election drove them to war and secession will assume office, and the measure of their overthrow will be indeed complete. Those, however, who know the place best bid one hope that this rancorous spirit will wear away ere long; and at an evening party given a night or two ago at one of the leading houses on the Government side, signs of a *rapprochement* between vanquished and victors are said to have been visible.

Meanwhile the light begins to fade and a slight mist rises up from the river—these early spring evenings are chilly and treacherous—and now the holiday-makers come pouring into town again. The streets, which seemed quite deserted an hour ago, awaken once more to their customary bustle and rattle ; the windows and balconies are full of stay-at-home folk watching their friends go by with many a nod and salutation ; at the gateways of every other house the carriages are setting down or dropping people ; there are effusive partings and greetings at the entrances to the *patios*, with an accompaniment of rustling silks and quick short sentences and laughter rising strangely clear above

all the street clatter; at each step one gets odd
little glimpses into the everyday habits of a life
spent, as it were, almost in the open gaze—simply
and unaffectedly and without trace of *arrière-pensée*
—and in so many ways curiously foreign to our
own rigid, and somewhat narrow, ideas of propriety,
above all to the holy horror in which we hold all
demonstrations in public.

Very soon all these artless, loud-spoken people
will be at their dinners—that sacred meal taking
place here at the fairly civilised hour of from six
to seven; the clubs and restaurants will be full,
and two hours hence so will be the numerous
theatres and places of amusement, where all will
meet again—or in each other's houses at *tertulias*,
to which one may drop in unbidden. Thus will
close for the day the round of gaiety in this
sociable little Transatlantic world, of which it can
hardly be said, as in the title to the witty French
play, ' Qu'on s'y ennuie.' Certainly if one does, it
is not for lack of opportunities to the contrary.

CHAPTER IV.

PRESIDENTIAL INAUGURATION—LEVÉE AT THE PINK HOUSE—
DIPLOMATISTS IN DIFFICULTIES—BUENOS AYRES BOTH DE-
THRONED AND EXALTED—A POPULAR FÊTE.

THE accession to office of the new President was,
as I have said, imminent, and, important as such an
occurrence is at all times in republican communities, the grave series of events which had followed
upon the nomination of General Roca gave an exceptional interest and significance to his assumption
of power. General Roca, no doubt, mainly owed
his election to the reputation he had acquired by
the well-planned campaigns against the Indians,
which had led to the conquest of the Rio Negro,
and had added twenty thousand square leagues to
the territory of the Republic. But he was still
better known as the subduer of two rebellions, the
last of which had been directed against his own
election. To the Buenos-Ayreans, above all, who
had so bitterly opposed his elevation to the supreme
magistracy and had so recently succumbed to his
strategy, he might well appear in the light of a

stern conqueror bent on revenge.   It seemed as if
the dread shadow of the sword were once more
about to descend on the path of the easy-going,
money-seeking metropolis; as though under the
hollow disguise of legal constitutional forms the evil
days of militarism were again at hand.   A vague
uneasiness pervaded all classes, and men watched
for the 12th of October with much distrust and
heart-sinking, for on that day the outgoing President was to resign his powers into the hands of
his successor, in the presence of Congress assembled
in solemn session.

The morning came round—fair and cloudless,
ushering in the new reign with floods of sunshine.
From an early hour the whole population was astir,
and thronging the streets which lead to the Plaza
25 de Mayo, where stand the House of Congress
and the Casa del Gobierno, or Government House,
and filling them with true Southern movement and
ebullition.   But, although things bore outwardly
the most cheerful and festive aspect, it was well
known that the battalions that lined the roads and
hemmed in the surging crowd had been strengthened in the last few days from outlying garrisons,
and it was whispered about that, in the dead of the
previous night, a number of the more hot-headed
opponents of the National Government had been
quietly arrested, and at the same time the printing-

E

presses of the principal opposition journals seized and placed under lock and key. Sinister rumours were soon afloat that these high-handed proceedings were due to the discovery of a plot to assassinate the new President, and there was considerable anxiety as to what the day might bring forth. There was much exaggeration in these reports. In reality, the measures taken, although sharp, were purely precautionary. The Government may have had, or affected to have, intimation of some design to disturb the public peace; but, at any rate, the few persons whom they thought it prudent to detain were set free again in less than twenty-four hours, and the hostile papers allowed to appear as usual the next morning.

The building where Congress holds its sittings is small and insignificant, and barely affords room for a few hundred persons. On this occasion every nook and corner in and about it is crowded to excess. A numerous, but by no means imposing, assemblage is packed inconveniently close in the dark, stuffy Hall of Session itself, the sombre effect of the mass of Congressmen and spectators, all clad in plain black clothes, being only just relieved by a few—a very few—ladies' dresses (society sulking, as before observed, in opposition), a sprinkling of military uniforms, and the gold embroideries and decorations of a dozen or so unfortunate foreign diplomatists, who have donned their official attire in honour of the solemnity, and look uncomfortably out of keeping with these severely simple surroundings. The heat is perfectly suffocating, and the function, with the indispensable speeches that form part of it, seems interminable; and is decidedly uninteresting up to the moment when the hero of the hour steps forward to take the oath and deliver his inaugural address to the representatives of the nation.

The new President is a young-looking man, of middle height and spare delicate build, prematurely bald, with thin fair hair at the temples, and slight beard and moustache. At first sight his is a refined rather than a powerful face; it bears, however, an unmistakable stamp of determination, and there is a glitter, as of steel, in the cold grey-blue eye. What perhaps strikes one most about it is an air of great lassitude and a deadly pallor. The General has only just recovered from severe illness; but his health is at no time robust, and he has something of that dim look of depression and apathy so noticeable in the third Napoleon, and which, to those who knew, told so sad a tale.

His demeanour on this trying occasion is singularly impassive. Standing there, as he does, at this perilous but triumphant hour, with the fortunes of his country just placed in his grasp, it is impossible to discern in the worn, colourless countenance the slightest vestige either of exultation or disquietude. Clear proof there is here, at any rate, of no ordinary nerve and self-control. He begins reading his address in a low voice and in studiously measured tones; but when he reaches the passage which expresses his unalterable resolve to use, to the utmost, the powers vested in him for the repression of any attempt against the unity of the nation, and calls upon all to support him in the task, there is a sudden vigour—almost a ring of defiance—in his accents that goes straight home to the listeners. Short, fierce bravoes answer his words; in an instant he is in complete sympathy with those whom he addresses, and receives full consecration as the man appointed to do a certain thing, and who, it is felt, is both willing and able to do it with an inflexible determination. Altogether the President scores a success of the best kind. None but the most confirmed cavillers can deny that the sky-blue and white scarf[1] sits well and gracefully on this pale, quiet soldier of unassuming but resolute mien. A feeling as of relief after great tension spreads through the densely crowded audience, and when the General bows and withdraws, to the sound of the National Anthem—

---

[1] The presidential insignia (*banda presidencial*), of the national colours, worn diagonally over the shoulder like a *grand cordon*.

a poor, commonplace melody struck up by a military band outside—the entire assembly rise to their feet and again cheer him right cordially.

There is no time to be lost now for those who would get across to the *Casa Rosada*, or Pink (a very dirty pink) House, at the opposite and further end of the square, whither the President, in the Government coach, surrounded by a cavalry escort, has gone to hold his first official levée and receive the congratulations of all who choose to attend. The police, for some inexplicable reason, will not allow any carriages to enter the square for the purpose of taking up at the Hall of Congress, so that all, without exception, have to make their way across on foot—our foreign friends like the rest—the result being that the envoys of some of the biggest Powers of the earth are reduced to elbow their way, in their official frippery, through the very rough, and decidedly irreverent, throng, amid the cheerful banter of the rising generation of citizens, and are thus placed in a most awkward predicament. But there are worse difficulties in store for the worthy diplomatic body, and the privileges and dignity supposed to be attached to it.

On leaving the House of Congress, they form, with their respective attachés and secretaries, to some extent a compact group representatively covering the best part of the globe; but a buffet here and a push there soon break them up into separate and geographically incorrect knots, so that they ultimately reach the entrance to the Government House split up into the most fragmentary condition, *sans* neighbours, *sans* allies, *sans* everything, like a Congress that might have issued forth distractedly from some diplomatic Tower of Babel. As they severally straggle up to the entrance, with feathers ruffled, both literally and figuratively, they hail with joy the well-known faces of a couple of Government functionaries who have been told off to look after them. A fresh courage now pervades the nations; one by one they rally at the foot of the rickety old wooden staircase, and prepare to ascend it, and to make an imposing entry *in corpore.* Their experiences in the open, however, are as nothing compared with what awaits them here.

Every inch of standing room on the narrow stairs is flooded by a torrent of *hijos del pais,*[2] of all ages and all ranks and conditions, working their way up as best they can; they hang in clusters over the banisters, and some of them are almost climbing them astride in acrobatic fashion. In vain the friendly officials strive, partly by force, partly by expostulation, to clear a passage for the

[2] Natives; literally, sons of the country.

dignitaries committed to their care. The crowd, to say the truth, is wedged so tight that it is hardly possible for it to yield, even if it would; but there is not the slightest inclination on its part to do anything of the kind. Meanwhile the cry is 'Still they come,' fresh contingents surging in from the outside and effectually cutting off all retreat. There is nothing for it but to go forward. By dint of desperate efforts, some of the unfortunate big-wigs contrive to hoist themselves through this mass of struggling, unlovely, and all too pungent humanity, as far as the first landing. Here there is a door leading into a waiting-room, which one of the officials aforesaid, with great presence of mind, opens, quickly and unceremoniously shoving in his charges and closing the door upon them. Not exactly a dignified predicament this for their Excellencies, but better than having their coats torn off their backs. A flurried conference is, no doubt, now held by the indignant and perturbed plenipotentiaries, at which the resolve come to is probably the prudent one not to attempt any more battling with fate and a rampant democracy, for they beat a retreat, and get home as best they can through a suite of empty government offices and so out at a back door. They thus wisely escape the additional slights which await one or two more adventurous spirits of their number who have persevered in the attempt to reach the apartment where the President, looking dead beat, poor man! patiently stands shaking hands with his fellow-citizens as they file past him. There is a story told of the Papal delegate—a most courteous and highly esteemed ecclesiastic, who took a very leading part in the mediation which terminated the late civil conflict—being treated with the greatest rudeness and contumely, not by the rough un-tutored crowd, but by functionaries who ought to have known better—an unpleasant experience he shares with the representative of a leading Protestant Power who, by an odd juxtaposition, is doing his best to help him through the throng.

Altogether the reception ends, as far as the foreign representatives are concerned, in a *scandalum magnatum*, and ultimately, it is said, leads to a very sharp correspondence with the Argentine Foreign Office. No doubt the Government are to blame for not making proper arrangements for the reception of the diplomatists who have come officially to congratulate the new head of the State on the part of their respective Governments; but a severe regard for etiquette is hardly to be expected in these young republican countries. No deliberate disrespect has, of course, been intended, although with the regret somewhat charily expressed there may mingle just a shade of malignant

satisfaction—what the Germans call *Schadenfreude*
—at the discomfiture of effete monarchies and
aristocracies in the person of their representatives
in all their official splendour. At the same time, I
must say that, in my humble opinion, uniforms are
decidedly out of place at these democratic functions, only making those who wear them unde-
sirably conspicuous, and needlessly exposing them
to disagreeable incidents such as the one just
related.

It must, too, in fairness be added that the
building in which these receptions take place is
utterly unsuited for the purpose. It is a tumble-
down concern of very mean proportions, built on
the site of the old Spanish fort of the Trinidad,
which was held by Beresford and his small force
for some weeks, and where he was finally forced
to capitulate. In those days the square on which
it stood bore the unpretending name of *Plaza de
Perdices* (Partridge Square),[3] and game and poultry
were sold on the spot where now General Belgrano
curvets on high, on his charger, in imperishable
bronze. There is some talk of pulling down this
old Government House and replacing it by an
edifice of greater dignity which would not con-

[3] It is now called *Plaza 25 de Mayo*, from the date on which
Buenos Ayres first proclaimed itself independent of the Crown of
Spain.

trast so unfavourably with the massive and very handsome general post office recently erected next door—to my mind by far the most satisfactory public building in Buenos Ayres.

The passing excitement which had been produced by the presidential inauguration very soon wore away, and the city resumed its ordinary aspect and occupations. But for the state of siege, which was maintained for a short time longer, things in general might be said to have returned to their normal condition, and certainly no outward trace of the recent civil dissensions was discernible.

The new administration, however, in no way relented in their policy of unification. A most important step in that direction had already been taken in the shape of a bill laid before Congress for the incorporation into the national army of all the forces hitherto kept on foot by the provincial governments, those governments being further forbidden to raise in future any new local corps under whatsoever denomination. The measure was unquestionably a wise and necessary one, for among the many evils entailed on this country by a Federal system originally, and, most unfortunately, borrowed from the United States, this right of the provinces to provide themselves with military forces of their own was perhaps the greatest.

It had been all along a fruitful source of civil war
and discord, and had more than anything else
contributed to make the Confederation the pan-
demonium of military tyranny and the prey of
contending chieftains and factions it had been for
so long a period. It remained, of course, to be
seen how far the other provinces would acquiesce
in a measure really directed against Buenos Ayres,
but which involved such a curtailment of their
own State rights and autonomy; but the general
current in favour of national consolidation was so
strong that no very serious opposition was to be
apprehended.

For the province of Buenos Ayres it was a
bitter pill to swallow; but far worse was the Act
of Congress by which the city was federalised and
declared to be the permanent capital of the whole
republic, the provincial authorities being required
to hand it over to the National Government, and to
provide themselves, as soon as possible, with a new
home elsewhere. Practically Buenos Ayres had
already been the national metropolis for a number
of years, but, remaining at the same time the seat
of the powerful government of the province, she
had grown to look upon herself as the arbiter and
mistress of the Confederation; granting, it is true,
hospitality within her walls to the central authorities of the nation, but taking good care in return

to make her influence felt in their councils. Indeed, at times it might well have been doubted which was the stronger of the two—the President of the Republic or the Governor of the Province thus residing side by side.

This proud position Buenos Ayres was now called upon to surrender at one stroke, while her own authorities were ejected from her midst and driven to seek shelter in some obscure third-rate town. The province, in fact, was simply asked to submit to decapitation for the benefit of the nation at large. Legal forms were, however, so far respected that the decision of the National Congress was submitted to the Provincial Legislature for ratification. The debates on the question came on late in the month of November, and extended over a week, although their result was a foregone conclusion. The small minority who opposed the surrender in the Chamber of Deputies spared no oratorical efforts, one of their number speaking on three successive days. In the small hours of the morning of the 25th the division was finally taken, and the Senate having already unanimously adopted the bill, the dethronement of Buenos Ayres on the one hand, and her exaltation on the other, became accomplished facts. A glowing presidential proclamation announced the event and its momentous bear-

PLAZA VICTORIA AND CATHEDRAL.

ings to the population, and set apart the 8th of December as a day of general public rejoicing.

For December, in this hemisphere, read June. The festive day, when it came, brought with it great heat and insufferable glare and dust. Gratefully cool and restful to the eye it was, therefore, under the lofty arches of the cathedral, where a solemn thanksgiving ushered in the appointed festivities. This cathedral is a very spacious structure, surmounted by a cupola some hundred and thirty feet high, and is profusely decorated inside in the debased style of florid ornamentation prevalent in Italian and Spanish churches of the middle of last century, at which period the present edifice was raised on the site of the decayed fabric first designed by Juan de Garay in 1580. A somewhat heavy portico with marble columns, crowned by a sculptured pediment, adorns the front facing towards the Plaza Victoria, and at first sight vaguely recalls the Church of the Madeleine in Paris. It is a fine building on the whole, but, although it has been extolled as the grandest of its kind in South America, is not to be compared with the cathedral at Lima.

The *Te Deum*, chanted at full length and with due solemnity, in the presence of the President and all the principal authorities, both National and Provincial, was followed by a still longer pulpit oration delivered by a brawny friar from some distant province in the interior, Catamarca or Tucuman, in great repute for his eloquence. There was something about this swarthy, uncouth monk, of half-military aspect, which brought to mind those of his brethren who, some sixty years before, had trudged with the liberating armies across the giant Andes down into the smiling Chilean valleys beyond, and, by lending the countenance of the Church to a contest waged against the Most Catholic King, had helped to secure for its clergy so strong a hold on the affections of the people. Of that influence there is, in truth, little left in these days; but the South American priesthood nevertheless showed much sagacity in the attitude they at once assumed towards the revolutionary movement against Spain, and for a time reaped very substantial benefits from it.

The preacher gave us what was in reality a political address, couched in rudely effective and somewhat barbarous language—oddly interspersed here and there with short extemporary prayers—and dealing with recent events from the strictly national autonomist point of view. For a *discours de commande*, such as might have been preached by one of Louis XIV.'s chaplains before the *Grand Monarque*, it was not amiss, and must have been highly gratifying to the chief listener. To other ears it may have been less grateful, for it contained decidedly uncomplimentary, and perfectly uncalled for, allusions to monarchical principles and monarchical States. Our distinguished foreign friends — for whose comfort the most perfect arrangements had this time been made — were destined, it seemed, not to escape the *amari aliquid* in some form or other at the public functions they had to attend.

After the religious ceremony there came a march-past of the troops. Those favoured persons who had been asked to witness it from the windows and balconies of the Town House, or Cabildo, which stands at right angles to the cathedral and overlooks the Square of Victory (so named from the triumph over Beresford and his diminutive army), followed the President thither on foot through the protecting lines of the soldiery. The force assembled was not a large one—probably some four or five thousand men—but the 'attenuated battalions' had a decidedly martial air, and went by with a swinging step, their bronzed skins and lean, wiry frames plainly showing hard service and excellent condition. With their red-trousered uniforms, which are almost exactly copied from that of the French infantry, they might well have been taken for African *troupiers* just home from Algeria. Altogether the force, though far from smart—especially the cavalry and artillery—looked very serviceable and workmanlike, and the cheers the men gave as they filed past showed how well affected they were to their chief. If closely analysed, their ranks would no doubt have shown a curious medley of nationalities, and a good many of their officers were of foreign extraction, amongst others one of their most distinguished leaders bearing a good old English name. It was well that the review lasted but a short time, for the powerful midday sun seriously affected several of the men, one poor fellow being struck all of a heap, and falling down just in front of the Cabildo. Fortunately the troops were rapidly dismissed to their quarters, and spectators of all classes were glad to get away from the fierce white glare and to take refuge at home in carefully darkened rooms.

The full glory of the fête was reserved for the evening, and I must say that I have seldom seen anything prettier or more striking in its way. Again the Square of Victory—the old Plaza Mayor—was the centre of attraction. It was most effectively lighted up with garlands and pyramids of coloured lanterns, intermingled with devices of gas which followed the outlines of the surrounding buildings, wound in luminous spirals round the central obelisk, and cast their refraction on the diamond spray of the large fountains adjoining. Several excellent military bands relieved each other at intervals, and filled the air with familiar strains from Marchetti or Verdi— just the kind of melodies for a popular fête; while above the whole was spread out a canopy of deepest, blackest blue, all quivering with the glitter of stars innumerable—the Southern Cross, and all the myriads that bear it company in this, the richest, half of the celestial chart.

The large square—so big that although illuminated *a giorno*, its contours were softened by distance and lost in a more subdued radiance— was filled to overflowing with sightseers. It was no easy matter to elbow one's way through so dense a crowd, especially in the neighbourhood of the fountains, where, to the sound of orchestras placed on raised platforms, dancing was going on vigorously; but there was no kind of hustling or roughness, no rude horse-play or signs of intoxication. Nothing could be more orderly or good-tempered than this really vast assemblage, left to look after itself, and with but little visible police supervision. In the stillness of the warm breathless night the hum of the many voices formed a deep continuous bass to the bright clear tones of the wind instruments, while now and then a loud crash of brass or a roll of drums covered the whole, to

F

be presently succeeded by a shrill peal of female laughter, alternating with some quick Southern exclamation in Basque or Italian. Wandering through the serried throng, with one's cigar as an indispensable protection against all too powerful whiffs of onion and garlic, it was amusing to note the variety of idioms that struck one's ear in turn. Every tribe and nation under the sun, excepting those of the Eastern world, seemed represented here, and you were able at once to realise the intensely cosmopolitan character of the population. However much I at all times dislike a crowd, this one at least offered infinite variety and interest. For the outpouring of all the humbler classes of a busy and populous capital, nothing could less resemble the mobs we are wont to see and dread on similar occasions at home. The inference could hardly be avoided that this difference of demeanour was greatly due to the keener sense of self-respect and personal dignity which is one of the best points of republican training. To this, however, must in fairness be added the habits of greater sobriety that distinguish Spaniards and Italians of the lower orders. At any rate, the result was a really exemplary crowd, and, but for the intense heat and the wearying process of wandering round and round in a relatively confined space, I might have been tempted to linger on much longer.

It was high time, however, to think of effecting
a retreat, so, after a last glance at the gaily draped
windows of the Municipality, filled with beautifully
dressed ladies, on whom the patriotic inscriptions
in flaring gas that ran just beneath them beat
crudely, and almost indiscreetly, I wended my way
home along streets which looked like continuous
arcades of light. This was perhaps the prettiest
and most original feature of the whole illumination,
and was produced by the simple device of stretching across from roof to roof, at frequent intervals,
slender arches of gas-piping from out of which
sprang the jets enclosed in small globes. Between
the darkness of the sky above and of the houses
beneath, these looked like strings of opals hanging
in mid-air, and had quite a fairylike effect.

CHAPTER V.

RAILWAY DEVELOPMENT AND ITS EFFECTS—THE INDIAN SCOURGE
—A TRIAL TRIP ON THE 'GREAT SOUTHERN'—NEW PUEBLOS
OF THE CAMP—THE GAUCHOS.

THE excellence of its soil and climate, which has
done so much to attract immigration, and a con-
figuration of ground which seemed specially to in-
vite railway construction, have been main factors in
the sum of material development hitherto reached
in this country. Of the actual Argentine railway
system it may fairly be said that it has been created
by English enterprise and English capital, although
to a French engineer of the name of Ringuelet is,
I believe, due the credit of having laid down the
oldest of the existing lines—the Western of Buenos
Ayres, running to Chivilcoy and Lobos—the first
section of which was opened barely twenty-five
years ago. The Provincial Government of Buenos
Ayres, be it said by the way, work this line themselves, and do so very creditably, their management,
and especially their freights, contrasting favourably
with those of some of the other railroads.

Certainly the progress achieved in this direction in the space of less than a quarter of a century is in every way remarkable, some fifteen hundred miles having already been handed over to traffic, and about nine hundred more being now in course of construction—a liberal allowance for a population not exceeding three millions. But here—as in other young countries—the locomotive precedes population instead of following it, plunging like a pioneer into the wilderness and creating its traffic as it goes.

Villages and towns spring up in its wake with mushroom growth, and stud in an incredibly short space of time, those vast empty tracts which on the map were marked before only with the sites of former Indian encampments or a few simple names indicative of barbarian chase or travel. Such picturesque appellations as ' the one-eyed deer,' ' the ten trees,' ' the red mule,' ' the tiger's head,' are rapidly swamped by patriotic dates, or the titles of National triumphs which their founders love to bestow on the aspiring new *pueblos* of the desert.

The process of settlement and colonisation is, of course, a much slower one than in the newer regions of countries like the United States or Canada, where there are denser masses at the back to feed the necessary full stream of immigration and impel the more adventurous forward ; but it is nevertheless surprisingly rapid. To the West and South, more particularly, the iron horse is penetrating more and more deeply into the ancient patrimony whence only yesterday the redskin was cast out, never to return.

Perhaps no greater contrast can be conceived than the sudden change from the old methods of locomotion to the new. In old-world countries the railways were preceded by a more or less organised system of posting, which, in Western Europe especially, had almost attained perfection. Here the engine is the immediate successor of the bullock-cart, or at best of the lumbering *galera* or diligence. It may in fact be said that within the last century the means of communication had rather deteriorated than improved—certainly in the more distant provinces. Previous to 1776, when Buenos Ayres was erected into a separate viceroyalty, the intercourse between the province and the centre of government in Perú made it a necessity to keep open some direct mode of approach across the entire breadth of the continent from sea to sea. Thus in those days, when the *Audiencia Real,* the supreme tribunal for all these regions, had its seat six hundred leagues away at Chuquisaca (now become the capital of Bolivia under the name of Sucre), a delegation from it travelled backwards and forwards periodically every five years over roads which lay through the now almost impenetrable fastnesses of the Gran Chaco, the home of the Tobas and other fierce Indian tribes.

The worthy magistrates moved across slowly, but in perfect safety, with an imposing retinue, and a whole *posse* of advocates and *procuradores*, clerks and *alguazils*, under the escort of an armed force, and as majestically returned when they had disposed of the arrears of judicial work that accumulated between their progresses, granting, let us hope, a speedy delivery to the poor wretches whose fate or fortunes had been at stake all through the dreary interval. Along these routes too—for such were the almost incredible fiscal arrangements of Spanish colonial rule—travelled the entire proceeds of the local customs, which had all to be remitted to Lima, whence were brought in exchange all that numerous class of Spanish goods which it was strictly prohibited to import through any other emporium. These old tracks, which stretched across the barren plains of Santa Fé and were hewn through the thorny thickets of the Gran Chaco, have long been obliterated, and some of the more recent exploring expeditions sent to the last-named region, with a view to establishing a permanent trade route to Bolivia, have met there with a tragical fate.

The thin glittering lines of steel have not yet penetrated thus far, but in other directions they reach a long way into the old Indian territory, and the trains are whirled smoothly along almost in the same furrows which, but a few years back, marked the *rastrilladas* of the warriors of Namuncura and Pincen.

These *rastrilladas*, which may still be traced in many parts of the Pampa, were the rough-worn tracks along which the mounted savages habitually advanced in their raids and incursions. The commonly received idea of the order of Indians on the march is the single file to which they have given their name, but it is erroneous. The wild horsemen rode indeed singly, but in close *échelon*, one rider following the other at a short distance to the right, so as to leave each man's bridle-hand perfectly free. Seen coming towards one from afar, the formation, as it has been well described, seemed that of a mounted Macedonian phalanx, while in shape it in reality resembled a set of Pandean pipes. On these *rastrilladas* as many as forty furrows may be counted, showing the frontage of the advancing column. In this order, followed by troops of spare horses and raising huge columns of dust as they rode, the savages came sweeping over the plain in their moonlit night-marches, till by dawn of day they had broken into some *pueblo* slumbering in fancied security within the frontier line, murdering or ravishing the wretched inhabitants, and vanishing again into the desert, with their spoil and their captives, long before the sun was high and the alarm could be given to the nearest fort or guardhouse.

At last came the final day of retribution in the campaigns, first planned by Alsina,[1] but carried out by Roca, in which the tribes were systematically and remorselessly hunted down, and their shattered remnants driven either across the Rio Negro or to the foot of the Cordilleras, some of the principal Caciques and leaders—among others the redoubtable Pincen—being carried away into captivity, and such of the tribesmen as were not shot down sent to work on the sugar estates in Tucuman, or drafted into the Argentine army and navy.

The capture and final destruction of the tribe of the Cacique Catriel, among others, has been admirably described in the 'Revue des Deux-

---

[1] In 1833 Rosas commanded in person an expedition, the object of which was to occupy the whole Pampas as far as the line of the Rio Negro. He established his head-quarters on the Rio Colorado, his lieutenants sweeping the country up to the Chilean frontier. This military promenade was not followed up, though the terror it struck into the Indians kept them quiet for a good many years (Mulhall, *Repúblicas del Plata*).

Mondes' by M. Ebelot, who, a few years ago, contributed to that periodical a series of very interesting sketches of life on the so-called Argentine frontier, by which is meant the artificial line of defence which had been raised against the Indians of the Pampas some years before the finishing stroke was dealt to them. Specially severe punishment was awarded to this tribe, on account of the breach of faith it had committed in absconding from the cantonments in which it was located under Government protection near Azul, and betaking itself again to the lawless life of the desert. This same Catriel, by the way, is the only chieftain who is ever known to have indulged in the luxury of a carriage, for which every genuine Indian professes the greatest contempt. During his long residence near Azul—then only an advanced border post, but now one of the most important stations on the Great Southern of Buenos Ayres Railway, and the head of its proposed extension to Bahia Blanca—he had got so used to that form of locomotion, that when he raised the standard of rebellion and fled to his native wilds, he did so in a splendid equipage borrowed from some unsuspecting landowner of the neighbourhood.

The entire change produced within a few brief years by the conquest, and by the immediate

extension of railroads and opening up of the
country that followed it, is so wonderful that, in
order to realise it—and that only in a faint degree
—one must almost imagine to oneself railway
enterprise in the United Kingdom as already existing in the days of Rob Roy and his caterans, and
its civilising and subduing effects being brought to
bear on the Highlands before 1715. I need not
add that, in venturing on so bold an illustration,
nothing is further from my thoughts than to set
up any comparison between the stout-hearted clans-
men who gathered round Charles Edward, and the
licentious, half-tamed Gauchos of the border lands
—still less the debased barbarians who have been
so recently swept off the Argentine map.

There was indeed little left of the 'noble
savage' about the Indian of the Pampas in the
decadence that preceded his final expulsion. Even
those among the tribes which, like the more distant
Pehuenches, were of Araucanian origin, had sadly
degenerated from the formidable warriors sung by
Ercilla. They had lost all the bolder traditions of
savage warfare, and had sunk to the level of mere
marauders, though their inborn ferocity too frequently showed itself in cowardly murders committed on the defenceless. Unfortunately their
tolderias, or encampments, served as a refuge to
the more lawless elements among the native Argen-

tines or Gauchos, and they were often led, as well as instructed in the use of firearms, by deserters and criminals flying from justice. Still, considering the paucity of their numbers—Catriel's tribe, for instance, was only reckoned at 900 lances some two years before its destruction—and the poorness of their armament, it seems almost a national disgrace that they should have been allowed to hold their own so long, and indeed to derive tribute, as they did, from the treasuries of civilised communities like Santa Fé or Buenos Ayres. It is the more surprising because, like their kinsmen in North America, they were an expiring race, and at the time of their final overthrow had been reduced to a state of semi-starvation by the iron barrier of the frontier, which put an end to cattle-lifting on a large scale, and prevented their replenishing the herds of horses which alone made them formidable. The internal dissensions, which so long distracted the Confederation and paralysed its energies, must account for the lack of vigour shown towards these intolerable savages, and the radical manner in which they have now been dealt with is a happy augury that this country has at last reached the era of stable, well-ordered government.

General Roca's campaigns at one stroke added some 20,000 square leagues, or something like 140,000,000 acres, to the domain of the Republic, and these immense tracts were forthwith thrown open to the settler. The original Government price demanded for a square league of land [2] (upwards of 6,600 acres) was 400 hard dollars, equal to about 70*l.* Much of the land was at once snapped up at that price, and it has since so increased in value that in some districts—especially those to the west and southwest of Azul, which were almost immediately tapped by the Great Southern Railway—it is already worth from 2,000*l.* to 3,000*l.* a league. Round the old Indian centres of Guamini and Sauce Corto, good land is at present let at upwards of 200*l.* a year per league, on short leases of at most three years. All this country, which is now well covered with cattle farms, was a wilderness in the hands of the Indians barely eight years back. Much of the land is of the highest quality for pasture, and the climate being very temperate and admirably adapted to European constitutions, these new districts can be highly recommended to English settlers bringing with them sufficient

---

[2] In 1878 a loan of 1,600,000 hard dollars was decreed, in bonds of 400 dollars each, which entitled the subscriber to one square league in the conquered regions. The cost of the expedition was to be defrayed by this loan. I am indebted for much of the above, and other valuable, information to a report by Mr. Egerton published in the series of commercial reports by H.M.'s Secretaries of Embassy and Legation for 1881.

capital to purchase and stock a league or two. A large extent of country has, however, been already taken up.

Shortly after my arrival at Buenos Ayres I had an excellent opportunity of seeing for myself how railroads are laid down in these regions. A new extension on the Great Southern system, from Dolores to a place called Chacabuco, was almost ready for traffic, and, before handing it over to the Government inspectors, the manager and engineers of the line were about to make a trial trip over it, in which they kindly asked me and one or two friends to accompany them. The important district to be opened up by this branch railway extends, in a straight line from Dolores, over more than one hundred miles to the south coast, and contains some of the best land in the province of Buenos Ayres. The Great Southern, which is favourably known to the investor in England, is, I need not say, a purely British undertaking, and noteworthy for its success and able management.

We started at about three o'clock in the afternoon from the chief terminus of the railway, which is situated quite at the end of the town, near a very large square (Plaza de la Constitucion) that serves as the principal market for the wool from the southern districts. Here may be seen row upon row of the immense wains or wagons in

which the fleeces are brought up to town—great
Noah's arks, mounted on formidable wheels that
have groaned and creaked over many a long mile
across the Pampa, and covered with tilt roofs made
of hides stretched across wooden frames. Our
train was simply composed of an engine and tender,
to which was attached a long saloon car, furnished
with unusually wide leather cushions on either side
that made up into most comfortable beds. The
saloon could, if required, be turned into separate
compartments by curtains drawn across it, and,
without having any pretensions to luxury, made
as capital a travelling-carriage as could be desired.
There is no need, however, to describe it any
further, for it figures in one of the most popular
narratives of yachting adventure that have been
given to the world of late years.

We were off for forty-eight hours at least, and
the capacious hampers that were stowed away in
a corner of the carriage showed that our hosts did
not intend us to starve on the road. We quickly
settled into our places, the favourite cocktails of
these regions were duly handed round, and we
soon shook down into an extremely cosy party.

Gliding smoothly out of the station, we soon
attained a very fair rate of speed, and when we
were clear of the town, and had left behind us
Lomas de Zamora—a favourite health resort snugly

embosomed in plantations of poplar and *paraiso* and peach-trees—and a few other suburban stations, such as Glew and Lanús and Temperley, which are all called after the principal neighbouring *estancieros*, we plunged into the great empty plain, and at once fully realised its character. It was like spinning across a billiard-table, so green and so level was it on either side, the telegraph posts alone breaking the field of vision as they whizzed past us in what seemed to be a helter-skelter race for the town. In the zone more immediately surrounding Buenos Ayres there had been signs of husbandry in the market-gardens, and in the fields of maize and wheat and flax that broke the monotony of the meadow-land; but agriculture soon ceased, and we got into continuous pastures thickly covered with cattle and sheep and horses. These rich pastoral tracts lasted as far as Altamirano, some fifty odd miles from town, at which point the main line divides into two branches, the one running to the right down to Azul, and the other to the left on to Dolores. We pulled up here for a minute or two, and then ran straight into Chascomus, doing the entire seventy-five miles without a single stoppage but for this one slight break.

After Altamirano the country had so far changed its aspect that it showed fewer flocks and herds, and thus betokened less occupation. The land here, however, is not so much cut up as it is round the city, and the stock on it is less conspicuous, having a larger expanse to roam over. The clumps of trees on the line of the horizon, which mark the sites of the *estancias*, were somewhat wider apart, but as yet sufficiently numerous. Still, we were passing into newer regions, and by very fine gradations the settled camp was roughening into the vast solitudes beyond.

At Chascomus we were to dine, and while our repast—a very excellent one—was being got ready, we went up to a terrace on the roof of the station, and in the last rays of sunset surveyed the boundless prospect, the dull flatness of which was here relieved by the shining waters of a large lake at some short distance from the town, celebrated for its *pejereyes*—an excellent little fish, in size and flavour much resembling our smelt, that fully deserves the regal title bestowed on it, so superior is it to the mostly tasteless finny tribe which peoples the Argentine rivers. We dined luxuriously by candle-light in the spacious waiting-room of the station, and then returning to our special, made another straight run of fifty-six miles through the dark to Dolores, which was to be our night quarters.

The Great Southern Company have rented a

good-sized house here for their engineers working on this extension, where I and my friend E—— were put up in clean, whitewashed rooms, the remainder of the party going to the local hotel, where their rest was by no means unbroken, to judge by the account they afterwards gave us of their nocturnal experiences. Having reached Dolores late in the evening and left it again at a very early hour next day, the place remains almost a blank in my memory; but the impression I gathered of it in driving down to the station was of the dullest of small provincial towns, and as dismal a sojourn as is bound to be a place named, in good old Spanish orthodox fashion, after Our Lady of Sorrows. Its terminus, however, where we waited for some time in the early sunlight while our special was getting up steam, showed it to be the centre of considerable traffic, the sidings being filled up with trucks laden with the first wool of the season and other produce of the country-side. There are some very large and flourishing estates in this neighbourhood, among others the immense *estancia* of Anchorena, which extends over miles between Dolores and the sea. In this, and still more in the adjoining *partido* (department) of Chascomus, the foreign element gathers very strong, the Scotch and Irish being especially numerous. The country is well watered by the Salado and Samborombom rivers, and agriculture is by degrees supplanting pure stock-farming.

Our inspection tour began at this point, and we therefore now proceeded at a very leisurely rate, feeling our way, as it were, carefully along. At frequent intervals we came to a standstill, the engineers getting out and walking a few hundred yards along the metals. The rails are made of steel, and rest on iron sleepers (of the Livesey pattern, if I am not mistaken), these being much cheaper than wood in this timberless country; and on a bowling-green line like this they are laid down with wonderful rapidity and at very little cost. I have not got the exact figures, although they were given me at the time, but they struck me as quite remarkable. The older portions of the Great Southern system cost over 8,000*l.* per mile, while the outlay on this extension did not, I believe, reach 4,000*l.* per mile, or something like one tenth of the cost of some of our best-known railways. On this side of the river Salado, however, it was all plain sailing, there being no real engineering work to be done.

In between our frequent halts we put on an extra spurt, and, during one of these, by far the best way of judging of the line and the country it passed through was to take one's seat on the cow-catcher in front of the engine. This we did by turns, and it was both a novel and a delightful sensation to feel oneself propelled into vacant space through the keen morning air across the boundless prairie. It was the next best thing to an early gallop, with the additional excitement of charging now and then into troops of horses that scampered away on the line in front of us, at the sound of our warning danger-whistle, and scattered right and left just as we were upon them.

The plains now appeared decidedly emptier and less full of life than they had been before Dolores, and the *montes* of the *estancias* were less frequent. That they were amply stocked, however, was proved by the bones of the victims of the great hurricane that had swept over these regions a month before. Shortly after leaving Dolores, my eye was attracted by the carcass of one of these poor creatures, which was lying across a shallow ditch by the side of the permanent way. A few yards further on I noted another, and yet another, and, the sight producing a sort of morbid fascination, I took to counting them. Watch in hand, I reached something like four or five hundred of them—I forget now which—in the space of three quarters of an hour, when I got wearied and gave up the gruesome task I had set myself. All these lay within a very short distance—at most a couple of hundred yards—of the line, and of

course only on the side I was watching. Stock of
all kinds, though mostly cows, and in every stage
of decay—from the dried-up carcass to the clean-
picked skeleton. Some of these poor remains
were still singularly well preserved, and lay in
groups of two and three in pathetic attitudes;
others again had taken strange twisted shapes in
their last contortions. Altogether it was a piteous
sight, and showed that there was little exaggeration in the accounts first published of the extent
of the disaster.

By eleven o'clock we had reached Maipú, a
station about halfway to Chacabuco and thirty-
five miles from Dolores. Here we stopped for
some time, and breakfasted sumptuously in our
car. The place is a good specimen of the new
centres of population that seem to crop up by
enchantment wherever the railway reaches. Although only a year or two old, it is already
marked out in regular streets, with high-sounding
names, running at right angles from a central
plaza. Like the generality of these *pueblos nuevos*,
it has no doubt sprung from a few huts gathered
round a *pulperia*[3] on some old wagon track across
the Pampa, where, probably, first a wheelwright

---

[3] The *pulperia* is a kind of combination of provision-shop and
public-house, which supplies the wants of the population in the camp
for miles round.

and then a carpenter had squatted and found employment. When placed like this in a promising locality, the primitive hamlet soon expands into a village. Authority then steps in and sends down an *agrimensor*, or Government surveyor, to lay it out in approved fashion and measure the various allotments. Next appear law and discipline in the persons of a *juez de paz* and a commissary of police. The place having thus acquired official dignity is considered entitled to a church and a school, and the priest and the schoolmaster now come on the scene, though for yet a while the school-benches may remain empty and the church have no worshippers. But the whole system being a forcing one, these are quite secondary considerations. In this embryo condition the new *pueblo* may continue to vegetate for a short time and then relapse into nothingness, or it may suddenly develop into a busy local centre: everything depending on the quality of the land that surrounds it. Maipú is said to be favoured in this respect, and possibly has a future.

At present it is hardly a cheerful-looking spot. The conditions attached by law to the grant of any building lot are that it should be enclosed, and a house constructed on it, with a proper side-walk towards the street, within a year from the date of the concession. As few of the settlers have suffi-

cient capital to build at once such a house as is
contemplated by these somewhat ambitious regula-
tions, the difficulty is often turned by running up
a structure which in size and shape resembles
an enlarged dog-kennel, and surrounding it by a
rough enclosure of *adobes* (sun-dried bricks). The
effect of a lot of these pigmy, whitewashed cabins,
standing each in its little square, in formal rows, is
decidedly depressing, and of such the half-dozen
carefully designed and duly christened streets of
Maipú are largely made up. There is, of course,
a sprinkling of *bond fide* houses, mainly round the
plaza, and a *fonda*, or inn, as well as the indispensable *almacen*, or general store for food and drink,
and a *tienda* (shop) or two, where the Gaucho can
procure his simple requirements, such as the most
ordinary house utensils and rough tools and implements, as well as the gaudy clothing and horse-
trappings to which he is partial, and the various
articles that go to make up the ponderous *recado*,
or native saddle. Here, however, as elsewhere,
the picturesque in dress is rapidly disappearing,
dingy trousering and common cotton shirts taking
the place of the bright *chiripa* and graceful
poncho.

As is Maipú so is Chacabuco, which we reached
early in the afternoon after an easy run—the names
of the two *pueblos*, by the way, recalling the twin

triumphs of General San Martin in Chile. A break with four horses and a couple of carriages were waiting for us, and conveyed us, over excruciatingly bad roads, to the inn where we were to dine and sleep. The sky had been lowering since midday, and we had hardly got to our quarters when it began to rain—a steady downpour that left no prospect of amendment for the rest of the day. Under these circumstances there was no attempting to see what Chacabuco might have to show, and one had to possess one's soul in patience indoors, although the ' Hotel Libertad ' was not precisely the kind of inn one would have selected for taking one's ease. It had its resources, however, and, fortunately for some of us, a billiard-table among others. Presently a *galera* came rumbling up to the door and landed a stray passenger or two, and as the afternoon wore on the choicer spirits of the place dropped in one by one.

In these small localities the *fonda* is the general rendezvous for gossip or local business. Here the *estanciero* meets the country woolbroker or cattle-dealer and strikes a bargain with him over a glass of *hesperidina*, and here, between two games of billiards, the village medico prescribes for his patients. The *sala*—dining-room, smoking-room, and billiard-room all in one—is in fact a kind of club, where, after the evening ordinary, the company settle down to cards till late into the night. The Gaucho is an inveterate gambler, and, next to horse-racing and cock-fighting, play is his favourite excitement.

I had an instance here of the people one unexpectedly comes across in the remotest regions. Early in the evening a youngish man, in well-cut European clothes that had long seen their best days, sauntered in and stood watching the players with evident interest. Under pretence cf asking for a light for his cigarette he soon got into conversation with the younger men of our party, with the clear intent of getting them to join in the game. Failing in this he presently sat down to the table himself. He was evidently no native, spoke several languages, and had all the manners of good society. We were not able to find out his name, beyond the familiar ' Don Pedro,' or ' Don Juan,' by which he was addressed, so put him down as a Polish refugee count; but we afterwards heard from the civil landlord that he was a nightly guest and lived more or less on his play. Clearly a waif from the Homburg or Monte Carlo gaming-tables, whom it was curious to find stranded in this *pays perdu*.

But by far the most characteristic time for seeing one of these *pueblos* of the camp is on a Sunday or church festival, when the wild gentry of the neighbourhood for miles round come riding in for the day. Outside the *fonda* the gaily caparisoned horses are tied up to the palings in a row, or their fore-feet hobbled in true Gaucho fashion. The *sala* and every other available place inside are full of smoking and drinking and card-playing, the venue being now and then changed to the square round the corner, where a horse-race has been got up on the spur of the moment. Towards evening the fun grows fast and furious, and ends with singing and dancing to the noisy accompaniment of squibs and rockets. Fortunate is it when the revels do not culminate in a drunken brawl, with knives unsheathed, and murder, or at least manslaughter. By daybreak the carousers are off again, galloping wildly back, too often with empty pockets, to the distant *ranchos*, where the poor drudges that stand them in stead of wives have been watching listlessly for their return, without any attempt at employment all through the weary hours, beyond preparing the indispensable meal or looking after the squalid offspring of these *mariages interlopes*—almost the only ones known in the camp.

This is no place for attempting to go at length into the manners and customs of the half-tamed children of the Pampas, which have been described with true French finesse and gift of observation

by M. G. Daireaux, of the 'Union Française' of
Buenos Ayres, in some charming sketches he contributed to that paper.[4]   It may, however, be said
that among the unlovely homes of the peasantry
of most countries none perhaps is more dreary
or repulsive than that of the Gaucho—if home it
can properly be called, having in most cases for its
basis an illicit union with a poor creature devoid
of all feminine charm or grace, and steeped in
utter ignorance and slovenliness.   The typical
Gaucho woman, in fact, has little of her sex beyond
her untidy garments and sharp tongue; and but
for the powers of endurance which enable her on
occasion to vie with the men in the hardest work,
such as sheep-shearing or cattle-driving—in the
saddle she is of course at home from her infancy
—and a certain rough fidelity that makes her stick
to the chance partner with whom, after many a
previous experience, she has finally mated for good,
she has no redeeming qualities.   Of things above
these she has neither knowledge nor instinct, and
it is no wonder, therefore, if her companion is
driven from her cheerless society by sheer *ennui* to
seek a solace elsewhere in drink and debauchery.

[4] I gladly take this opportunity of acknowledging my indebted-
ness to this gentleman and his brother editor, M. Ebelot, for many
traits of local character I have put down in these pages. M. Daireaux
is, besides, the author of a very interesting volume, entitled *Buenos
Ayres, la Pampa, et la Patagonie.*

It is difficult to say who is to come to the rescue of these hot-blooded, untutored men, who, for all their vices, attract sympathy by their fearless bearing and a certain native dignity and courtesy. The priest has never had any hold on their dark heathenish homes, for the pure Gaucho has but the faintest tinge of Christianity, his religion being made up of childish and degrading superstitions, mainly derived from Indian sources; the schoolmaster so far has hardly reached him, and he has yet to be redeemed if he is to be worked up into a useful element in the new fabric of civilisation that is growing up around him. The National Government have an arduous task before them in this direction.

We left Chacabuco early in the forenoon, after a sleepless night, as far as I was concerned. The accommodation being very limited, E—— and I, with another of the party, had shared a three-bedded room, the ceiling of which proved to be anything but water-tight. It rained steadily all through the night, and the walls and the floor of beaten earth became so damp that it was very like bivouacking in a wet ploughed field. The beds, however, were clean, and the worthy Basque landlord, who, by the way, had managed to give us a very fair dinner, eked out by the provisions we had brought with us, was most attentive, and in ordinary weather one might be worse put up than at the Hotel Libertad.

The heavy downpour on this stiff, clayey soil had made the roads almost impassable, and it was with the greatest difficulty, and at imminent risk of upsetting, that our team contrived to drag us up the slope that led to the embankment where our train was waiting for us. Our inspection being now over, we made very good time, and, including stoppages at the water-stations, covered the two hundred and odd miles in about nine hours. We loitered somewhat at the Rio Salado, a few of us getting out and crossing the iron railway bridge—a fine work—on foot. It was blowing a stiff *pampero* after the rain, and the structure seemed to sway in the violent gusts that swept up the river—which here is broad enough and runs between two steep banks—so that it was rather giddy work getting across, there being no footway, and the swirling current below being visible in between the bare rails and sleepers. On a slight rise above the stream a biggish *estancia* house was pointed out to us as belonging to a rich family, a most tragical event in whose history is commemorated by the handsome church of St. Felicitas, erected some years ago in the Santa Lucia suburb of Buenos Ayres;—a wild tale of Southern passion and revenge, the full particulars of which were given me afterwards.

Soon after dark we reached the city, and parted with much regret from our kind entertainers of the Great Southern, and especially Mr. C——, the energetic and *muy simpático* manager of that eminently prosperous line.

BUENOS AYRES GAUCHO.

CHAPTER VI.

IMMIGRATION—THE FOREIGN COMMUNITIES.

ACCORDING to a calculation made in February 1881, the city of Buenos Ayres at that period contained upwards of 270,000 inhabitants. It was ascertained on the same occasion that the population was increasing at the rate of over two and a half per cent. a year, more than 13,000 souls having been added to it in two years. The increment was, of course, largely due to the steady flow of immigration which is rapidly converting the Argentine metropolis into the most composite, if not cosmopolitan, of cities.

But, in addition to this influx from abroad, other causes had been at work in the same direction for years before. I take up a book of statistics, published under Government supervision some ten years ago, and find there the following figures, derived from the general census of the Republic taken as far back as 1869. The population of the town was reckoned at that time at a little under

180,000 souls, of whom only one half were put down as Argentines. Of the other, or foreign half, nearly one half again were Italians, another quarter being made up, in almost equal numbers, of French and Spaniards, and the last quarter of half a dozen other nationalities, among which British subjects figured for some three thousand, and Germans for some two thousand.

The most startling fact, however, revealed by the figures from which I am quoting was that, while the excess of males over females in the entire population was in the proportion of five to four, the females among the purely Argentine population outnumbered the males in the ratio of about seven to five. It appeared, in fact, as if the native population, left entirely to itself, must ere long have reached a point that would almost, if I may permit myself the pleasantry, have justified the introduction of polygamy or Mormonism, had not the foreigner providentially stepped in and restored the proper balance between the sexes.

But this was not all. It further resulted from these figures that the births among the foreign inhabitants were fully three times more numerous than among the natives, and this without counting the children born of foreign fathers and Argentine mothers. It was likewise shown that of the illegitimate births that took place two-thirds were to be put down to the natives. Finally it appeared that the death-rate among infants (*parvulos*) had attained the alarming figure of fifty per cent.; a fact which, it need hardly be pointed out, was in undeniable correlation with the preceding data as to the large proportion of illegitimate unions. Everything, therefore, went to show that an alarmingly steady process of deperdition was going on in the native race—accelerated, no doubt, by the ravages of civil war and pestilence, but mainly due to the fearful waste of infant life resulting from ignorance and laxity of morals.[1]

I hasten to apologise for these dry statistics, than which nothing can be more repugnant to the general reader; but the figures I have used illustrate in a remarkable manner the rapid transformation taking place in the country, and more especially in its capital. Under the conditions they indicate, and which have been intensified by the marked increase of immigration in the last few years— probably half a million of intending settlers having landed here in the course of the last decade—the *bonâ fide* Argentine element must necessarily sink to a minority ; and though all children, of whatever nationality, born on the soil are claimed as Argentines, the character of the Buenos-Ayreans of the

---

[1] The mortality seems, according to an official statement, to be greater among infants of the male sex.

H

future cannot but be essentially modified by so large an infusion of foreign blood.

Up to the present time, as I have hinted before, the foreign communities have kept very much to themselves, and, unlike the settlers in the United States, have not blended with, or been absorbed in, the native population. It is both easy, therefore, and interesting to note their distinctive traits and individual character.

The sons of Italy—mostly Neapolitans or Ligurians—take by a long way the first rank as to numbers among them. They are pouring in now at the rate of over fifty thousand a year, and although a considerable percentage of them return to their homes after having made a little money, those who remain behind are so many and so ubiquitous as to have already given their stamp to the city. Chiefly recruited from the humblest classes, they are numerous rather than influential, and, thus far, constitute a kind of dormant force, which might, however, at any moment assert itself, and have to be reckoned with by the natives, who, up to the present time, have kept both government and administration almost exclusively in their own hands. The Italian colony have indeed at their head a highly intelligent and respectable class of merchants, shipbuilders, lawyers, and so forth ; but the great mass are labourers and artisans, and take to a variety of useful industries and occupations. Together with the equally laborious Basques, they almost monopolise the river coasting trade, and their boats ascend the mighty affluents of the Rio de la Plata far up to the remoter borders of Brazil and Paraguay.   Both in town and country they are largely employed in the building trade, as masons and as bricklayers.[2]   They are expert gardeners and agriculturists, they work as navvies on the railways and as porters in the towns, making themselves thoroughly useful wherever they go, and giving a bright example of thrift and persevering labour.

There is, of course, a rough element amongst them, and the better class contains not a few unquiet spirits whom political discontent or advanced social views have impelled to seek a refuge here. The great name of Garibaldi, and the traditions of his strange romantic career in these regions, no doubt originally contributed to attract them hither. They are almost all organised in philanthropic clubs and benevolent societies, which, under the cloak of charity and mutual help, are said not

---

[2] 'A friend of mine,' says Mr. Egerton, 'who bought land in a distant part of this province—but lately in Indian possession—told me that the Italian bricklayers made their appearance there nearly as soon as the person whom he had sent to take possession, and at once offered to build his house, the soil being in most parts of the province suitable for making flat bricks.'

entirely to exclude political aims and aspirations; but they are nevertheless always ready to acknowledge the authority of the official representatives, consular or diplomatic, of their country, and, in the hands of the able men whom the Italian Government have generally employed here, their very organisation affords a valuable means of control over them. One of the most respected of these officials explained to me one day that in cases of emergency he had only to send for the presidents of these associations, some of which reach very far down in the social scale, and talk matters over with them, in order to secure the most complete harmony in the colony. There is no doubt that this method was most beneficially resorted to during the recent civil commotions.

The love of country strongly pervades this well-ordered and praiseworthy community. Striking evidence of this was given on the occasion of the death of King Victor Emmanuel. The entire colony then turned out in full force and marched in procession, with their national flags and the banners of their several associations, to the church where a funeral service was held in memory of the first sovereign of United Italy. Although formed in serried ranks, they took up a dozen of the *cuadras,* or blocks of 150 yards square, into which the city is divided, the dense column extending to upwards

of a mile in length. In the same way they gathered
in their thousands at the death of General Garibaldi. These imposing displays of organised force
on the part of a foreign, however peaceable,
element residing in their midst are said to have
greatly impressed the native population and authorities.

Some parts of Buenos Ayres, and more particularly the outlying districts of Barracas and the
Boca, are in fact almost exclusively Italian. The
Boca—so called from its being built at the mouth
of the Riachuelo, a small river that falls about five
miles from the city into the River Plate—might,
with its swarming population of shipwrights and
fishermen and carpenters, be to all appearance a
suburb of Naples or Genoa. A tramway, as well
as the railroad to Ensenada, unites it to the city,
and it well repays a visit. The stream, which for
many years literally ran with the gore and was
choked with the offal of the thousands of beasts
slaughtered in the adjoining *saladeros*, has been
canalised since the terrible visitation of so-called
yellow fever [3] that afflicted the city in 1871,[4] and

---

[3] It is very doubtful whether this plague can be properly termed
yellow fever. Its reported importation from Brazil was never, I am
assured, actually proved, and it is far more likely to have originated
in local causes.

[4] These *saladeros*, where as many as 10,000 head of cows and
mares were sometimes slaughtered in one day, were then closed by

the origin of which was attributed to its putrid waters. To its quays the craft employed in the river traffic are moored in such numbers as almost entirely to conceal the channel, and you wonder, as you walk along and scan all these closely packed barques and schooners which are disgorging baskets of fruit or bales of *yerba maté*, or taking in cases of wine and beer and preserves, how they will ever manage to get out and slip away into the broad waters beyond. It is a singularly bright and busy scene, and, were it not for the uniforms of a *vigilante* (policeman) or two who are lounging on the quay, might well be laid in some Italian seaport. The shouts and vociferations of the men at work, the names and inscriptions on the ships and stores, the whole character and colouring of the scene, foster the illusion. A more perfect bit of dear, untidy, picturesque *marina* is hardly to be found on all the fair Ligurian coast, or on those still lovelier shores where 'Vesuvius shows his blaze.'

Adjoining the Boca are the populous suburbs of Barracas and Santa Lucia; the latter standing on a gentle slope which leads to the higher level of the town. The lower part of Barracas, with its great warehouses of hides and wool, is likewise

the authorities, and transferred to Ensenada and other distant points (Mulhall, *Repúblicas del Plata*).

almost purely Italian; while the upper part, as well as Santa Lucia, principally consists of villa residences belonging to rich natives. Here stands the striking church built in expiation of the murder of Doña Felicitas Alzaga. It was pointed out to me by E——, who told me its story, which, although of comparatively recent occurrence, is fast growing into a dark and mournful legend of the past.

The victim was a young and very beautiful creature, belonging to one of the best families of the country, who had been made to marry against her will—her affections being already bestowed elsewhere—a man much older than herself who owned a very large fortune. She was soon released from this ill-assorted union by the death of her husband, who left the whole of his immense property at her absolute disposal. With her recovered freedom and the fortune that made her independent of all control, her thoughts naturally turned to the man whom she loved, and she shortly became engaged to him.

Meanwhile, however, another admirer, a man not of the best repute, began persecuting her with his attentions, and repeatedly urged her to marry him, though she as persistently refused him.

One evening he called at the house at Santa Lucia and asked to see her alone. She left an aunt, who lived with her, in the dining-room where they were having their evening meal, and went to join him in the drawing-room upstairs. What passed between them at this interview no one can tell; but before long two shots were heard, and the aunt and servants running up in alarm found the wretched girl and her assassin dead or dying, the villain still holding a revolver in his hand. There is some obscurity as to the manner in which he came by his death, one version being that the accepted lover came in on hearing the fatal shot fired, and at once avenged the deed, the theory of suicide on the part of the murderer being allowed to obtain currency in order to screen the avenger. In the grounds of the house where the terrible crime was committed, the heirs of the victim erected this beautiful church to her memory.

But to go back to this cursory review of the foreign communities. The next in numbers and importance are the French and Spanish, and these two have a common bond in the Basque element from both sides of the Pyrenees, of which they are largely composed.

The Basques form so conspicuous a group by themselves that they are well entitled to separate mention. They furnish one of the most energetic and valuable ingredients to be found among the many races and nationalities which are represented here. As a rule, they come out with their families

and household goods, and resolutely settle down to
their work without any of the *animus revertendi*
with which a number of their fellow-immigrants
arrive here. It is indeed curious to note how
kindly these men from mountainous regions take
to the insipid plain. Their natural bent is towards
cattle-tending and rural industry, and as dairymen
they have secured one of the most lucrative branches
of the latter, and are almost the only retail vendors
of milk and butter. The figure of the brawny
lechero, with his typical flat blue *béret*, perched
astraddle between his milkcans on a very sorry
steed, and ambling on his rounds along the streets
and country roads, is the first that strikes one on
landing. The Basque also works, however, at
rougher and more repugnant trades, and, thanks to
his great physical strength, his services as a formidable slaughterer and *cuartero* [5] are both highly
prized and highly paid in the staple industry of
the country. A simple and somewhat dull race of
men, of frugal habits and few wants, the Basques
have a marked capacity for patient toil of all kinds,
and in some instances have amassed considerable
wealth as a reward for their industry. Among
other things they are capital gardeners. I had

---

[5] *Cuartero* is the technical designation given in the *saladeros* to
the *peon* who, after the beast has been felled and half cut up by
the *desnucador* (literally neck-, or nape-breaker), finally dismembers
its carcass with the axe.

one in my employ for some time who was the most painstaking and hardworking of men, but, alas! too, the dirtiest. He was devoted to his flowers, and such fustiness in constant contact with such fragrance was a standing puzzle to me.

The Basque immigration—which is said to have greatly fallen off of late as regards the French side of the mountains—is of old standing in the River Plate. The first of them must have come out within a very few years of the declaration of independence, and at once have shown great enterprise, for, as early as 1826, they are reputed to have founded the now rising little town of Tandil, far away in the south, in what was then, and remained till quite lately, a purely Indian zone. Possibly they may have been attracted thither by the range of hills which traverses that district and the old Indian territory as far as Curamalal, under the name of Sierra de Tandil and Sierra de la Ventana, and is the only excrescence to be found on this side of the continent from the Rio de la Plata down to the Straits of Magellan. These hills contain, by the way, that singular phenomenon of natural equilibrium, the *piedra movediza*, or rocking-stone—a huge boulder which stands on end and sways to and fro with the least breath of wind. Mulhall states that Rosas tried to throw it down by harnessing ' a thousand horses' to it ; all the king's horses and all the king's men failing in the attempt as utterly as they did in their more laudable efforts on another occasion.

Talking of Rosas, the Basques of French nationality had evil times to go through, with the rest of their countrymen, in the days of that Dictator, with whom everything that was French was in great disfavour, on account of the hostile attitude taken up towards him by the July monarchy. In one of his craziest moods he actually issued a decree for the solemn military degradation of the old patron saint of Buenos Ayres, St. Martin of Tours, on the ground of that warlike apostle of the Gauls being a Frenchman—which, *par parenthèse*, he was not, having been born in Pannonia, or, as we should say now, Austria. He likewise habitually headed his proclamations (printed in flaming red characters) with : 'Death to the Unitarian [6] savages ! Death to the filthy (*asquerosos*) French ! Death to the unclean pig (*chancho inmundo*), Louis-Philippe !'

After the tyrant's fall in 1852, the immigration from France took a fresh start, and at present the French hold an important rank among the foreign communities. There are probably some 40,000 of

---

[6] There is no need to remind the reader that the Dictator was the incarnation of Federalism as opposed to the consolidation of the different states under one national government.

them in the town and province of Buenos Ayres, and the natural leaning of the natives being towards French forms of civilisation and luxury, the capital has in consequence acquired, in some respects, a decidedly Parisian aspect. The community stands, too, on a much higher level than other offshoots from the mother country elsewhere. Physicians and lawyers, professors and literary men find a ready welcome and lucrative employment here, and help to imbue the Porteño upper class with French modes of thought and French habits and tendencies. The principal shops for articles of dress or furniture and the many other requirements of a rich and luxurious class are, as a matter of course, kept by Frenchmen, as are also most of the numerous confectioners' shops, restaurants, and hotels—the last, I am bound to say, doing them but little credit. French capital is, besides, invested in a variety of undertakings, such as carriage-works, dyeing-works, steam grinding-mills, manufactories of linseed and other oils—none of them on a large scale, but all fairly profitable. Bieckert's Brewery, on the other hand, is a very big concern indeed, conducted on the model of the largest establishments of the kind in Europe, and capable of turning out thousands of dozens of beer a day. At the foot of the slope on which it stands is a large public garden, where a charity fair—

called 'la fête de St.-Cloud,' after the well-known popular fair near Paris—is held every year, the very large proceeds of which are divided among the different philanthropic associations, of which, like the Italians, the French have a most creditable show.

French industry in this place has been seriously threatened since 1870 by German, and more recently Italian, competition, but it still manages to hold its own; and in fact the whole history of the community goes some way to prove that it is a fallacy to look upon the Frenchman abroad as being wanting in the spirit of enterprise or disinclined to the exertions which have made other settlers so valuable in new countries. The French Basques were among the first to devote their attention to the improvement of the breed of almost wild native cattle. They were also the first to export the rough native wool, which at that time (in 1842) was considered so worthless as only to fetch five centimes (a halfpenny) a kilo, and now, thanks of course to an immense improvement in quality, is worth from one to two shillings in the place of production. It is claimed too, with what reason I cannot say, that M. Antoine Cambacérès, a relative of Napoleon's Arch-Chancellor, was the originator of the *saladeros*.

The natives of Spain are numerous, both in the

town and province, but owing to their close affinity with the indigenous element they are scarcely to be distinguished from it. Many of them are small shopkeepers or publicans, and most of the *pulperías* (country taverns) in the camp are owned by them. They are also great market-gardeners and tillers of the soil. Besides those who settle in the country, without, however, giving up their nationality, there is a large migratory class—chiefly Catalans—who of late years have taken to coming out for the spring and summer field-work of this Southern Hemisphere, going back again in time to resume the same labour in their native homes. Many of the Southern Italians come out in the same way, the new line of steamers from Genoa carrying them backwards and forwards at extremely low rates. These adventurous husbandmen thus obtain lucrative employment all the year round, at the cost, it is true, of a journey of three weeks twice a year across the broad Atlantic.[7]

The Germans have a rising community out here, which is well looked after by the official representatives of the empire, and presents the creditable national traits of concord and good-fellowship which are generally to be met with

[7] Mr. Egerton, in his report before quoted, states that the return third-class fare in these Italian steamers costs about 14*l.*, the men coming out here in October and going home in March.

among the sons of the Fatherland in foreign countries. They are engaged almost exclusively in trade, and can therefore scarcely be accounted as colonists in the same sense as the Basques or the Italians, or our own people from the Three Kingdoms. The German sticks almost entirely to the towns, where he trades very carefully, making considerable profits against a relatively small expenditure, and leading a life of studied self-denial, relieved by cheerful social meetings at choral unions, gymnastic clubs, and such like, which do much to keep up the tone and harmony of the community. A quiet, unobtrusive, but by no means uninfluential body of men, who steadily act up to the punning precept inculcated by the Iron Chancellor on one of his diplomatists whom he was sending out to South American regions :—' to seek trade and beware of (international) difficulties' (*suchen Sie Handel, aber ja keine Händel!*)

This, I much fear, tedious survey of the foreign communities must be concluded with our own people, who, obeying, it would seem, the same influences that keep the different nationalities out here apart in so marked a manner, themselves form three distinct groups, and have to be separately classed as English, Scotch, and Irish. And here one is at once bound to give precedence to the Irish, who, besides being the most numerous, are unquestionably the most successful, of all our settlers in the River Plate. In some respects indeed they are more prosperous than any of the other foreign bodies. There are among them men who, having originally come out with scarcely a shirt to their back, are now the owners of league upon league of well-stocked land, and rank with the largest proprietors in the country. The Irish were the first to take seriously to sheep-farming out here, and they have so successfully developed that branch of rural industry that it is claimed that their flocks produce one half of the wool which is exported from this province. Yet, barely forty years ago, the sheep was looked upon as relatively worthless,[8] and to Irishmen is mainly due the credit of having reclaimed that valuable animal from the contempt and degradation into which it had fallen. The native breed had so degenerated under the neglect of three centuries,[9] that among the Gauchos not only was the wretched sheep utterly despised as an article of food, but no better use was found for him than to kill him—after stripping him of his fleece—in order to dry his carcass and throw it as fuel into the brick-kilns. To this day, it may be observed, the prejudice against mutton still

[8] As recently as fifteen years ago the current value of sheep was about half a crown a head, and of cattle sixteen shillings a head.

[9] It need not be pointed out that the sheep, like the ox and the horse, was introduced by the Spaniards.

survives among the pure natives, whose exclusively
meat diet consists entirely of beef.

There is little doubt that the Irish owe their
fortunate beginnings in a great measure to the
good influence and judicious direction of their
clergy. Submissive as they always have been to
the voice of their pastors, they were positively
blessed in some of the priests who first came out
with them. One of them, Father Fahy, seems to
have wielded much the same kind of authority
over them one reads of in the story of the missionaries who accompanied the first French settlers in
Canada, or of the Jesuit fathers who, much about
the same time, began to work such wonders among
the Guaranis of Paraguay and the adjacent regions.
Father Fahy appears not only to have been the
trusted adviser of many of his countrymen, but to
have constantly acted as their banker and agent,
and, owing to his shrewd counsel, their investments
became from the outset so profitable that prosperity
seems never to have deserted them since. The Irish
have, in short, proved as great a success and as
valuable an element in the River Plate as they have
been in so many ways a failure in North America.
They own almost entire districts in the north and
centre of the province of Buenos Ayres, where
they have endowed chaplaincies, and founded
schools of their own with libraries attached to

them ; and altogether they present an aspect so different from that of their brethren in 'the distressful country' at home, that one cannot but think that a providential outlet is offered to them in these regions. A distinguished compatriot of theirs, who is one of the principal church dignitaries at Buenos Ayres, warmly advocates their coming to this country, and a short time ago undertook a journey to Ireland with the view of furthering emigration from thence on a large scale. He did so in part at the instance of the national Government, who are very desirous to induce more Irish settlers to try their fortunes on Argentine soil.

In so well-to-do a community there is but small scope for political agitation. The little Ireland we have out here, although intensely national in feeling, is by no means disloyal. An attempt made a short time ago by an emissary from the Fenian organisation in the United States to form a centre in this country entirely failed. Nor has the Land League, so far, been more successful in its efforts to obtain funds and support from hence. There is good reason to believe that the priests at once set their faces against all such schemes.

It would, at the same time, be absurd to pretend that the national movement finds no response among the Argentine Irish. Indeed, the leading foreign newspaper, which is in well-known and able Irish hands, lately opened its columns to a subscription in aid of the Parnell Defence Fund. It so happens that one of the contributors to this fund, an Irish *estanciero* on the borders of the province of Santa Fé, had the full significance of the movement forcibly brought home to him shortly afterwards by threatening letters from his Irish tenants demanding a reduction of rent, which were soon followed up by the burning down of buildings and stacks on his property.

Next to the Irish come the Scotch, who, as a rule, have done well, as they do wherever they go. The majority of them are prosperously settled in the southern part of this province, though a certain number who tried their hand in Northern Entre-Rios, and lighted there upon pastures not so well suited for sheep, have not been as successful. The Scotch, above all, count in their ranks some of the most distinguished *estancieros* in the country—men who from the beginning devoted themselves to improving and refining the native breeds by the importation of the choicest stock from Europe, and have thus produced herds and flocks that can compare with the finest of their kind anywhere.

The Englishman must come last, I fear, on the list, and take rank after his fellow-subjects of the sister kingdoms. Not that he has been wanting in those qualities which everywhere else have made him the prince of colonists. On the contrary he was to be met from the first at the advanced posts and in the most exposed situations, tilling the ground and raising cattle, rifle in hand, in the evil days when the Indian plague was still at its worst. But the very daring of his first ventures in some instances led to disastrous, and sometimes tragical, failure, as in the massacres at Fraile Muerto.

Many of the young Englishmen who were first tempted to come out were perhaps scarcely fitted, by birth or education, for a hard life of unremitting toil and severe privation. Some of them went home in disgust, while, of those who struggled on, not a few took to drowning their cares in whisky, or *caña*,[1] or fell into the toils of the native *chinas*,[2] and speedily sank to the level of the ordinary Gaucho. These failures threw for a time an unfavourable light on English immigration, and somewhat checked it; but though the English hardly form a compact and flourishing community as clearly marked as in the case of their Irish and Scotch fellow-subjects, they hold their own both in trade and farming. Of their great services as engineers and railway contractors enough has been

[1] An inferior kind of white rum made from the sugar-cane and imported from Brazil.

[2] The name commonly given to women of the lower orders, mostly of half Indian descent.

said elsewhere. In Buenos Ayres itself all the Queen's subjects now happily amalgamate more and more in literary and debating societies, or for purposes of sport, as in the cricket and boating clubs, or in philanthropic institutions, like the British Hospital or the Charitable Fund—the latter of very recent foundation. Only the other day, too, the entire community, without distinction of class or country, united in giving a thoroughly magnificent reception to the flying squadron with the young princes.

More than enough has been said to show how important and all-pervading the foreign element has become in this republic. When it is further considered that its peaceful invasion commenced barely thirty years ago, and that already two-thirds of the soil, in this province of Buenos Ayres alone,[3] may be safely said to be in its hands, some idea will be formed of the rapidity and extent of its conquests. Previous to the advent of the new-comers, most of the best land was held in immense estates by the descendants of the original colonial owners, who either dwelt on it in very primitive fashion, without any attempt at improving it or developing its resources, or, if—as was frequently the case—they preferred the charms of city life in

[3] The area of the province is 63,000 square miles, or more than one half of that of the entire United Kingdom.

Buenos Ayres, left it, like the old Russian Boyards, to the mismanagement and rapacity of their stewards and major-domos.   With a few exceptions these large properties have now been broken up, and have passed into the hands of the foreign colonists. The transfer of real property, and with it the transformation of this province in particular, has in fact been almost complete, and it coincides with the enlightened rule of President Sarmiento (1868–1874), which did more than anything to attract the vast influx of productive capital and productive labour, thanks to which a country, which up to then was relatively poor and torn by internal dissensions, has been launched on its present career of peace and great promise.   For not only has the foreigner the greater part of the soil and of the commerce of the country in his hands, but he controls the exchanges, regulates the markets, and provides the capital for nearly all the industrial and financial undertakings that have been started of late years.

Such being his means of influence and the material stake he holds in the country, it seems at first sight unaccountable that he should abstain so carefully from any interference in its public affairs.   The explanation is not far to seek. Although the Constitution admits all aliens to the same civil and municipal rights as natives, only those who have become naturalised citizens are eligible for office under the State or are entitled to sit in the National or Provincial Legislatures. The immigrant is thus practically debarred from any share in local politics, and he has hitherto only too gladly kept aloof from the party intrigues and the corrupt wire-pulling by which they are too often characterised. It may be questioned now whether, in justice to their interests, the foreign communities should rest content much longer with such a state of things. Recent events have shown that the era of civil contention cannot with absolute certainty be said to be closed for good, and it might perhaps be well that the leaders of the foreign bodies should claim the full privileges of citizenship, and frankly throw in their lot with the country they have adopted and are fashioning more and more with their hands. Their weight would be infallibly thrown on the side of order and concord, and would be more than sufficient to check the restless spirit of change, and the tendency to military *pronunciamientos* which still survive among the natives and have ever been the bane of that strange Spanish race, so incomprehensibly made up of noble, indeed heroic, qualities and glaring weaknesses and defects.

The local press has itself lately started a discussion as to whether the time has not come for modifying the naturalisation law, so as to induce a greater number of immigrants to apply for Argentine citizenship. Some writers go the length of proposing that naturalisation should be to a certain extent compulsory after a given period of residence. The Government are wise enough to withhold their countenance from these projects. A very high official, with whom I conversed on the subject, told me that he would consider it highly impolitic to touch the question at present, for it would only check the immigration of which the country still stands in such need. The persons, he said, who were in favour of, to some degree, forcing the Argentine nationality upon foreigners, always quoted the example of the United States, which was absurd. Great numbers of those who emigrated from Europe did so to avoid the burdens of military service, and they naturally went to, and became citizens of, a country where no such service was required of them. This he believed to be one of the main causes of the United States being the favourite resort of the European emigrant. When this country could show a clear era of twenty years' peace, the same inducements would exist for emigrating to it and adopting its nationality. But this could not be expected at present, with the unfortunately well-founded reputation of the republic for disorder and civil strife.

A period of peace and quiet would modify all that, and meanwhile the sons of foreigners born on the soil brought fresh blood into the nation and certainly became very patriotic Argentines.

These remarks struck me by their fairness and candour. At the same time, it must be borne in mind that the number of foreigners over here is already so large that they are unquestionably viewed with suspicion by the natives, and an attempt to confer the full rights of citizenship on them by some comprehensive measure would probably meet with considerable opposition.

Nevertheless, the foreign question must surely ere long come to the front. There is some talk of a so-called gathering of the Latin race on the occasion of the projected Italian National Exhibition to be held here. It is said—of course with some exaggeration—that the different Italian, French, and Spanish societies and corporations will take that opportunity to march past to the number of from eighty to one hundred thousand. It is difficult not to believe that at no distant period the destinies of this country must be in great measure controlled by other races than the native.

CHAPTER VII.

BELGRANO—MY GARDEN AND ITS NEIGHBOURHOOD—SAAVEDRA.

I WAS of course anxious to be out of stuffy quarters, in what was at best a second-rate inn, as soon as possible.   Unfortunately it is no easy matter to lodge oneself in Buenos Ayres, and summer now drawing on apace I was strongly advised to look for something suitable outside the town.

Even there, however, the choice is almost limited to one or two places like Flores or Belgrano, which, although at some distance, are practically suburbs of the city, so conveniently are they joined on to it by trams and railways. There is a still greater difficulty in getting a furnished house, which, in my case, was an absolute necessity, as I had come out altogether in light marching order, reckoning with some certainty on my residence in the River Plate not being a very lengthy one.

One fine Sunday afternoon in October I started, in company of mine own particular friend and adviser, in quest of what I needed, and, having previously explored Flores in vain, we bent our steps towards Belgrano, taking one of the tram-cars that run to that place from the Plaza Vittoria up the Florida. I had heard of two houses there which had lately been in the occupation of members of the British community and seemed likely to suit.

After ascending the busy Florida and skirting the gardens of the Retiro, the tram plunges into a poorer part of the town, passing along interminable streets, lined with low houses devoid of any character, till it emerges on a broad and ill-kept highway, and, after a run of five or six miles or so, terminates in the main street of Belgrano. The first house we went to see in this thoroughfare proving not available, we struck across into narrower streets of villa residences, all laid out as usual at right angles, and running towards the *barranca* or cliff—if cliff a shelving height of some fifty feet can be rightly termed—on which the town is raised in full view of the giant river, the banks of which lie about three quarters of a mile off. These villas, or *quintas*, are each of them enclosed by crumbling walls of sun-dried bricks, with here and there an aperture revealing the buildings and grounds within. Besides these dead walls, most of the streets are lined with trees, so that the whole place, with its sombre, neglected avenues, in which hardly a soul is to be seen stirring, at first conveys the impression of a large necropolis, the frequent cypresses which rear their funereal heads above the enclosures still further lending themselves to the lugubrious fancy. Passing glimpses, however, through gateways or gaps in the walls, reveal a wealth of flower-beds inside these dismal enclosures. The porticoes and house-fronts are thickly hung with the brightest of creepers—the scarlet and purple bougainvilleas, the wistaria, or clusters of banksia roses—and the air is full of the rich scent of the double jessamine and the magnolia. As yet it is too early, according to the seasons of the Southern Hemisphere, for the gardens to be at their best—mid-October answering here to mid-April—but the abundant rains of spring have made what green there is singularly fresh, and have kept down the dust, in which all will soon be smothered for months. Passing through *cuadra*, or square upon square of these depressing avenues, we at last get to the edge of the *barranca*, which forms a natural terrace, fringed with a row of much more cheerful *quintas*, whose frontages face freely riverwards, or rather ocean-wards—for such is the effect produced to the eye by the huge and ever-changing estuary.

A corner, one-storied house here, surmounted

A VILLA AT BELGRANO.

by a low square turret, is the one to which we
have been directed, and at first sight it seems to
be the very thing we seek. Its present occupier
happens to be at home and at leisure. The rooms
are convenient in size and number, as well as comfortably furnished, and as everything as it stands
—including plate, crockery, and linen—can be had
on fairly reasonable terms, the bargain is concluded
in a very few minutes. The house, by the way,
is not without a history, having been built by
an Argentine who had held very high office in
the State, and who spent his last days under its
roof. It has a charming marble portico, divided
from the pavement by an elaborate ornamental
iron railing. and, above all, a delightful enclosure at
the back—half flower-garden and half orchard—a
peep into which at once puts an end to any doubts
I may have had as to the excellence of the arrangement I have entered into. A broad, stone-flagged
verandah, resting on wooden pillars and partly
covered in by a trellised and vine-clad roof, runs
along the back of the house and leads *de plain pied*
into this garden, which has no trees of any great
size to show, with the exception of a few fine
acacias and laburnums and a couple of magnificent
magnolias, but is laid out in trim narrow walks,
bordered by luxuriant flowering bushes sufficiently
high to afford ample shade from any but a vertical

sun, and with its wealth of roses and heliotrope and verbena is as fragrant a little spot as can well be imagined. There seems to me to be a special sweetness in the scent of South American flowers, just as on the other hand there is a decided want of flavour in South American fruit. My garden to be is at the same time a most abundant orchard, stocked with strawberries and currants and raspberries, not to mention numerous cherry and pear trees. A Basque gardener attached to the house keeps the bright cheerful spot in very fair order.

Why, I wonder, away here at the Antipodes, does it remind me so of the fatal garden in 'Faust'? Yet it somehow does, and in the long moonlit evenings, as I lounge and muse in my verandah, and watch the tremulous shadows cast by the tall currant-bushes across the white, glistening paths, I almost expect to see the pair of lovers come round that turn by the magnolia tree, a silver ray just glancing off the tresses of Gretchen as she passes on, with bent head, listening to the words murmured into her all too ready ear.

But these dramatic reminiscences might almost, I fear, lead to the conclusion that my *jardinet* has a stagy appearance: its characteristic charm to me, as well as the reason of its conjuring up the scene of that far-off German love-tragedy, on the contrary being a certain prim formality, a simple old-world air which would well befit that quiet nook, nestling in the shadow of frowning mediæval ramparts, where Frau Martha doubtless had her garden and her *Laube*, and whither the orphan neighbour's child must have come back day after day with heavy heart to dream and weep when ' her rest was gone,' poor soul ! for ever.

One real eyesore the place, on the other hand, contains, in the shape of a large ornamental fountain of cast-iron of most pretentious design, which, besides being a wretched sham to begin with—since it is waterless and does not perform its proper functions—is utterly out of proportion and harmony with its surroundings. A memento this of the original owner, by whom it had no doubt been ordered from Europe for the adornment of some public square, and finally forgotten here without even trouble being taken to turn it to useful account. But queer stories could be told of similar and more lavish orders for ' works of art ' given abroad, and of the fate which sometimes attends them.

Another and more pleasing feature my garden has, which, however, is likewise not in keeping with the *mise en scène* of that tragic story, playing, as it does, under sober Northern skies. In the hottest hours of the day, when even the shrill *cicada* holds its peace, there will flash across the broad patches of sunlight what seems the sparkle of a gem. Keep quite still and watch, and you will see it again. There it goes darting over the path into that pear-tree. Some humming-birds have built their nest in a corner of the garden, and the timid little creatures show themselves now and then, though very seldom. So far south as these latitudes I believe them to be rather an uncommon sight, and, at any rate, they invest my modest little cabbage-garden with an air of tropical splendour it certainly could not otherwise pretend to.

Against these brilliant little beings must be set the leaf-cutting ants, who, to the despair of my Basque gardener and of his ally E——, who takes a deep interest in the garden, play the very mischief with it. These extremely destructive, but remark-able insects carefully build their nest—an enormous one—in the most inaccessible places underground ; in this instance under the foundations of the house. The only way of driving them out and getting rid of the plague is by constantly pouring tar down the holes—when you have found them, which is no easy matter—by which they issue forth from their stronghold. E—— did this persistently, and finally succeeded, but not till after they had ac-complished wonders of destruction in their way. The little rascals entirely stripped a pomegranate tree in one single night. They worked divided in two bands; the leaf-cutters proper going up the tree and letting the strips of leaves fall down, while the carriers below picked them up and bore them away on their backs to the granary.

One more feature of the garden, and I have done. The house, as I have said, is not in the least raised above its grounds at the back, but on a complete level with them, which is in many ways a serious drawback to it as a habitation. In the not unfrequent days of wet *pampero*—dirty *pampero* (*pampero sucio*), as it is termed—or in the still more evil days when it blows from the north and it rains in torrents for hours together, the broad verandah is more than half flooded, the water reaching the doors of some of the living-rooms, and a hot, steamy dampness pervading the whole house, to the ruin of one's clothes and especially one's boots. But the rooms are thereby exposed to far more repulsive inroads than those of damp and mildew. One night, just as I had got into bed after one of these heavy downpours, I was disturbed by a horrid sound—half bark and half croak—which clearly proceeded from somebody or something inside the room. I struck a light, and, after a careful search under the bed and the furniture, at last traced the unearthly sound to a corner where stood a large clothes-basket, near the outer door, which had only been shut late in the evening.

K

I moved this basket aside, and to my utter horror and disgust found myself face to face with an enormous spotted yellow toad—certainly as big as the inside of a soup-plate—which had strayed into captivity, and was uttering these mournful appeals for delivery from behind the rampart which shut it in, like the 'buck-basket' of that other noisome creature the fat knight of Windsor. I seized a stick and drove the loathsome monster out into the garden, which, as a set-off to its other denizens, the dear little *picaflores*, unfortunately harboured plenty of his fellows, though I never again got sight of any of such portentous size and hideousness.

One of these violent storms from the north in summer is a thing to be remembered. The sheets of water that come down perfectly straight, all through the day and night, without a break, are accompanied by equally continuous thunder and lightning, which seem to work their way right round the heavens and to box the entire compass. The thunder is one unceasing muffled roll, out of which burst sudden fierce claps of deafening violence; the lightning playing meanwhile almost uninterruptedly at every point of the horizon, and leaping forth now and then into a great scorching flame, which for a moment lights up the whole world with a lurid blue and yellow. The darkness,

too, is very striking, and almost equals that of a
dense London fog ; while the heat seems to increase
rather than to yield with the storm, and one sits
as in a prolonged vapour-bath, with the most
trying sense of physical prostration and depression
of spirits.   These storms, in fact, do not in the
least clear the atmosphere, and relief only comes
when the wind veers round to the south-east, and
brings with it a renewed feeling of vigour and
elasticity, as marked as were the languor and de-
jection before.

Far more appalling, however, than these tempests of rain must have been the dust-storms, which
now, thanks to the enormous increase of cultivation, have almost ceased to visit the neighbourhood
of Buenos Ayres, but in the memory of the older
residents used periodically to sweep over that city.
It so happened that, going into town by train one
sultry afternoon to attend to some business, I came
in for a small sample of what one of these tor-
nados must have been like. As we drew near the
terminus, I noticed a remarkable bank of cloud of
inky blackness, which hung very low down over
the city in a south-westerly direction.   I got out
at the Retiro station, and before I had walked up
the short distance of some eight hundred yards
to the house I was going to at the top of the
Florida, the blackness had already spread nearly

over the entire sky, while the air, which up to then had been strangely and oppressively still and motionless, was agitated by sudden gusts of wind of great violence.

On reaching the door, and before turning in to go upstairs, I could see that the neighbours in the houses opposite were all busy fastening their windows and shop-doors. In a couple of minutes more the darkness had deepened to such an extent that it seemed to be a rapid dying-out of the very principle of light. The buildings over the way faded almost out of sight, the room in which I stood was as dark behind me as if the shutters had been closed, and a moving mass of solid, and yet impalpable, matter whirled mightily past the windows, and, as it went by, seemed to fill up all space. This lasted, fortunately, only for a very short time. The wind ceased as suddenly and completely as it had risen, and presently shifted round to the south-east, and in less than an hour all was bright and clear again. The tables and furniture, meanwhile, were completely covered by a thick layer of the finest dust, and this work of a few minutes sufficiently showed what must have been the effect of one of these visitations of old on the inhabitants, kept pent up for hours in their dwellings, with everything tight closed and barred, and as good as stifled by the whirlwinds of

tangible Cimmerian darkness rushing in through
every hole and crevice, which could only be compared to the rain of ashes that engulfed Pompeii,
or the dread simoom by which so many a stout
caravan has been overwhelmed.

The range of low sandy hillocks, rising at the
most some fifty or sixty feet above the water-level,
on which Belgrano stands, must in former times
have marked the wash of the great river which,
ages ago, receded from it, leaving an intervening
space or valley, in some parts from one to two
miles broad. These heights are, in fact, the abrupt
edge of the huge plateau which stretches away to
the rear and finally merges into the boundless
Pampa. Running with varying elevation, and in
broken outline, from the outskirts of the city to
the waters of the Tigre, some thirty kilometres off,
this paltry ridge produces, by sheer force of contrast, all the effect of a range of real hills or cliffs·
From the railway, that skirts its base, it offers
indeed a decidedly picturesque appearance. Substantial old Spanish manor-houses, with square white
towers that remind one of the *casini* of Northern
Italy, or more modern villas with terraced gardens and colonnades all covered over with vines,
crown the summit at frequent intervals and in
well-selected spots, each one standing in its little
grove or clump of trees, with sloping orchards and

meadows straggling down the hill. All these rural retreats get the full benefit of the river breezes, and on this account, and from their being within easy reach of the stores and offices in town, are much sought after by the foreign business community. Were the railroad that works the district only better managed—and although an exclusively British undertaking, it was in my time, I am sorry to say, a rare specimen of how things ought not to be done, what with its unpunctual trains, dilapidated rolling-stock, heavy tariff, and irrational time-table—there is little doubt that this neighbourhood would be still more thickly peopled. As it was, the morning and late afternoon trains were crammed with passengers going to and from their daily business in hides and wool, and the traffic at those hours would have done credit to any suburban line in one of our great mercantile centres at home.

The prospect one has from these houses perched up on high is, for so essentially unpicturesque a region, decidedly pleasing. In fine weather, when I did most of my reading and writing seated at a marble table under the front portico, the scene that lay stretched out before me when I looked up from my work was certainly not without attractions. Half a dozen very large *ombús*,[1] the only

[1] *Pircunia dioica*, according to the nomenclature given in the

indigenous tree that grows to any size in the Pampa region, studded the broken foreground and gave a park-like aspect to its declivity. These trees make up for their utter worthlessness as timber by the beauty of their spreading foliage and their strangely gnarled and rugged trunks. They are frequently quite hollow—mere shells of trees, harbouring legions of ants and other insect tribes—the soft, white, fibreless wood being hardly fit even for making matches: in fact, splendid shams that would scarcely be tolerated in any but so treeless a country as this, although, with their weird and tortured shapes, they are worthy of the pencil of a Doré, and would make admirable studies for some enchanted forest such as the 'wild woods of Broceliande.' At the foot of the hill a pretty villa or two with brilliant flower-gardens are grouped round the railway-station, the line of rail itself being marked by a green fringe of *paraiso* trees and stunted willows and eucalyptus, with *ceibo* bushes all hung with bright scarlet flowers. Beyond this, again, comes a long flat reach of rank grass, with shallow pools of stagnant water here and there, stretching down to the edge of the gleaming river. A straggling settlement of low, whitewashed cabins, and of *ranchos* thatched in with branches, lies

official handbook of the republic compiled for the Philadelphia Exhibition.

scattered all over this low, swampy ground, and between them roam and browse at their free will a seemingly countless number of cows and horses.

But the ocean-like river itself, and the constantly changing sky above it; the splendour of the sunsets; the wondrous colour of the deep-blue arch mirrored in the smooth majestic tide, or the wild shadows cast on it by tempest-driven clouds; the fiery glory of noontide on the burnished waters, or the marvellous transparency of the cool starlit nights—in these was the one never-failing attraction. Nor were life and movement wanting to complete the picture. The outlook over the river took in all the outer anchorage of Buenos Ayres where lay the big ocean-bound steamers; all the intermediate expanse of dancing, glistening water being crowded with white-winged craft speeding to and from them with living freights of traders or emigrants, or cargoes of hides and tallow and wool. It was a bright and busy scene, and I might well have gazed at it with placid content but for those big hulls in the far distance, which, one by one, moved off and sank 'beneath the wave' on their way back to the land whence I had so lately come —not all too readily perhaps—and where I had left all I cared for and thought of as I gazed.

There is no denying that life at Belgrano was on the whole contemplative, and would have been slightly monotonous but for the frequent visits to town and an occasional excursion along the line to San Isidro or on to the Tigre, which helped to diversify it.

The latter spot is the head-quarters of the Buenos Ayres Boating Club, and in hot weather it was delightful to run down there in the fore-noon and spend the day sculling lazily upon the river, which, with its numerous creeks and chan-nels and the countless green islands embosomed in its placid waters, is the freshest, most restful spot I know of in the whole of the River Plate region. It is the abode, too, of myriads of wildfowl, and as such the paradise of the Porteño sportsman. Much bigger game used to frequent it, and up till quite a recent period the jaguar, or tiger as they miscall him here, found his way down from the Gran Chaco to these waters in such numbers as to give his name to the district. It is now infested by nothing more dangerous than a plague of mosquitos, of exceptional size and ferocity, that must be a terrible drawback to the many charm-ing *quintas* built here of late. Nevertheless it is thickly inhabited, among others by the French colony of Buenos Ayres, and up the quiet reaches of the river are to be found restaurants and *buvettes*, kept by enterprising French Basques, with shady gardens down by the water's edge, where one can land and indulge in a *friture* or a *matelote* not unworthy of the Île de Croissy or other Parisian suburban water resorts.

The walks in and around Belgrano itself are unfortunately few and insufferably dusty. The small town, besides its lonely grass-grown streets, has the usual *plaza*, with a *cabildo*, or town hall, which was the headquarters of the besieging forces during the late troublous times, and a big church, distinguished by a cupola of most ambitious proportions, fondly believed by the natives to be second in size only to the dome of St. Peter's. Either from lack of funds or a dying-off of religious zeal, the building remains in an unfinished condition, looking forward possibly for its completion to the day when Belgrano shall have established its claim to the honour it is competing for with several other townships of becoming the new capital of the Buenos-Ayrean province.

One of my most frequent stretches when the worst heat of the day was over was to a place called Saavedra, distant a couple of miles off. A ragged, ill-defined high road led to it across a wild bit of common, and thence along an avenue bordered by a row of eucalyptus trees of recent growth, and by the shrubberies of a few tenantless country-houses. At one part of this road it was advisable to walk fast and hold one's breath, for here stood one of the many noisome slaughtering sheds that form part of an industry which, although a source of great riches to this country, at the same time has a brutalising influence on the inhabitants, and at any rate, far and wide, taints the pure health-bringing breezes. At a corner, a little past this *matadero*, the road turned sharp round to the right by a sluggish canal, and, after a few hundred yards, brought one abruptly to a large public garden surrounded by a wet ditch.

Of all places of its kind this park or garden is, I think, the dreariest and most depressing I ever beheld, and when I came upon it unawares for the first time it produced upon me almost an uncanny impression. So oddly is it placed here, and so entirely without *raison d'être*, on the verge of the open half-desert country, in this quiet rural district a good many miles away from the town, that it looks as if it might have been left there years before by some community that had been driven out of the neighbourhood by war or pestilence. In fact, to stumble upon it like this was, in a very mild way, to experience the sensations of the traveller who, in the midst of primeval woods, suddenly falls in with the ruins of some long-forgotten city. In reality it is simply a striking instance of the wanton manner in which money is thrown away in these regions ; for having, it is said, cost no less a sum than 120,000*l.*,[2] it has already, thanks to its uselessness, more even than to neglect and consequent decay, acquired the forlorn aspect of some bankrupt and deserted Cremorne or Vauxhall. Its tangled, untended shrubberies, and dismal, meagre walks of *paraiso* and Italian poplar, decorated at intervals with plaster casts of statues with maimed limbs and defaced features, are melancholy to a degree. In the centre of a kind of *quinconce*, surrounded by benches, there stands a moss-grown monument erected in memory of the godfather of the place, Cornelio Saavedra, who was one of the leading men in the struggle for independence, and the first of the native governors of the country. In another open space further on there is a tumble-down stand for an orchestra, and a dilapidated merry-go-round. Besides a couple of artificial lakes half choked with weeds, the extensive grounds are intersected by sluggish watercourses, spanned by rickety rustic bridges leading to deserted kiosks and summer-houses, which the lizard and, I doubt not, the slimy toad have long made entirely their own.

At a cottage lived in by the custodian there are indeed refreshments for sale, but this, as far as my experience goes, is the only sign of the gardens being a place of any resort. I used to go thither

---

[2] Fifteen million dollars (paper currency) according to Mulhall — *Manual de las Repúblicas del Plata.*

frequently in my walks in the late afternoon, and scarcely ever met a soul. In fact there was to me a curious charm, which I can with difficulty account for, in the utter loneliness of the spot. In the low, slanting rays of the setting sun I have often wandered about by its green moat, amid a perfect nebula of midges, and watched the shadows creep over the darkening plain, with not a sound to break the stillness beyond the shrill chorus of innumerable frogs, and now and then, perhaps, a snatch of song—one of those strange, quavering South American ditties—the Indian grafted on to the Spanish—always plaintive, and always in a minor key—sung quite softly to himself by some young fellow who had come out there with his *china* for a quiet evening stroll. It felt—what in truth it was to me—like standing at the outer edge of the world, and one's thoughts and fancies had ample scope to roam as they listed over the silent solitudes.

But the sun has almost touched the low horizon, a slight shiver passes through the poplars and wakes us from our dreams. It is time to trudge home to one's evening meal through the all too short twilight of these latitudes. By the time we reach Belgrano the night has almost closed in, and the lamplighter is going his rounds through the quiet sleepy townlet.

CHAPTER VIII.

DEPARTURE ON A TRIP UP THE URUGUAY—THE 'COSMOS'—
FELLOW-PASSENGERS—MARTIN GARCIA.

EARLY in November I was asked to join a party about to visit the Upper Uruguay. The opportunity was an excellent one—indeed unique. The river was unusually full, and a light-draught steamer, which had just been placed on it, would take us up, on a trial trip, far beyond the course of the few boats that ply on its higher waters. Our party, too, was as pleasant a one as could be got together amongst Englishmen in these regions: our creature comforts had been carefully considered: we should have the steamer all to ourselves, as yet unpolluted by traffic—and what such pollution is, let those say who have ever journeyed up the River Plate and its mighty affluents: we should see a country but seldom visited; every possible temptation, in short, being placed before me, I gladly accepted the invitation.

And first as to our party. We were ten in all,

four of whom joined us after we left Buenos Ayres, and, though we did not include in our number any 'remarkable men,' like those paraded for the benefit of Martin Chuzzlewit, our pursuits and avocations were sufficiently various to make us agreeable and interesting company to each other. Commerce and engineering, railway enterprise and farming—all the main sources of wealth in this promising country—were represented among us; not to mention a couple of officials—fairly intelligent, travelled men, who, we venture to hope without presumption, made themselves as pleasant on the whole as the general run of the British *tchinovnik.*

We left Buenos Ayres on a Thursday morning in my old friend the 'Cosmos,' which was to take us up as far as Concordia, some 220 miles from the Argentine capital, and, as I had to join the steamer in town from my suburban station on the Northern Railway, I was obliged to make a very early start. My train sped along through the flat meadow-land, with on either side a thin border of weeping-willow and *paraiso* and eucalyptus, relieved here and there by the lovely red blossoms of the *ceibo* tree, till presently it slackened as we drew near the station of Palermo. After stopping here to take in and set down a few passengers, we went on and soon reached the outskirts of the town, passing the gasworks and the—as yet, alas! unfinished—water-works, and in a few minutes more were deposited at the Central Station, within fifty yards of the passenger mole and of a narrow belt of public garden where Italian and Argentine democracy have joined hands in raising a marble statue, of the clever realistic school of modern Italy, to the arch-conspirator Mazzini. '*Agli Argentini ospiti e fratelli gli Italiani*' is inscribed on one side of the pedestal, and on the other '*A Mazzini gli uomini di sua fede.*' At the further end of the garden stands, raised on a meagre little pedestal, a far less imposing effigy of Christopher Columbus—the moral almost to be drawn from it being that, with his countrymen over here, in this enlightened nine-teenth century of ours, the genius of revolution and destruction is more highly honoured than that of discovery. But these be the pet gods and heroes of our passionate half-instructed democracies—not the strong man of simple earnest faith, who, sailing into the unknown ocean, ended by doubling the patrimony of mankind; but rather the mystic plotter, steeped to the lips in treason, who from some safe retreat sent deluded victim after victim to the dungeon or scaffold—all in the hallowed name of freedom. Alas, poor freedom! and alas, poor Columbus!

This garden, by the bye, which bears the name

of *Paseo de Julio*, in memory of the date of the final
declaration of national independence, was first
laid out by Rosas, and must be put down to his
credit as one good deed at least.   It is but a
narrow strip running a short distance along the
river front, but, small as it is compared with the
original design of its founder, who would have
made it something like the Villa Reale at Naples,
it is a pleasant little oasis by the waterside.   It
contains some good trees and shrubs—beautiful
mimosas with yellow and scarlet threads; Japan
medlars, splendid magnolias, and luxuriant castor-
oil plants; and the views of the town and roadstead one has from it and from the long pier
beyond are extremely striking.   Owing to the
peculiar conditions of the trade in this place,
caused by the absence of any harbour in which
larger vessels can unload, the traffic carried on
from the beach by means of boats and carts is
busy in the extreme, and the sight one gets of it
from the two long jetties, which form a kind of
inner haven, is one not to be forgotten.

At high water the big *lanchas*, or lighters, get
within easy reach, and an armada of smaller boats,
laden with goods and passengers, plies between
them and the shore; but when the tide is low,
their place is taken by huge carts, on monster
wheels, drawn by several mules or horses, the

L

driver perched on the shafts, that wade out, like so many bathing-machines, through the slush a long way beyond the pier ends, where the barges lay bobbing up and down waiting for them with idle, flapping sails. When this traffic is in full swing, the slimy foreground looks in fact like some great amphibious fair full of animation and colour, the sun shining on the bright red of the carts, and on the white of the canvas and of the piles of linen which a tribe of washerwomen are making believe to cleanse in the turbid little pools of water that are scattered all along the shore. From out of this busy scene there rises a cracking of whips and jingle of mule-bells, mingling with the more distant cries of the boatmen hauling in or setting their sails. Nor is the circus element wanting to this fair, for on either side of the jetties the fishermen are going out to their morning work—not wading, nor in boats, in ordinary piscatorial fashion, but on horseback, and often standing on the backs of their horses. Thus they advance two by two, in double line, each man holding up one corner of a gigantic seine-net, some three hundred feet square, the furthest end of which is sunk well out of depth, and then dragged again in shore, the more distant horses, with their acrobatic riders, having often to swim for it on their return.

But there is no lingering this morning to take

in all the curious features of this charming scene, which I have often watched before in my afternoon strolls on the passenger mole. The 'Cosmos' is blowing her dismal fog-whistle with a persistence peculiar to these river-boats; so we hurry down the steps, and are quickly pulled on board by two stout Basque boatmen. We greet our companions, are shown to our cabin on the upper deck, stow away our luggage, and soon are under way.

Our steamer is the crack ship of the company named *Mensajerías Fluviales*, whose seat is at Salto on the Uruguay, and the founder of which is a shrewd French Pyrenean of the name of Rives, better known in these waters as Don Saturnino. A big undertaking he has made of it, and next to his own native habits of thrift the intelligent co-operation of two British partners does not make it prosper the less. Certainly it is conducted on highly economical principles. It is indeed whispered of the head manager that he is not above counting over the soiled linen at each journey's end, and we half suspect him of weighing the food placed aboard, so accurately is it calculated, as to quantity, to keep the passenger from starving, and as to quality, effectually to quell his appetite—except he be what Mr. Hardy, in one of his cleverest books, calls 'a nice unparticular man.' But these are minor matters. The 'Cosmos' is a fine steamer, well adapted for her work, and luxuriously fitted up, and reflects credit on her British builders and the British flag she sails under.

When we have had our last gaze at Buenos Ayres, which looks at its best as seen from the river, and are well in mid-stream, with no sign of land on either side, we begin to take stock of our fellow-passengers. They seem as uninteresting as they are numerous; but one family, or rather tribe, composed of a benevolent-looking old gentleman with a shiny bald head, a round dozen of exceedingly fat women, and a boy, somehow attract one's attention in a perverse sort of way. First one attempts to count them—but never succeeds, for just as they have been carefully ticked off on one's fingers' ends, another turns up so undistinguishable from the rest that one is at a loss to tell whether she has already been reckoned, and so has to begin all over again. Then, as to size, which is the fattest and greasiest?—a still fatter and greasier one upsetting the award just as it has been carefully arrived at. On the whole they are harmless people enough in their way (though rather trying at meals, when they indulge in alarming knife-jugglery), and, excepting when they show signs of sea-sickness—hardly surprising, considering the amount of tight-lacing they must have undergone—they are extremely cheerful. They

sit on deck and chatter unceasingly, without as
much as an attempt at working or reading, and
they all worship the boy. The latter, a brat of
about eight years old, in a South American edition
of a Highland costume, is, of a slightly exuberant
race, the most irrepressible infant specimen I ever
beheld. From the moment we start, till late at
night, when I lose sight of him with the comforting assurance from the captain that he is to be put
on shore with his sisters and his cousins and his
aunts somewhere in the small hours of the morning (to be melted down in the nearest *grasería*,[1]
brutally suggests one of our party), this dreadful
boy never for a second stops yelling, and singing,
and dancing the fandango, and going through
the most extraordinary clown-like antics, nor do his
female relatives tire of admiring him, periodically
clasping him to their capacious bosoms and passing him on like a sort of loving cup. A boy to
exasperate the greatest lover of children, and to
whom, one cannot help uncharitably thinking, a
gentle switching would be of the greatest benefit—
and, Lord! as Mr. Pepys might have said, the
good it would do him!

About one o'clock we sight Martin Garcia—the
Gibraltar of the Plate, as it has been modestly

---

[1] Establishment for melting down the carcases of the sheep and
oxen slaughtered in the *mataderos*.

termed—and soon pass close to the southward of it. A big Argentine flag floats over some low buildings—barracks and storehouses—and a few guns are in position on the barren, treeless shore. These defences are, it is said, not strictly in conformity with existing treaties, like some fortifications that might be quoted in very different regions; but the Brazilian Government, while outwardly protesting against them, must have laughed in its sleeve, having known all along that the narrower, unfortified passage between the island and the oriental (Uruguay) coast—the so-called *Canal del Infierno*—although supposed to be navigable only with small craft, in reality affords a passage for much larger vessels. What fortifications there are on Martin Garcia are of no formidable order, and bring to mind the bitter saying attributed to an Argentine statesman, who, being asked why he did not put the island in a proper state of defence, replied that he knew no one 'above one thousand ounces' (about 3,000*l*.) to place in charge of it. Fortunately *nous avons changé tout cela*, as was conclusively shown by the perfect staunchness of the national forces during recent events.

There are a number of convicts here who are kept usefully at work on the stone quarries which have furnished the pavement of the streets of Buenos Ayres—such as it is. The island has also

been used of late years as a prison for the principal
captives made in the last Indian campaigns.   It
became in fact the St. Helena of the famous
cacique Pincen, the bravest and wiliest of the
desert chieftains taken by Roca: and one can
picture him to oneself fretting out his Indian soul
as he gazed on the waste of waters, haunted
by the memories of his barbarian reign on that
other, inland, ocean the Pampa, and—in the
splendid words of Manzoni, which, allowing of
course for the difference between the *infiniment
grand* and the *infiniment petit*, are in some ways
so applicable here that I cannot refrain from
quoting them—conjuring up

> ' Le mobili
> Tende, e i percossi valli,
> E il lampo dei manipoli,
> E l' onda dei cavalli,
> E il concitato imperio,
> E il celere obbedir.'

But our stay here is very brief.   A boat comes
off from the shore to pick up mails, and we quickly
move on again, not stopping till about four o'clock
at a place called Higueritas, or Palmira, on the
Uruguayan side.

There is nothing to be seen here, and we begin
to be troubled with doubts as to the real merits of
the trip before us.   Nor does anything of note
occur till after dark, when the lighting of the

deck-saloon with the electric light brings our party together again over a rubber of whist. As an advertisement in this land of *progreso* the light no doubt answers well enough, but I can hardly imagine anything more disagreeable than its flickering, unsteady, cold glare in the confined space of a cabin; so, not playing whist, I take refuge from it in the darkness outside, and leave my book—a volume of Eugène Labiche's plays—behind me. Great is my amusement when, presently returning, I find it in the hands of a stern-looking, middle-aged Spanish female, who is reading it attentively with knitted brows. After some time she guesses I am the owner, and returns it with the simple words: 'Es francés!' I should think so, my good woman! Palais Royal French of the most perfect kind; 'Edgar et sa bonne!' I wonder how she liked it and what she made of it!

But the fog-whistle begins screeching again, and a small steamer comes alongside to fetch passengers and cargo for the town of Mercedes, a favourite watering-place of these regions, situated some three or four hours up the Rio Negro. This operation takes some time, and not very long afterwards we stop again off Fray Bentos, which boasts of a monster *saladero*, and is yet more distinguished as the home of the highly scientific and renowned, but to my mind villainous, compound

known as 'Liebig's extractum carnis.' The nature
of the operations carried on here is clearly enough
revealed by the whiffs that come borne to us on
the night breeze. We are, however, to some extent inured to this, for even in the balmy shade
of our own garden similar incense has occasionally been wafted to us from the *mataderos* all
round the city. Once more, to borrow the vigorous and terrible words used by Vicuña Mackenna
in speaking of it under the rule of Rosas, this
country is literally a huge slaughter-shed, making
the air hot and heavy with the smell of blood,
and men callously unconcerned at its sight. A
profitable trade and occupation for a nation
doubtless, but one that keeps alive in it those
inborn human instincts of cruelty and savagery
which in our older civilisation have long been
curbed and softened down. One of the ugliest
traits of the uneducated native of these countries
is his perfect indifference to the sufferings of
the brute creation; his comparative disregard of
human life is, with such a training, not unintelli-
gible. We are not sorry now to turn in, in search
of slumbers which are sadly broken into by the
steam-whistle as we stop at Concepcion and Paysandú, and, later on, by the effusive farewells of
our jabbering fat friends as they are passed down
into the boat that lands them at their journey's end.

CHAPTER IX.

CONCORDIA TO MONTE CASEROS—A SPECIAL ON THE EASTERN
ARGENTINE—A GOVERNMENT COLONY.

A LOVELY morning, not all too hot, brings us on
deck again after the luxury of a capital bath, for
which we are indebted to our worthy and obliging
skipper, who hails from Newcastle-on-Tyne, and,
although he has spent his life in these regions,
sticks manfully to his British nationality and British habits. The night has wrought a favourable
change in the aspect of the river. The stream
hardly exceeds two miles in breadth, and its banks,
now clearly visible on both sides, have become
higher, more especially on the Uruguayan side.
On the Argentine shore, too, the level pasture-lands
derive character from a thin belt of palm-trees
which runs, for miles and miles, at some little distance from the river and parallel to it, at intervals
almost as regular as those of telegraph-posts. The
montes of the *estancias* seem richer in wood than in
the neighbourhood of Buenos Ayres, and several

large estates are pointed out to us on either side, some of which are owned by Englishmen, one of them being under the management of a gentleman who later on joins our party at Concordia.

After breakfast, as the sun gets high, I weary of looking across the glare on the water and following the sails of the Italian schooners that are beating up stream close under the shore, and for a change take to the eloquent pages of Sarmiento's *Civilizacion i Barbarie*. I am deeply immersed in them when my attention is called to a bluff or headland, of exceptional boldness for this tame river scenery, known as the *Mesa de Artigas*, respecting which a ghastly legend is told of the partisan general of that name having, during the War of Independence, flung all his Spanish prisoners from thence into the broad current below—sewed up in hides, adds one source of information. There is little in the tale that is surprising to those who have heard anything of the savage ferocity of the time and of the race; but the interruption happens to chime in so well with Sarmiento's epic, and somewhat complacent, narration of the exploits of the ruffian whom he has strangely chosen for his hero in the person of Facundo Quirogua; of that hero's barbarian contempt for all civilisation, of his insolence and ignorance, of his cold-blooded cruelty and brutal viciousness, that I cannot help closing the book with something like disgust. It is all the more vexing to be brought into so uncharitable a frame of mind, that, independently of the extreme beauty and charm of the pages in which the ex-President depicts the poetical and picturesque aspects of the Pampas, I have just been indebted to him for a very hearty laugh over the parallel he draws—surely not seriously?—between the party fights of Davilas and Ocampos in Rioja (a remote and obscure province, to this day probably not numbering one hundred thousand souls) and the struggles between the Orsini and Colonnas of mediæval Rome! But it is a singular faculty of South American writers honestly to see all things American through a magnifying-glass. Especially is this the case with their short and generally disagreeable national histories, insignificant incidents in which are in perfect good faith put on a level with events of real moment in the annals of the world. But, the full materials of history being as yet wanting to these countries, the most must be made of that which is available.

The first stage of our journey is now near its end. At about half-past two we sight Concordia, the houses of which being scattered for some distance along the bank make it appear a far bigger place than it is in reality, a slight bend in the river throwing the remoter houses of Salto on the higher opposite shore into the same prospect and the whole producing the effect of a good-sized city rising in tiers from the water's edge. Concordia itself has about seven thousand inhabitants, of whom thirty-three per cent. are said to be Italians. Our attention is at once arrested by a large building, not unlike a church with two square towers, from which the British and Argentine colours float on high in happy harmony. This, we are told, is the terminus of the Eastern Argentine Railway, the bunting on it being displayed in honour of our party. As soon as we have dropped our anchor, the manager of the line, Mr. S——, comes on board to welcome the friends he has among us and take us ashore. Our landing having been effected, and, what is far more important, that of our packages—some thirty odd in all, save the mark! and deeply interesting from a victualling point of view—we are driven to the station up a grassy slope, and then along glistening, pebbly roads, which, on closer inspection, are seen to be full of rough agates, and onyxes, and cornelians. The air is keen and fresh and has a smack of our English downs, and we readily believe Mr. S—— when he assures us that Concordia is a singularly healthy spot. A smart-looking special train is waiting for us in the station—which, by the way, is far more substantially built than the majority of similar buildings in this country—so, after a hurried lunch, we climb into the saloon-carriage and are off.

Our carriage is built on the model of those in use in India, with round wooden shades, in shape like coal-scuttle bonnets, painted white and blue, projecting over the windows; but our speed is plain honest British, for, starting at four o'clock, we get over the 99 miles that divide Concordia from Monte Caseros in very little over three hours. As we rattle along, Mr. S——, who goes with us as far as Chajary—the halfway station—gives me some account of the vicissitudes of the Eastern Argentine Line, which, after a hard and patient struggle for existence, is now, according to him, developing hopeful signs of prosperity.

Like almost all the railway undertakings to which this country is indebted for so much of its progress, it belongs to an English company, of which Mr. Ashbury was, I believe, the founder. Its main scope and intention was to connect the lower and the upper sections of the Uruguay, the navigation of which is effectually interrupted by the rapids of Salto Grande above the towns of Concordia and Salto. This it, to some extent, does now, though it would far more completely accomplish its object but for the suicidal competition of an opposition line running parallel to it on the

Uruguayan side of the river.   It seems hardly credible that, in regions so sadly in need of railway communication as these, capital which might be beneficially employed elsewhere should be foolishly embarked in rival schemes that can but damage each other.   But this is not the only instance of aberration in railway enterprise to be noted hereabouts.   Mr. S——, nevertheless, takes a sanguine view of the undertaking for which he has done so much.   He thinks the tide of ill-luck has turned for it, and quoted to me the steady advance it shows from 1877, when it was worked at a loss of 10,000*l.*, and 1878, when that loss had decreased to 4,000*l.* ; to 1879, when it yielded 1,200*l.*, and the current year, when a clear return of 10,000*l.* may be expected from it.

But, *faut de la statistique, pas trop n'en faut.* I turn to the window, and am at once made aware that the country we are speeding through has a decidedly different aspect from that of the ' camp ' of Buenos Ayres, which happens to be the only one I am as yet acquainted with.   It has considerable undulations, and is not unfrequently broken by deep *arroyos* running down to the Uruguay, the steep sides of which are clothed with dense thickets of *espinillas* and other tree-like shrubs, among which the *ceibo* hangs up its clusters of richest scarlet ; here and there, too, it is dotted with clumps of larger trees, of the ever picturesque *ombú* chiefly, while further afield the palm-trees skirmish in open order across the swelling ground. There is none of that oppressive sense of un-broken distance here; even the gentler undulations affording a rest to the eye, and allowing the mind to trick itself with the hope of agreeable little surprises lying in wait for one in the dips beyond the range of vision. Still it is wild and steppe-like enough, in all conscience, though by no means devoid of life. A *rancho* here and there; a mounted herdsman pausing on a knoll; number-less cattle and horses roaming freely about; a troop of buzzards rising ponderously behind the bushes; a hawk or two swiftly swooping down from above—and yes! by Jove! not a hundred yards from the line—three ostriches trotting away with wings extended and craned necks, scared by our rushing, whistling train. Such are some of the pictures framed in by our window-sash as we glide along. Yet these vast solitary tracts are all taken up; though agriculturally, or rather pastorally, speaking (Mr. S—— still obligingly informing us), the land is not to be highly commended, the grasses being as yet too coarse for sheep, and requiring to be fined down by cattle. What few flocks we note on it are the property of Irish sheep-farmers, and are not as good ventures as those of their countrymen in other parts of the Republic, especially in the northern districts of the Province of Buenos Ayres.

Shortly before five we slacken and draw up at the crossing at Chajary, where we take in water, and are sorry to part with Mr. S——, whom business compels to return to Concordia. We get out to stretch our legs and have a look at the place, which seems to have nothing to show beyond the meanest, untidiest of human habitations—in painful contrast with the square, substantial, English-looking station, round which they straggle in squalid lines. Chajary is a Government colony of recent foundation, and, from what we hear of it, far from a thriving one. It is made up of a mixed, heterogeneous lot of Germans, Swiss, Belgians, and Italians—mostly petty tradesmen and mechanics, with no idea of farming—who have been put down here in the heart of distant Entre-Rios to try their fortunes at purely agricultural work. In addition to the inexperience they bring to their task, these poor people have had a full share of the trials to which both agriculturists and stock-farmers are so terribly exposed in this country, and which, be it said *en passant*, are all too lightly glossed over in the flaming incentives to immigration with which the press—more especially the foreign press—of Buenos Ayres at this time more than ever abounds. Their first year was one of exceptional drought, followed by two consecutive years of that truly Egyptian plague, the locust. This year they have contrived to save their wheat crop and are just able to subsist. Mr. S——, who takes an active interest in them, and has been endeavouring to help them in every possible way, tells me he allows them the lowest Government freights, and even sends them bands of music to enliven and draw purchasers to the periodical fairs at which they seek to get rid of their produce. But their utter helplessness and inertness discourage his best efforts ; nor are their prospects likely to be improved by what one hears of the action of the Government inspector of the colony.[1]

Grouped round the station and watching our train with a languid curiosity, they certainly gave me the impression of a dejected, inelastic lot. The most conspicuous figure amongst them was a tall German doctor, with long sandy hair and ragged

---

[1] Other Government colonies have fortunately been more prosperous than the one mentioned above, not to speak of the numerous and well-known settlements founded by private enterprise in the provinces of Santa Fé, Cordova, and Buenos Ayres. Among others there is at Olavarria, in the south of the latter province, an interesting colony of Russian Mennonites, who are said to be doing remarkably well, although some unfortunate delay occurred at first in handing over to them the title-deeds of their lands. I had no opportunity, however, of visiting any of these settlements during my residence in the country.

beard, spectacles, a very dirty wisp of a quondam
white necktie, and splendid jack-boots of bright
yellow leather that might have reminded one of
Wallenstein's Lager had they not been so much
more suggestive of Renz's circus. The man's face
was familiar to me, for I could remember its almost
exact counterpart in the medical authority of one
of the best-known Swiss water-cure establishments.
As for this *fruit sec* of some German university, he
certainly did not believe in hydropathy in any
form as applied to himself, to judge by his linen,
his tipsy talk in atrocious Spanish, and his general
air of beeriness. But the guard sings out : ' All
on board, gentlemen ! ' and off we are again.

Our original number of seven had now been
raised to ten by the adjunction of two railway
engineers and an *estanciero*. Mr. B——, one of the
first named, has been specially employed on this
line for some years, but is still quite a young man,
and is gifted with a flow of spirits that soon makes
him the life and soul of the party. He is as full
of keen humour and fun as I am assured he is of
professional knowledge, and I am specially grateful to him for much hearty amusement during the
trip I am chronicling. Indeed, it seems almost
unfair that such social talents as his should be
buried for any length of time in these South
American wilds. His brother engineer, Mr. W——,

is employed on the wicked rival scheme across the water, and we are therefore bound to look upon him as a secret enemy, and to assume that, under a mask of undeniable cheeriness, he is darkly plotting against the prosperity of the Eastern Argentine. He is, however, so ready a draughtsman and caricaturist that he is far more likely to be taking mental notes of our several physical weaknesses and peculiarities.

This being on the whole essentially an engineers' expedition, I might well have introduced here a few complimentary remarks about the British engineer in general, 'coupling them,' as they say of toasts, with the senior engineer of our party, a man of great experience, and a thoroughly genial as well as instructive companion (we dubbed him 'the amiable and experienced' on this trip); but I will content myself with observing—although it may well seem a truism to those who travel as much as I do—that nothing can be more creditable, and from a national point of view more satisfactory, than the achievements of our C.E.'s in this country, as indeed all the world over, or more pleasant than their company. All honour, I say, to them as a body.

We were now rattled along at an increased rate, no longer having any train to cross, and, as the light decreased, our whistle was sounded almost unceasingly to drive the straying horses and cows from the line, which seems to have a perverse fascination for them, for they scamper off just as the cow-catcher is upon them. One wretched mare runs it too fine and is knocked over—a piteous sight—her poor little foal just getting clear of us. Mr. B—— told us that not far from here they ran into a lion (*read* puma) a few weeks ago, and killed him on the spot. By the time we had crossed the limits between Entre-Rios and Corrientes it was getting dark, and soon afterwards we reached the terminus at Monte Caseros, where an excellent dinner—if anything, too copious—was waiting for us. This Monte Caseros, by the way, may pride itself on being the site of the crowning victory gained by General Urquiza on the 3rd of February, 1852, over the forces of Rosas, and which decided the fall of the Dictator. A memorable day for this country, and indeed for mankind, which never, in our times, witnessed a more brutal tyranny.

After having done full justice to the meal provided for us, we got into our saloon carriage again, and a ten minutes' run on an extension lately completed to a point called the Ceibo on the Uruguay River, brought us abreast of the ' Mensajero,' which lay waiting for us, with her steam up and lights in all her cabins, presenting a very festive appearance in the dark sultry night which had now closed in. Mr. B—— at once took us on board and showed us all over the little vessel—a miniature copy of an American river-steamer—with a not unnatural pride, for she is really more his work than that of the well-known firm of builders who are answerable for her. She was sent out from England in pieces, altogether making up some seven hundred packages, and put together here, a work of several months. As she stands now she has from beginning to end cost about 8,000*l.*, and may perhaps prove rather an expensive bargain, not quite answering all the expectations entertained of her. Of this, however, it is needless to speak, and certainly, as far as I am concerned, I was so comfortable on board that I can record nothing of her but praise.

While our things were being transferred to her, the moon had risen and revealed the proportions of the little creek in which we were moored. The gleaming water looked invitingly clear and cool, but we were assured that it was full of alligators and of a kind of electric eel (*gymnotus*), called here *rayo*, or lightning, of the effects of contact with which very curious and unrelatable stories are told. It was getting late, however—towards the witching hour of twelve—and when once we were fairly under way and had glided into the main stream, I was glad to withdraw to my berth in the stern of the vessel, where, although tired, I lay awake a long time, watching, through the open door, the shower of sparks driven from our wood fires by the cool south wind, and which formed a fiery network across the broad silver band of moonlight outside.

CHAPTER X.

URUGUAYANA—RIVER SCENERY—SUNDAY AT ITAQUÍ.

IN the early morning we stopped off Uruguayana, a town in the Brazilian province of Rio Grande do Sul, and came to an anchor close into the shore. It had rained heavily in the small hours, and when I put my head out of the cabin door to survey the place, I saw before me a perfect sea of mud, beyond which the shelving ground grew harder as it rose, half a dozen miserable *ranchos* filling up the middle space, the dreary, uninviting prospect being bounded by a few ordinary flat-roofed houses backed by a curtain of green trees. Behind this, and not visible from where we lay, extends the town— at one time a tolerably flourishing place, now slowly recovering from the effects of the Paraguayan war. It was well spoken of by those of our party who visited it, but I myself was not tempted to do so. The position it occupies is a very strong one, and was seized upon and stubbornly held for a considerable time by a Paraguayan division, which finally surrendered to the

Emperor of Brazil in person. The unfortunate commander of this force was ruthlessly shot by Lopez on his return to Paraguay.

So deep was the mud on the beach, that the only mode of approach to and from our steamer was by a series of planks laid on trestles, at the end of which a cart, on immensely high wheels and drawn by three mules, waited to receive passengers and convey them up the slimy slope to the town on the top of the ridge. While I was having my bath below, one of these vehicles came jolting down with a load of natives intent on visiting our vessel, and, the bath-room being devoid of window-blind or curtain, they must have had an excellent view of my toilet operations, which, indeed, seemed to gratify them. Later on, too, when they were going the round of the ship, they paused one by one at the window of the cabin where I was dressing, saluting me most amiably, and audibly expressing their approval of the arrangements of my quarters, which, I must say, were quite luxurious, and included a mosquito net of a delicate pale blue! Harmless people, who, for all their rusty black clothing and stove-pipe hats, have not as yet got much beyond the initial, fig-leaf stage of civilisation.

As the hours wore on, the beach became more alive. Coloured women, with long, black, plaited hair, scanty clothing, and gaudy kerchiefs, lazily emerged from the *ranchos* and hung out a few white rags to dry in the bright morning sun ; naked little boys came racing down through the slush, from which their brown bodies were barely distinguishable, and paddled about in the turbid stream with yells and shrill laughter ; a yellow, wolf-like dog trotted up to the water's edge and watched them, whereupon they pelted him and pursued him halfway up the slope ; a Gaucho, with striped *poncho* and broad-brimmed hat, heavy silver spurs and stirrups, leading a spare horse, rode down to the riverside, where he dismounted, and, clambering into a boat, shoved off for the opposite shore, swimming his cattle in tow behind him ; presently, too, a Brazilian officer of some rank—to judge by the amount of gold lace on his uniform—came ambling down on a dun-coloured charger and rode majestically backwards and forwards taking a stern survey of our brand-new craft.

It was amusing enough to note these humours of the place from under the shade of the awning, but I was principally interested in watching two small schooners that were moored side by side close astern of us. The French tricolour showed them to be Basque boats, and their business was scarcely less evident than their nationality. In the triangle formed just here by the meeting of the three territories of Brazil, Uruguay, and Argentine Corrientes, the facilities for smuggling are so great that half the population live by contraband. My Basque friends had probably no other errand up the river. At this early hour they were just emerging from the dark little cabins where they huddled together at night beneath the poop. The first to show was a young woman with delicate features and the becoming national *fichu* tied round her head. She at once set about lighting a fire and preparing the morning meal; next a curly, half-clad urchin crawled out from under a heap of tackle, and then, one by one, three men appeared, yawning and stretching their arms—one of them doubtless the husband—but which, it was difficult to say, for they were all young, and seemed to form one family. A shaggy white dog completed the *tableau*, which, with all the loose gear and casks and chests strewn about the decks, and the wet sails drying in the sun, was effective enough, and kept me amused till breakfast time, after which we made a fresh start, crossing the river to the Corrientes side to the town of Paso de los Libres, or Restauracion, as it is officially designated.

We did not feel tempted to inspect this very mean-looking *pueblo* more closely, but, one of our party having to go ashore to attend to some business with the local authorities, we were detained here for some time, being invaded during our enforced stay by a crowd of noisy, unmannerly natives who insisted on being shown all over the ship. The amazed remarks of these unsophisticated, but extremely disagreeable, people at the fittings and arrangements of the steamer, and still more at the rapidity with which we had performed our journey, were diverting enough in their way. They could not believe that we had left Buenos Ayres but little more than forty-eight hours before. We were heartily glad to be rid of their vulgarity and noise and chatter, and to find ourselves this time fairly on our way up stream.

Truly a perfect afternoon! As the sun began to decline on the Correntine shore, a cool, south-easterly breeze sprang up, just giving a crisp curl to the broad, swift current against which we were steaming. We hugged the Brazilian side, keeping about a stone's throw from the water's edge. The bank was high enough here to cast a grateful shade over our course, and now at last, too, it began to show a far more vigorous vegetation. A few forest trees stood out here and there from the thick, rank undergrowth, and presently, when they became sufficiently frequent to form substantial patches of real sylvan scenery—how grateful to the eyes of the dweller in Buenos Ayres!—revealed a clothing of strange creepers and parasites; soon too we could discern air plants swinging from their boughs, and coils of brilliant flowers wound around their stems. Downwards the shrubs and plants came creeping into the dark, cool water, mingling with the rushes and slender, willowy bamboos, pushing their tangled roots far out into the stream, and forming charming, mysterious little pools that looked so deliciously inviting that one longed to stop and wade into them and sit down in their eddies in the shade of the broad-leaved plants that wove a green roof above them, the swift tide bathing one's feet and the smooth, glossy foliage fanning one's brow. In these tiny bays the amber stream rushed in and out at such a pace, that it was possible to realise how rapid and mighty was its current—a sadness coming over one as one watched each bright little wavelet hurrying on from its first home in the beautiful upper waters, where it had been warmed by tropical suns and had reflected the glories of tropical scenery, only to be lost in the turbid, shallow flood—gigantic, yet devoid of grandeur—hugest of drains, rather than of streams—which bears the delusive name of the Silver River.

To our left the whole expanse of water—all but the narrow shaded belt through which we held our course—was glowing in the slanting sun-rays, a mirror of burnished gold framed in by the low western bank of emerald green, all pasture without a tree or shrub to break its level line. This, Mr. B—— assured us, was in a great measure due to the ingenious fiscal legislation of Corrientes, which levies a tax of one *patacon* on every tree that is planted in the province. Perhaps the most striking features of the scene were its stillness and the almost complete absence of animal life. We had dreamed of alligators basking on reaches of sun-baked mud, and had not even quite despaired of a glimpse of a jaguar slaking his thirst at the stream's edge, but, beyond a few startled water-fowl that rose from among the reeds in front of us, we beheld not a living creature. A large-sized duck or two, of the breed called *patos reales*, strong of wing and of gorgeous plumage ; a heron poised on a big stone above the current ; a kingfisher skimming in and out of the rushes, were literally all we saw. Nothing but the silent, tangled woodland stretching far back, and growing, we liked to fancy, into those virgin forest solitudes of Brazil which hide in their recesses the rarest beauties of creation. It was something to imagine to oneself these things as being concealed by the verdant curtain past which we were gliding, even though we beheld them not.

At dusk we came in sight of the twinkling lights of Itaquí, a place of some consequence, where the Brazilians have their principal naval

station on this river, and where they own an
arsenal. Some time before coming to an anchor,
we distinguished the lights at the mastheads of
their monitors, and now as we neared the town,
which is built on the cliff-like river-banks, we
could see the inhabitants gathered in knots in the
fading light, in front of their low-roofed dwellings,
and watching our unexpected advent with evident
interest. Soon they began letting off rockets in
true South American sign of welcome. But it was
too dark to land that evening, so we most of us
remained on board and sat down to the rubber of
whist over which our 'amiable and experienced'
was nightly called upon to preside. One or two
of the younger members of the party, however,
made an exploring expedition on shore, and presently returned with half a dozen queer-looking in-
dividuals, whom B—— introduced as artists of the
'compagnia drammatica Italiana,' which was touring
it in the principal towns of Rio Grande. There
was a 'lean and hungry' look about these gentry
which did not say much in favour of the nightly
receipts they made; and they not only looked
hungry, but unquestionably were so, and it was too
absurd to see the incorrigible B—— ply them with
ham sandwiches, with mustard half an inch thick,
which they swallowed with watering eyes and beads
of perspiration on their foreheads—perfect internal

sinapisms some of them must have been, all mustard and no ham! Poor wretches! though they may have thought the food peculiar to these *indiavolati Inglesi*, they seemed to appreciate its substantial qualities, and washed it down with so much beer that it at last became somewhat difficult to get rid of their uproarious cordiality.

Sunday morning broke in with a cloudless sky and intense heat. The dwellers in Itaquí, barring our dramatic friends, keep early hours and rise with the lark, and we were hardly dressed before our deck was invaded—literally swept this time— by visitors of the fair sex—one a decidedly handsome girl—with endless trains and square-cut open *corsages* of brightest blue and pink. But fairer sights than these were in store for us. Mr. R——, who was the botanist and horticulturist of our party, had stolen a march on us and made at early dawn a raid on some of the Itaquí gardens, whence he returned triumphantly with a plant, among others, which seemed to me one of the most perfectly beautiful objects I ever set eyes upon. It may—I suppose so, at least—be classed among the *cannœ* family, but none of us ever remembered to have seen it before. It had a grape-like cluster of buds—each in shape and size something like a small elongated plover's egg—of a white so dazzling and so glossy that they seemed made of porcelain or

the purest wax, the opening of the bud being
tinted with a blush of the loveliest pink. Two of
the buds had burst open and revealed a cup-like
flower of a brilliant orange colour with pink
streaks. In its loveliness it seemed almost unreal
—a dream of a flower or the flower of a dream.

This discovery Mr. R—— had made in the
garden of a Brazilian lady, who had kindly told him
he might dig up one of the plants to take away with
him. After breakfast, therefore, he and I sallied
forth in search of it. Climbing the *barranca*, and
walking some little distance up a hot dusty road,
we got into one of the main streets—if so it could
be called—of the town, and soon found ourselves
in the *praça*, or public square. To our left was a
diminutive, barn-like building, evidently very old,
and surmounted by a rough kind of cross, which
had probably been one of the original Jesuit chapels
of the country. Next to it stood a curious structure
composed of two wooden posts and a cross beam,
which at first sight bore a ghastly resemblance to
a gallows, but, as we afterwards discovered, had
filled the office of bell-tower. The bell was gone,
and the disused chapel had long been replaced by
the much larger church which faced it at the
upper end of the square, its doors thrown wide
open, gaily dressed women passing into it and
groups of men loitering about it, as is the custom

N

on feast-days in all these southern latitudes. While we were crossing the *praça*, a female school debouched into it from one of the side streets and filed into the church straight up to the altar, to the right of which it halted in column, remaining in that formation, as we presently saw, all through the service.

We did not then enter the building ourselves, mass not yet having begun, but passed on to the garden of the beautiful flower, which was situated just beyond. A quiet, thin Brazilian woman, with a pale olive complexion, and dressed in a loose white wrapper, greeted us on the threshold of the house and accompanied us into the garden, which lay behind: a mere strip, into which, I grieve to say, all the rubbish and refuse of the dwelling seemed to have been shot indiscriminately for months past. Close under the wall, in a corner of this uninviting pleasaunce, grew the fairy plant, and while R—— was engaged in digging it up, our gentle, mild-visaged hostess insisted on presenting me with some lovely gardenias, several large bushes of which grew hard by. It was all I could do to prevent her from plucking all the flowers. We soon took leave of this simple, civil creature. Whether it be due to languor, induced by greater warmth of climate, or not, these Brazilian women have more repose of manner, and thus to an

English eye seem, at first sight, better bred than their more joyous, impulsive Argentine sisters.

As we again entered the square, a company of marines marched up, to the sound of a bugle, and halted just outside the church. Here it was first put through a summary sort of drill by a very small officer with an exceedingly big voice and great sternness of aspect, after which there was a kind of inspection of arms and accoutrements, which gave us an opportunity of ourselves examining the men. A fine lot, scrupulously clean and well clad, but curiously made up of negroes, mulattos, and whites, while their armament apparently varied as much as the shades of their skins, including the last pattern of Henry-Martini as well as the obsolete muzzle-loader. Suddenly they came to attention, the word of command was given, and filing off by twos they marched into the church, the bugle blaring away in front and not stopping till they were drawn up in two ranks across the building. Four files of men were told off as altar-guard, and the rest grounding their arms, the service began.

We had followed them in and watched the scene with some curiosity. The church was big and bare, with whitewashed walls and a rough roof of rafters of hardwood; but there was no lack of brilliancy in the altar, with its coating of sky-blue and gold, its tinsel ornaments and garish draperies, and the chromolithographic daubs that hung on either side of it; plenty too in the dresses of the women, who, not affecting the black church-going garb of Spanish countries, were clad in the brightest and crudest of colours. The noontide blaze came streaming in from the open doorway, lighting up all this flaring frippery, against which the central figure of the officiating priest stood out with some grandeur—a tall, brawny half-caste, with a powerful, melodious voice and considerable dignity of manner. There were no chairs or benches, so the women stood or knelt in little radiant groups all about the stone-flags; further back the men lounged carelessly, twirling their straw hats in their hands, their white clothes shining in sharp contrast to their dark skins; two or three dogs strayed in and chased one another undisturbed in and out of the worshippers; an old negress feebly tottered past and cast herself down, repeatedly striking the pavement with her forehead. It was but a shabby, commonplace scene on the whole, for all its local colouring, and my thoughts had strayed away to distant and more decorous services, when of a sudden there came the tinkling of the bell, and down the men dropped on one knee on a carefully spread-out pocket-handkerchief; down the female school squatted on their haunches, and there arose —not the muttered accents of the priest, but the

loud, high-pitched voice of the small lieutenant,
followed by the braying of that dreadful bugle. It
was altogether too startling and incongruous—not
to say grotesque—to have any but an irreverential
effect, and thus it went on throughout the celebration, each solemn portion of which was marked by
the word of command, with more too-tooing, and
the ring of the rifles as they were grounded or
brought to the present. From the church R——
and I took a stroll through the white glare of the
streets till we reached some thick orange groves
in the outskirts of the town, where we sauntered
up and down, moralising and botanising, till it was
time to go on board again. The heat at our moorings was most oppressive, and we were very glad
to get out of it and find ourselves once more in
motion on our way up the river.

CHAPTER XI.

UP STREAM TO SANTO TOMÉ—A WOOD-CUTTING STATION.

Two Brazilian passengers had been allowed to embark here for San Borja.   This special favour—for our trip was essentially private, and we formed what the Germans term *eine geschlossene Gesellschaft*—we suspected they owed to our *comisario*, or purser, a very perky, self-satisfied young native, whom we all disliked, and snubbed accordingly. We thought his asking these people a great piece of impertinence, the result being that our cordiality to the intruders was not excessive, although B—— jocosely would have it that one of them was at least a Conde and a near relative of the Duque de Caxias! (this in honour of one of our party who was known to have a slight failing for persons of rank), and when asked on what terms he had come on board, described his position as that of a first-class forward passenger, who was allowed the use of the spar-deck and the privilege of talking to the man at the wheel. Coals of fire were to be heaped on our heads before long by the poor Conde !

A breeze sprang up soon after we started, and we had just such another glorious afternoon as the day before, the vegetation yet further improving as we advanced, and acquiring a more marked sub-tropical character.　The bamboos grew thicker and higher, and large timber, in the shape of the *lapacho* and the *angito* and other hardwood trees, began to abound.　For a long time we kept close to the Brazilian side, gliding on through the same stillness almost under cover of the overhanging boughs. The hushed woods somehow brought to my mind the closing words of one of Lenau's most perfect sonnets.　Their silence was as 'that peace which parted for ever from the earth in the first dawn of Paradise.' [1]

So great was still the scarcity of life, that every living thing we caught sight of became an object of interest, and was at once noted down.　I amused myself for some time following the tactics of a couple of herons who flew away in front of us and alighted on separate branches of the same tree, where they grotesquely faced each other like two sentries, craning their long necks to the utmost and balancing themselves with flapping wings, till we drew nearer and they again took flight, to roost

---

[1] 'Mahnt mich leise an den Frieden,
　Der von der Erd' auf immer ist geschieden
　Schon in der ersten Paradiesesfrühe.'

again in the same fashion a few hundred yards further ahead. At a bend in the stream we came upon a wide reach, studded with low wooded islands, which closed in the prospect and imparted to the fast-flowing river the placid semblance of a lake. Here we steered across to the Misiones shore, which, now, was as thickly wooded as the side we had left. A clearing was to be seen here and there beneath the trees, and, in one of the arches thus formed, we just took in the motley figure of a solitary Gaucho peering curiously down upon us; but for miles and miles his was the only human form we set eyes on. Now and then a bigger arch of foliage came in view, spanning the green waters of some *arroyo* that broke through the river-bank, and affording a vista of infinite depth and mystery that sorely tempted us to stop and explore its recesses. There were spots here that seemed expressly made for the jaguar, or the alligator, or the *carpincho* (water-hog), but we had to content ourselves with the sight of a huge *lagarto* (lizard), whose scales glistened in the sun on the sandy beach.

We were now short of fuel, and hugging the western bank we passed up a narrow channel between it and one of the islands in search of some woodcutters' huts. Here we slackened our speed, and were able to gaze more leisurely on the charming prospect before us.   The stream was hardly wider than the Thames above Maidenhead, and though the woods that cast their purple shade across it, and left but a silver track in its centre, were not to be compared for loftiness or massive leafiness with glorious Cliveden, there was such an infinite variety in their foliage; each tree, with its rich drapery of creepers and twisting tendrils and swinging air-plants, formed such a vegetable wonder in itself; beneath, there was such an intricate growth of flowering shrubs and underwood, such a wealth of humbler ferns and reeds and grasses, that nature seemed really to have exhausted every form of vegetation in clothing the banks that hemmed us in on either side.   On the topmost branches of two, almost contiguous, trees that reared their heads beyond all this greenery, we noted a group of vultures and a few large parrots of brilliant plumage.   Further on, two Italian boats, that were drifting down the current under easy sail, mingled their slender masts with the nearer boughs, and imparted to the scene the human element which had been almost painfully absent from it.   These enterprising craft beat far up the rapid river with their more or less illicit cargoes, bringing down in exchange sugar-canes and *maté* from the great *yerbales* in the upper districts of Misiones.   Their owners are mostly countrymen of

Columbus, and worthy of his name, for they probably reach further into the heart of the continent than the men of any other European race.

At last our call for fuel was answered favourably, and we stopped on the Argentine shore close under a steep bank of red soil, strewn with logs of wood, up which we scrambled as soon as a plank had been laid across for us. There was a clearing above, with two or three rough log-buildings occupied by the owner of the place—an Italian, who had settled here and taken unto himself an Argentine wife, by whom he had a numerous and apparently increasing family. We found this meritorious matron seated on a bench under the pent-roof of the principal *rancho*, airily attired in not strictly spotless cotton garments, and approaching her, with all the exaggerated demonstration of respect for the sex which, to the European, seems one of the many *notes forcées* of Transatlantic life, we craved permission to visit her domains. She received our approaches with perfect ease and dignity, and with a sweep of the hand invited us to be seated and to consider the house as ours. We squatted down anyhow on planks of sawn wood and stumps of trees, but with something of the feeling attending upon a solemn audience, and underwent what seemed to me an endless amount of palaver in choice Castilian, B——, who is con-

OUR STEAMER AT A WOOD STATION ON THE URUGUAY.

sidered *muy fino* by the natives, acting as spokes-
man for the party.

These *belles manières* in the wilderness were too
much for me, and I soon strolled away, my example being speedily followed by the rest, and had
a ramble through the *chacra* that extended behind
the hut. It was wonderfully wild and pretty ; half
plantation and half garden, all cut out of the
primeval woods, with tracks just wide enough for
the low bullock-carts that brought the felled timber to the edge of the river-bank. The luxuriance
of the vegetation in these narrow winding paths,
and more especially the abundance of creepers
with brilliant clusters of purple and yellow and
white, was truly wonderful; but a sickly dampness and steaminess in the air and dark slimy pools
beneath the trees were not without their warn-
ings, especially at this hour of sunset, and for
my part I was not loth to get on board again. It
was long past dusk before we left our moorings, as
we had to take in as many as 2,400 logs of wood,
the charge for a hundred of these being, I was
told, six Bolivian *reales*, or about half-a-crown.
Their clatter as they were hurled from above on to
our iron deck, together with the stifling heat and
a perfect plague of mosquitoes, made us rejoice at
being in motion again, this time *en route* for Santo
Tomé, which we reached about nine o'clock, after

stopping for a moment off San Borja to land the
Conde and his companion. A few straggling lights
showed us where lay this *ultima Thule* of our expedition, but we could distinguish nothing further
from our steamer, the night being excessively dark
and threatening a storm, which broke over us with
tropical violence just about daybreak.

Notwithstanding the lateness of the hour, B——,
with the younger and more adventurous of our
party, went ashore, and somewhat mysteriously
found his way to a regular Guarani dance, of which
he afterwards gave us a highly graphic description.
It took place in a *pulperia* (half inn, half public-
house), in shape resembling a long, low barn, very
sparingly lighted, round the walls of which sat or
crouched such of the company as were not footing
it on the floor of beaten earth. The men were
all Gauchos of pure Indian or Guarani blood, and
each one had brought his girl with him. The ball-
dresses seem to have been of the simplest and
airiest description, consisting of the long Indian
chemise and a single petticoat, the feet of the
young ladies being bare, and their very perfect
and voluptuous figures, untrammelled by stays or
whaleboned bodice, showing to the greatest ad-
vantage and temptingly yielding to the pressure of
the arm that encircled their supple waists. The
men were all armed, and kept strict watch and

ward over their respective *belles*, but they nevertheless showed some hospitality to our friends by
allowing them to take a turn in the Paraguayan
dance called the Palomita, which is something like
a very slow waltz or redowa.

At this entertainment B—— made the acquaintance of an intelligent young Argentine, belonging
to one of the leading Corrientes families, whom he
brought on board next day, and who gave us an
interesting account of a journey of exploration he
had just been making through the interior of that
province and of Misiones, and across them from
the river Paraná to the Uruguay. A great portion
of this vast Argentine Mesopotamia is relatively
unknown, and he assured us that even the accurate
and painstaking Petermann was out in his topo-
graphy of it. As an instance of this, on his map,
the great Laguna of Iberá is represented by a
chain of smaller lakes, the fact being, said our
friend, that it is one vast sheet of water—half
swamp, half lake—some forty leagues, or 120
miles, in length. The bosom of these mysterious
waters is said to be covered with floating islands,
which, on examination, would no doubt be found
to be acres of reeds and rushes and other aquatic
plants, the queen of which is the colossal *Victoria
regia*, similar to those which choke the current
of the rivers of equatorial Africa. In the Indian

imagination these islands were peopled by a race of elves or fairies, whose habitations, says Mulhall, are sure enough visible to this day in the large conical mounds, upwards of three feet high, built by ants.

Throughout this region, which has now in many parts relapsed into the primitive, trackless wilderness, may yet be seen, at intervals of about fifteen miles, the remains of the old Jesuit settlements. The jaguar and the ounce crouch in their lairs where, a hundred years ago, stood the thriving plantations and *haciendas* of the mighty company. But we were soon ourselves to witness marked and saddening traces of their intelligent and beneficent rule, and of the comparative barbarism that has succeeded it.

CHAPTER XII.

SANTO TOMÉ—WHOLESALE DESTRUCTION OF JESUIT BUILDINGS—
SAN MATEO—A TROPICAL CLEARING.

AT Santo Tomé, as at Uruguayana, the beach had
become a perfect quagmire after the torrential
downpour that had deluged our deck at daybreak;
but a thoughtful friend, who afterwards turned out
to be the Correntine explorer mentioned above,
had obligingly sent horses to the landing-place for
us, and 'the amiable and experienced' and I
gladly availed ourselves of them. Santo Tomé is
built some little way back from the river on higher
ground, beyond the reach of the floods produced
by the rapid rises, or freshets, to which the Uruguay
is subject, and which are so considerable as sometimes to amount to twelve feet in the course of
a single night. Its well-chosen site, like those of
the other places of similar origin we visited, bears
witness to the sagacity of its Jesuit founders.

Picking our way across the swampy ground,
and cantering up a steep and muddy *chemin creux*,
we soon reached the brow of the hill and the

inevitable *plaza*, where we had hoped still to find substantial remains of the old Jesuit church, for we were assured by B—— that he had, a couple of years before, seen part of the stone walls, which he described as over fifteen mètres high in some places and thick in proportion. Not a remnant of these is now left standing, and the *administrador de rentas* (collector of revenue) of Santo Tomé—a forward and loquacious individual, of the French *commis-voyageur* type, who had joined us and volunteered his services as *cicerone*—informed us that they had recently been pulled down by order of the municipality, and sold off as building material at six reals a cartload.

Although this enlightened body had certainly done their work very completely, it was still possible to trace something of the outlines of the edifice in its foundations, which crop out among the orchards and enclosures and from between the dense flowering bushes—nature, *ædilitate adjuvante*, having most triumphantly reasserted her rights, and made a tangled wilderness of colour and verdure of the space where church and college once reared their massive buttresses. These buildings had evidently occupied a large extent of ground, and beneath them ran considerable vaulted passages—now choked up with rubbish, but still accessible in some places—which have been ran-

sacked time after time in futile search for the supposed buried riches of the fathers. Martin de
Moussy, in his *Description de la Confédération
Argentine*, states that these excavations led to the
discovery of veins of quicksilver in the soil; but I
did not hear that this find had ever been turned to
account. The only trace of ornament we lighted
on was a large fragment of red sandstone, adorned
with a rude carving of a passion-flower, and bearing the date of 1717, which may have formed part
of the keystone of one of the arches. A bell, with
the older date of 1688, still hangs on a gibbet-like
framework outside the modern church in the *plaza*.
We lingered for some time on the knoll, strewn
with all this wreck, which commands a fair view
of the rolling country beyond and of the ravine-
like dell which leads abruptly down to the landing-
place. The river, just below, was concealed from
sight, but some few miles further up it took a sudden turn and revealed its gleaming waters.

It required but little imagination to conjure up
the peaceful, but highly picturesque, scenes which
must have been witnessed by these solitudes on
great Church festivals. The broad bosom of the
stream furrowed by an armada of canoes that came
floating down with the Indians of the more distant
haciendas; the forest paths resounding with the
tramp of the village communities marching to the

sound of tambourine and fife;[1] along the leafy lane at our feet a winding procession of maidens and children bearing palms and banners and chanting hymns—all pressing onwards to the ridge above, where stood the great church, with portals flung wide open, and silver bells bearing their summons far and wide; its high altar in a blaze of tapers and decked with the rarest of flowers; while through the dusky reverent crowd passed the Jesuit fathers—half priests, half governors—practical, keen-eyed men of the world, who had tamed these savages and reclaimed them from their native barbarism and sloth, trained them to remunerative labour, and taught them a Christianity which, whatever may be thought of its soundness and purity, became very life and light to these children of darkness and superstition. While summoning up these pictures, one could not but be reminded that at this very time a fresh edict of proscription had gone forth against these sagacious trainers of infancy and infant races, and that they were being cast out of the city which the poet of the day, in a crazy flight of patriotic vanity, terms *la ville-soleil, la cité-lumière.*

In the midst of these musings I was interrupted

---

[1] Moussy and other writers, in their accounts of the Jesuit missions, all state that music was much encouraged among the Indians by the fathers.

by our self-constituted guide, Don Manuel C——,
who proposed to take us to where was still preserved
an ancient *bénitier* that had belonged to the church.
We assented, and, after riding half a mile along a
narrow lane, came to a rough *rancho*, in the back-
yard of which was deposited this relic. We had to
enter the enclosure in single file, B—— riding
immediately behind me, and Don Manuel behind
him. The latter had already revealed a more
than ordinary capacity for tall-talk, but now of
a sudden he charmed my ears with the following
exquisite sentence addressed to B——, although, of
course, intended for us dwellers in the great Buenos
Ayres. 'Yes!' he said, with a sigh, 'I see how it
is! *Ya lo veo! Cansados de palacios, Ustedes
vienen á las ruinas á buscar nuevas sensaciones!*' [2]
The poor ruins simply consisted of a block of red
sandstone, hollowed out into the shape of a trough,
and I much fear now subjected to trough-like uses.
It had evidently held the holy water, but the only
remarkable feature about it was the conduit fitted
to it, which, in place of lead, was made of solid
silver. But the simplicity of this relic of the past
only enhanced the sublimity of a remark worthy to
be classed with the finest sayings of the great
Monsieur Prudhomme, or the still greater Monsieur

[2] 'Weary of palaces, you come to these ruins in search of new
sensations.'

Perrichon. It reminded me, somehow, of the story of a friend—an extremely shy man—who, on the occasion of some ceremonial, had been sent for, much to his distress, in the State (glass) coach of the Republic. As he sat in this very handsome vehicle, in a thoroughly uncomfortable frame of mind, feeling very much as if he made up a Lord Mayor's Show all to himself, he addressed some harmless complimentary remark to the high official deputed to escort him, about the upholstery of the coach, which was of a tender blue and white—the Argentine colours—and was not a little startled by the majestic reply he received: ' *Si, Señor! muy simpáticos son los colores de nuestra bandera nacional!* '[3]

When the ruins had sufficiently *retrempé*'d our moral fibre, enervated by the Capuan delights of Buenos Ayres palaces, we turned our horses' heads and rode down the hill by the side of a very picturesque, tangled *quebrada*, or ravine, in the recesses of which lay a sugar-mill. Sugar planting is as yet in its infancy in these regions; but there seems little reason to doubt that it may prove a highly profitable speculation, and that the lowness of water freights to Buenos Ayres—not more than forty shillings per ton—ought to enable the planter

[3] ' Yes, sir! most sympathetic are the colours of our national banner!'

to compete successfully with sugar grown as far inland as Tucuman and brought mainly by rail to the port of shipment. On my return to Buenos Ayres I heard of considerable tracts of land having been purchased on the river, not far from Santo Tomé, for the account of a company about to try the experiment.

A council of war was now held on board as to our future movements. We were somewhat divided in opinion; I, for my part, being desirous to push up the river as far as possible. Some risk, however, attached to our doing so, on account of the very sudden falls to which the Uruguay is liable. It appeared, too, that our steamer was not insured for any point beyond Santo Tomé. More cautious counsels prevailed, therefore, and, at the suggestion of the Correntine explorer, who had accompanied us on board, it was agreed that we should content ourselves with going a few miles further up to the island of San Mateo (erroneously set down as a *pueblo* on Petermann's map), where we could replenish with fuel, and whence, in the afternoon, we might start on our journey home.

Steaming close to the Argentine shore, up a wide reach with numerous islands, we presently stopped alongside the woodcutting station, and, after a stiffish scramble up a bank of sticky red clay—which, by the way, proved fatal to poor

B——'s nether garments—found ourselves in the midst of a charming specimen of tropical clearing. The owner, a tall old Brazilian of extremely polished and dignified manners, in features not unlike the pictures of his respected sovereign, came forward to greet us, and led us inside his enclosure, which contained half a dozen huts, neatly put together with bamboos and strips of bark, and clustering under the shade of a gigantic ombú-tree. We were at once surrounded by two or three generations of the old gentleman's family, all more or less *en déshabillé*. The ingenious get-up of one small half-naked urchin, who came up to me confidingly with a bunch of flowers, made an impression on me. He had on a garment apparently made from an old tail-coat, sewed up round his waist, and cut out in front like a fashionable dress-waistcoat—so that he seemed to be in evening clothes, his little brown body serving for a shirt-front—and a dirty little cotton smock hanging halfway down his thin bare legs.

Besides felling wood and sawing planks, our host grew some sugar and *mandioca*. A rough kind of apparatus for manipulating both these was erected in front of the huts, but the women were busy crushing maize for the favourite dish of these regions called the *maza-morra*, which once furnished the Dictator Rosas with one of the apelike tricks

he loved to play on those whom he either feared or
hated. The victim on this occasion was the British
Minister, Mandeville. Rosas was expecting him one
evening at his house at Palermo, and had instructed
his daughter to stand pounding maize in the verandah when she saw the Englishman coming. The
courteous Mandeville, finding pretty Manuelita engaged in this menial labour and showing signs of
fatigue, offered to relieve her in her task, which,
'after compliments,' as they say in Indian episto-
lary style, she allowed him to do; Rosas, who had
been watching for this, suddenly coming on the
scene, with his usual train of courtiers and *bravos*,
to whom he childishly showed off the envoy of a
great Power employed in servile labour under his
roof.

Before leaving this very picturesque scene,
which, in many respects, reminded me of one of
my favourite boys' books, the Swiss Family Robin-
son, our botanists managed to secure several remarkably fine air-plants and orchids. One of the
latter grew out of the fork of the ombú some twenty
feet off the ground, whence it was brought down
by one of the woodcutters—a pure-bred Guarani
—who climbed, or rather walked, up the almost
perpendicular trunk in regular monkey fashion,
holding on by his big toe while he carefully dis-
lodged the plant.

It was now late in the afternoon, and much to my regret we made our final start from San Mateo down stream, only stopping for a few minutes opposite Santo Tomé to land our explorer. The river was so full and the weather so perfect that it was truly tantalising not to take a run at least as far up as San Xavier, which is situated, about sixty miles above, in the centre of the great *yerbales*,[4] in a district which in the Jesuit times yielded ample revenues, but now is seldom visited except by some stray Italian smuggler. Our engineers, however, shook their heads, so there was no help for it.

We were in a land of exceptionally beautiful sunsets, but this evening's was specially lovely, with softest tints of tender lilac and dove-coloured grey such as I don't remember to have ever seen before. We stood on deck, watching the amber light die out in the west in most delicate gradations, till we were driven by the heavy dew to take refuge in the saloon. To-night, for the first time since I had left Buenos Ayres, I was very glad of a blanket.

[4] Plantations of the Paraguay tea whence the *maté* is made.

CHAPTER XIII.

BRAZILIAN TOWN OF SAN BORJA—CONTRAST BETWEEN ORDER
IN RIO GRANDE AND LAWLESSNESS OF CORRIENTES—LYNCH
LAW IN ENTRE-RIOS.

SHORTLY after daylight we slowed down, and before
long were off the landing-place of San Borja.
This small Brazilian town, situated some seven or
eight miles inland, is of Jesuit creation, though
not so old as Santo Tomé, having been founded
about sixty years later, in 1690. It has an old
church, which we were particularly anxious to see,
as it was said to contain certain curious mecha-
nical figures of saints, which, in the days of the
Fathers, were made to roll their eyes or nod their
heads for the benefit of the credulous Indians.
We landed here by appointment with the poor
' Count,' who had volunteered to send carriages to
meet us. This time we had to clamber up a long
canoe, which lay at an excessively steep angle up
the bank and made a capital ladder. Above, we
came upon springy turf stretching far in front of
us, and, at a rise in the ground, saw, with no little

compunction, our ill-used, but unresenting, friend in person waiting for us with three very queer, shaky-looking conveyances. Into one of these—a kind of buggy—Mr. T—— and I climbed. A heavy, square-built mulatto boy seated himself on the footboard between our knees, and, with a yell and a crack of his whip, started the pony at a sharp canter. This did very well as long as he kept to a sort of rough track marked across the plain, but he soon took to devious courses across country, plunging in and out of heavy ruts and puddles, and plastering us from head to foot with mud, and jolting the very breath out of our bodies. Our remonstrances he simply answered with a jeer and a broad grin. At last I could stand it no longer, and seizing the young beggar by the scruff of the neck gave him a good shaking, after which he drove more carefully. The drive to San Borja was otherwise thoroughly uninteresting. We met one or two solitary *paisanos* on horseback, ambling across the open country—one of whom was fully done justice to by the skilful draughtsman of our party, and might have been the knight of the woeful countenance on his native plains of La Mancha—and crossed a couple of long, low bullock-carts drawn by a perfect procession of oxen. The air was as fresh as on an early English summer morning, and the sky above a speckless blue.

Three very large storks came sailing over our heads in single file and doubled backwards and forwards, escorting us most of the way.

San Borja struck me at once as quite different from any Argentine place of the same size I had as yet seen, and reminded me most of a small town in one of our West Indian islands. The houses are long and low and carefully whitewashed, with sashes to the windows as in England; the negro interest is fully represented; and when, at a turn of the street, I espied a warrior in scarlet, the illusion became complete. We were speedily rattled into the *praça*, one side of which is taken up by the church we had come to see, the barracks standing at right angles to it.

The building used at present as a church is built into the ruined remains of the more ancient edifice, which bulge out upon the square and form an imposing approach or forecourt to it. The original structure must have been of very considerable proportions, and had probably been wrecked in the great war between the Spaniards and Portuguese at the commencement of the century, when the latter conquered the whole of the territory belonging to the Misiones which was situated on the eastern bank of the Uruguay. The present place of worship scarcely deserves a visit, but we were bent on seeing the miraculous images, which a slovenly, ill-favoured priest volunteered to show us. He led us down some steps behind the altar into a dark passage, where, by the light of a taper, we simply found a number of life-size wooden statues, painted in what had been the brightest colours—of Italian origin I should think, and possibly dating back to the beginning of last century—but all made of solid, honest walnut-wood, in no way hollowed, and innocent of any internal clockwork. Such images, in short, as may be seen in any Italian village church, and which, all over South America, are still borne in procession on high festivals. I could well remember such a procession, in the great Alameda of Santiago de Chile, on Good Friday—and a beautiful sight it was, with such surroundings of colour and light and scenery, that even the poor images, carried on high in all their tawdry finery on rolling platforms or on men's shoulders, and tottering and staggering as they went, detracted nothing from its solemnity. Of all the rude, uncouth statuary which was now shown us, the only figure worth looking at was an entombed Saviour, the carving and painting of which was not without a certain amount of painfully realistic vigour and effect.

We soon had enough of this ecclesiastical property chamber, and gladly emerged into the ugly whitewashed church and the sunshine that poured down upon the double row of massive broken walls beyond it.   The old bells were still hanging outside on the usual gallows-like framework, the largest bearing the date of 1723, with the inscription ' *In oppido Sancti Caroli.*'   From the church we went on to the barracks close by, a low, vaulted building which had been used by the Jesuits as a college.   The troops quartered here were a squadron of frontier lancers, both showily and sensibly attired in a loose scarlet serge tunic, or blouse, with a belt, baggy white trousers, and a white shako. Besides their lances, they were armed with Westley Richards carbines, and both men and officers had a decidedly smart appearance.   Their arms and accoutrements were well kept, and altogether they looked quite fit to give a good account of any Argentine raiders who should attempt crossing the water.   The Brazilian Government keep a respectable number of troops in this frontier province of Rio Grande do Sul, *échelonné*'d all along the river, which, during the greater part of the eighteenth century, was the scene of ceaseless warfare between the colonial forces of the rival Crowns of Spain and Portugal.   A deeply rooted antagonism still survives between the subjects of the Empire and the citizens of the neighbouring Republic, and may very possibly some day lead to fresh conflicts on the battle-fields of old.

Although San Borja is but an insignificant *bourgade* with a few hundred souls, its clean, sober, and fairly thriving aspect conveys to the mind the idea of its forming part of a well-organised State and an orderly community. I was assured that there exists a striking contrast, in this respect, between the whole of this southernmost province of Brazil, and the specially lawless and disturbed Argentine provinces which are divided from it by the Uruguay. It would be too much to attribute the apparent prosperity and contentment of the people to their attachment to the monarchical form of government under which they live, for this very province of Rio Grande is said to be the head-quarters of the Brazilian Republican party, and to be ripe for secession from the Empire; but it is difficult not to believe that the order and security of life and property, which are as manifest here as they are wanting in the districts across the water, are in some measure due to the stability and un-questioned authority of the Executive. Notwith-standing this, there is no denying that a general impression exists that the present Emperor's de-cease, whenever that occurs, might be the signal for a disruption of the huge Brazilian State. It will be, I venture to think, a great misfortune not only for Brazil, but for the South American con-tinent at large.

On our return to our steamer, we acquired painful confirmation of the anarchical condition of Corrientes from the companion of the Count, whom we had taken up the river with us two days before from Itaquí, and who had now come on board again to beg for a passage back to that place. We found the poor fellow in a state of most pitiable excitement and distress, and with tears in his eyes he assured us he was now a ruined man. He had only just heard that a *razzia* had been made on some land he owned over the water on the Argentine side, and all his cattle and horses driven away by a party of marauders professing to act under the orders of the Provincial Government. There is little doubt that, since the recent overthrow of the Mitrista party in Corrientes, the adherents of the rival faction which came into power have added wholesale spoliation to proscription throughout that province. The live stock on many of the larger cattle-farms has been swept away by organised bands of caterans, and driven over the border, there to be sold. Some well-known persons at Buenos Ayres itself have even been publicly charged with being implicated in a nefarious speculation of this kind.[1]

[1] Agents were said to have been sent to buy up, at ridiculously low prices, a number of the stolen cattle. As every animal on an Argentine estate is branded with its owner's mark, there can be no manner of doubt as to its origin.

But far more serious than these acts of political brigandage is the amount of crime which, in these distant provinces, has been actually traced to the local government functionaries. During my residence in Buenos Ayres, no less than thirty murders of Italian subjects in Entre-Rios and Corrientes were reported to the Italian Legation in the course of six months, and, of these, nineteen were the work of persons in authority. In one instance an entire family of twelve persons was exterminated, under circumstances of peculiar atrocity, by the *Juez de Paz* (justice of the peace) of a place called Curuzú-Cuatia, in Corrientes, and his two sons. Other crimes were brought home to excise officers and commissaries of police, and in no instance were the criminals brought to punishment, all the efforts of the Central Government to cause justice to be done being frustrated by the much more powerful Provincial influences. The independence, not to say insolence, of the local authorities went so far that on the Central Government transmitting to the Government of Corrientes a copy of an official note from the Italian envoy at Buenos Ayres, commenting on the crimes committed with impunity on his countrymen, the Governor sent for the resident Italian vice-consul, and desired him to let his chief know that he would not put up with such language, and that in the event of

any of the persons whose punishment was demanded being arrested, he would use his pre-
rogative and pardon them, rather than allow
them to be condemned.

We talked over all these matters at breakfast,
and B—— gave us an illustration of the lawless spirit
reigning throughout these regions in an anecdote
of Lynch law in Entre-Rios, which, although somewhat lengthy and revolting in its details, I will
repeat, as nearly as I can, in his own words.

He told us that he was in charge, a few years
before, of the works on a bridge over the Mandirovi River, on the Eastern Argentine line, which
had been swept away by the floods and was being
rebuilt.   Late one summer evening an engine
arrived at the north side of the river, for the purpose of taking him and another engineer up the
line at daybreak the following morning.   There
was an encampment on the further bank of at
least 200 workmen of all nationalities, and as it
was frequently necessary to cross the water during
the execution of the work, a ferryman had been
hired for that purpose, who, besides, made his
profit out of chance passengers.   On the arrival of
the engine, the engine-driver and fireman got into
the boat in order to cross over to the encampment; but the wood-passer, who accompanied
them—a steady, well-conducted Frenchman, who

P

seems to have been a favourite with the engineers —not having any money with him, hesitated about using the boat, till assured by his companions that its owner was engaged by the Company at a fixed salary to convey their servants backwards and forwards. On reaching the opposite bank, the ferryman, notwithstanding this, claimed *un real* ($2\frac{1}{2}d.$) from him, and a considerable altercation took place between the two men, at the end of which the poor Frenchman skulked away, and, having no place to pass the night in, sat down upon some empty barrels outside a *pulperia*, where he soon dropped off to sleep. Meanwhile the boatman—a Brazilian negro of a very low, repulsive type—fetches his gun, draws the old charge, reloads with ball, and, at a distance of ten paces, shoots the sleeping man through the heart, killing him instantaneously. B——, who, with the other engineer, had turned into a railway wagon for the night, was roused by the report ; but shooting and stabbing were of such common occurrence amongst the various gangs of navvies, that he at first resolved to wait till the morning to know what new outrage had been committed. He was soon, however, knocked up by the engine-driver, who told him what had occurred, adding that they had secured the murderer and tied him up, and wanted to know what was to be done with him.

The fellow had been taken to a little hut on the edge of the river-bank which served as an office. 'Here,'[2] said B——, 'I found all the foremen, timekeepers, and others assembled, with revolver in hand, cursing and spitting at the repulsive-looking object, and each man particularly anxious that he should be allowed the privilege of despatching him.'   The proper steps were, nevertheless, taken, and an engine ordered to be got under steam to convey the prisoner to Federacion, a small town two leagues off, there to be handed over to the authorities. 'This pleased the prisoner very much, as, having money, he knew perfectly well that he could procure his release.' 'I returned to the hut,' continued B——, ' after giving my orders about the engine, and found that, in the general discussion which ensued, we unanimously agreed that the pathway in front of the hut was very narrow, and would be rather a dangerous place should the prisoner slip whilst being conducted to the train, and also, that, failing any such mishap, it would be equally unpleasant should he attempt to jump from the engine whilst crossing a sixty-foot iron bridge between Mandirovi and Federacion.

'The most indignant of the crowd was our

---

[2] The passages in inverted commas are taken from a written account obligingly furnished me afterwards.

cook (a North American nigger), who busied himself particularly in tying the fellow up.'   This
roused suspicion, and it was found that the knots
were so tied that with the least effort they could
be burst asunder, and further that the cook had
contrived to give the prisoner a knife.   'At last
the engine was ready, and the bulk of the men
were grouped about waiting to see the prisoner
embark ; but unfortunately on " the narrow path "
one of our men gave him a push, which sent him
down the bank into about thirty feet of water,
bound hand and foot.   We watched this revolting
spectacle without any other feeling than that of
having performed a duty.   The nigger cook made
an attempt to save the man, and was also pushed
into the river for his pains, and had great difficulty
in saving himself.   I was very much struck by
the cool manner in which the prisoner went into
the water without a single exclamation, and even
managed to swim for about half a minute.   Half
an hour after the occurrence we sent out a boat to
search for him in the dark, and came to the conclusion that he had made his escape and hidden
himself in the woods on the opposite bank.   After
burying the Frenchman, we took a stiff glass of
brandy-and-water and retired for the rest of the
night.

'On the third day after the event, and during

a thunderstorm, the body of the murderer rose to the surface, made a turn round his old boat, and then floated down stream. Shortly afterwards two "Napolitanos" were seen to take the corpse out of the river, rifle the pockets, and throw it in again. Then came the chief of the police to investigate the case ; but, finding that the murderer had been the owner of the boat, he quietly took possession of it and passed a verdict of "Ley de Lynch." So the affair ended.

'For some weeks the corpse was seen suspended by the waistband to some bushes on the river-bank, with face, hands, and feet completely devoured by the fishes. During this time we were very much inconvenienced by having to bring water from the neighbouring *bañados*,[3] as no one cared to drink the river water, and also by the vicinity of so disgusting an object. On the other hand the Napolitanos rather approved of it, as such fishing was never known before or after in this river. They were at it day and night, and no doubt looked on the nigger as ground-bait.

'This is a very ghastly narrative,' concluded B——, 'but I can assure you that the affair impressed the remainder of the men to such an extent that not another murder was committed, while before they had been of almost nightly occurrence.'

[3] Low lands permanently covered with water.

We now reached Itaquí, where we lay for the best part of an hour, while some of our party discoursed the local authorities about the future trips of the 'Mensajero,' which is intended to perform a regular service to this and other ports up stream. Here we parted, with great expressions of cordiality, from the Count and his unfortunate companion. The Count, it seems, is engaged in trade, Itaquí being the seat of his business. He is a most good-natured, civil creature, and long may he flourish and live happily in his far-off home by the bright, flowing river! In one respect he seemed to us an enviable man, for we saw him very warmly greeted on his return by an extremely attractive person, whom we of course assumed to be his Countess, and whose graceful profile was hit off very successfully by our artist.

Just before we started, a Brazilian man-of-war's boat drew up alongside, with the commander of one of the monitors, who had come to visit one of our officials. He was in full uniform, with cocked hat and spotless duck trousers, and looked very spick-and-span—indeed, by no means unlike a smart English naval officer. Unfortunately he spoke nothing but Portuguese; but we learned from him, through an interpreter, that the Brazilians take good care to keep up a naval force in these waters sufficient to ensure the command of the river, Itaquí being their principal station. Their officers are much given to copy English ways and customs, and they had even started a kind of cricket—which, I confess, I should have been rather curious to see. In fact, one of our party, a member of the B.A.C.C., on his return to Buenos Ayres, sent them a set of cricket implements of British manufacture.

A 'PAISANO' AT SAN BORJA.

CHAPTER XIV.

LA CRUZ—WRECK OF THE JESUIT MISSIONS.

AT half-past four we drew up opposite La Cruz—another place of Jesuit foundation, which we had been told was worth a visit—and went on shore in the dingy. Our road was up a gradual incline, and was skirted most of the way by rough enclosures made of rubble and the débris of older buildings, with here and there a larger block of red sandstone let into them. A little further on we came upon two biggish decapitated pillars of the same material still standing by the roadside. At the end of the rise we found ourselves in what is left of La Cruz—a good-sized *plaza*, of irregular shape, surrounded by a few very poor-looking houses and garden walls, and at its southern end the site of the ancient church. According to B——, the front of this edifice was still partly standing a few years back, a fact corroborated by Mulhall, who speaks of La Cruz as the only Jesuit mission still in a perfect state of preservation. But quite recently, as at Sànto Tomé, a utilitarian municipality has quarried out the ruins or turned them into cash. In their stead we found a very humble, barnlike building, devoid of all ornament and character, and without any decoration inside beyond a few hideously grotesque attempts at fresco-painting. A modern belfry-tower, of some pretensions, which, for a wonder, afforded orthodox shelter to the bells, overtopped the church and gave it a still more ignoble aspect.

Yet La Cruz, founded in 1629, had been one of the chief and most richly endowed centres of Misiones. The territory belonging to its jurisdiction extended to a considerable distance on both banks of the river, Itaquí being one of its dependent *estancias*. It was finally sacked and ruined in 1817 by the Portuguese Brigadier-General Francisco das Chagas, in a protracted struggle against the remnants of the Indians of Misiones, led by a half-breed—a native of Santo Tomé—of the name of Andrés Tacuary, better known as Andrecito, who, like his namesake Hofer in the Tyrol, seems to have fought for the independence of his country long after it had been abandoned to its fate by its former masters. For upwards of two years this humble guerilla leader maintained an unequal struggle, with varying success, against the disciplined forces of Portugal, till he was finally made a prisoner in 1819, and taken to Rio, where he died in captivity. In the course of this desperate contest das Chagas utterly destroyed the settlements of Yapeyú, Santo Tomé, San José, and others, and is reported to have carried off from them sixty-five *arrobas* weight (about 2,300 lbs.) of church plate and ornaments, all made of solid silver. Some of this spoil is said now to adorn the Imperial chapel at Rio de Janeiro.

Although all vestiges of the body of the Jesuit church had been ruthlessly removed, its ample frontage was clearly marked by the rows of broken stone steps which had led up to it. The destruction of the college, and other buildings grouped around it, is not as yet so complete, massive remains of masonry still extending back for upwards of a hundred yards. A few palm-trees and fruit-trees growing in the midst have turned these shattered refectories and cloisters into pleasant gardens.

Clambering over a low wall we found ourselves in what had been the spacious court of the college, in the centre of which still stood, erect and un-scathed, a solitary sundial of red sandstone fashioned in the shape of a pillar. It bears the date of March 27, 1730, with a monogram of the Virgin and the Sacred Heart beneath it. A little oven-bird (*hornero*)[1]

---

[1] These interesting birds build their nests—made of a rough lump

had made its nest of clay at the summit, and sat
fearlessly watching us from above.

I will confess that this rude fragment of a past
by no means so remote, awakened in me an interest
deeper than that of mere curiosity. *Tout est relatif*,
but, however insignificant it may be deemed, the
story of the labours and achievements of the dis-
ciples of Loyola in these innermost recesses of
the continent is to me a singularly picturesque
and fascinating one. The saddening reflection of
how utterly the tide of intelligence and practical
civilisation brought in by them has receded from
these regions, to be replaced by a barbarism trans-
parently veiled under the least attractive forms of
modern democratic teaching and so-called progress,[2]
gave this homely relic of a wise and beneficent
theocracy a pathetic interest out of all proportion
to its value or importance. I could not but remember that the poor sundial had marked many
hours of patient, humanising toil, and witnessed
energies which, even if misdirected, aimed at
improving and raising the lot of a benighted and

of clay, with a division in the centre leading to a sort of secret chamber
—as far away from the ground as possible. For this purpose they often
select the top of the telegraph posts, where they become, of course, a
nuisance. Such is their industry, that in the course of a single night
they are said to make a fresh home for themselves in the place of the
one pitilessly knocked down the day before.

[2] 'Corrientes,' said an intelligent Argentine to me one day, 'is
more than a century behind Buenos Ayres in civilisation.'

downtrodden people. The golden age of the simple Guarani was unquestionably under Jesuit rule, and it may be doubted whether the proud privileges of Argentine citizenship now enjoyed by the remnant of the race have brought to it advantages to be compared with the benefits of the firm and peaceful sway under which its forefathers throve and multiplied.

Meanwhile it so happened that one of the periodical manifestations of Argentine political life, in the shape of an election, was affording a passing excitement to La Cruz. We were crossed on the square by a number of mounted Gauchos—of a truculent type almost extinct in more civilised Buenos Ayres—armed with lances, and booted and spurred, and all adorned with sashes and ribbons round their hats of the bright crimson which, in the days of Rosas, was the badge of Federalism, and had to be worn by man, woman, and child under the severest penalties. These ill-favoured gentry were leisurely riding home, after voting in the church of La Cruz that morning for the electors about to nominate the new Provincial Governor. An ' intelligent native,' who joined us and gave us the benefit of his experience of the place, told us that about seven hundred voters had come in for the purpose from all parts of the *Departamento.* Some of these scowling *paisanos* may possibly have been lineal descendants of the Charrúa Indians, a peculiarly fierce tribe who gave the early Spanish invaders much trouble and inflicted serious disasters upon them.

Moussy says that the old settlement at La Cruz formed a parallelogram of four hundred metres, or three-fourths of a mile, surrounded by walls of rough, uncemented stone. Its limits coincided in fact with those of the plateau on which it stood, and it is easy even now to trace them. From the *plaza* which crowns the plateau the ground slopes imperceptibly all round to where this circumvallation had been raised. Beyond this, it takes a sudden dip to the river on one side, and on the others to the boundless, treeless plain, at the extreme verge of which, at a distance of at least a dozen miles, stand out three curiously shaped cones, simply known here as *los tres cerros*. B——, who had visited them, said they were pyramids of grass-grown granite some four hundred feet high, according to his description not unlike the tors which form so striking a feature of some of the Somersetshire valleys.[3]

It was getting towards evening when we re-

---

[3] Mr. Hutchinson, in his 'The Paraná, and South American Recollections,' quotes a letter from Bonpland suggesting that these hills should be explored for quicksilver, which in his opinion they contain.

traced our steps to the landing-place, being joined on the way by our horticultural friend R——, laden with lovely gardenias which he had got out of one of the gardens in the *plaza*. He told us he could not persuade the poor woman who presented him with them to accept any money, till he happily suggested to her that it might be applied towards a *cinta para la niñita*.[4] Perhaps one of the most pleasing traits of South American life, due no doubt to the deeply ingrained republican sense of equality and its accompanying self-consciousness, is a repugnance to remuneration for anything save real labour. The more trifling services are rendered freely and with an easy grace, and the odious institution of vails and tips is almost unknown. *En revanche* one has to put up with a trying amount of familiarity and hand-shaking, and I remember being much amused by the experience of a friend who, a short time after his arrival, was stopped one day in the street by a Frenchman, who shook him warmly by the hand, and passed on with a tender inquiry after his health. He knew the man's face well enough, but could not for the life of him put a name to it till some time after they had parted, when it dawned upon him that it was that of a Gascon chiropodist whose services he

---

[4] A sash for the little girl.

had required a few days before.   His impulse was
to run after the man and tell him ' Sachez bien que
ce n'est pas ma main que je vous donne, mais mon
pied ! ' but these happy inspirations unfortunately
always come too late.

CHAPTER XV.

SLIGHT HISTORICAL SKETCH OF MISIONES—PASO DE LOS LIBRES.

LA CRUZ being the last Jesuit settlement we visited, a slight and hurried sketch of the history of the Missions may perhaps not be out of place here. The Order first turned their attention to the territories watered by the upper affluents of the Uruguay and Paraná as early as 1580,[1] barely fifty years after their first conquest (1537) by Martinez Irala, the founder of Asuncion, which city remained for nearly a century the capital of all the Spanish possessions in these regions. It is an astounding fact, by the way, and most characteristic of the fearless self-reliance of the invaders, that, a mere handful as they were, they should, instead of contenting themselves with fastening upon the coast-line, have at once boldly sailed up into the heart of the continent, and established their centre of govern-

---

[1] According to some authorities the first missions were established even earlier than this (in 1557) by Father Field, an Englishman, and Father Ortega, a Spaniard.

ment at a distance of some two thousand miles
from the sea, which was their only secure base.
The daring spirit of adventure that marks the
exploits of the first Spaniards in America has, in
truth, never been surpassed, and of their leading
pioneers none showed themselves more intrepid
than the Jesuit fathers.

We first find them in the old province of
La Guayra, between the Y-Guazu and Tiete
rivers. Their stay here was, however, but of
short duration, all their earlier settlements having
been destroyed between 1620 and 1640 by the
Paulists, or Portuguese of San Pablo, and as many
as 60,000 of the Indian inhabitants carried away
into slavery. In 1631 a Father of the name of
Montoya led an exodus of 12,000 persons of both
sexes, flying from the inroads of these people,
whose savage brutality had gained for them the
nickname of 'Mamelucos.' The fugitives embarked
in seven hundred canoes, says the chronicler, and
floated down the Paraná as far as the big fall of
Maracayú, whence they dragged their boats by
portage roads through the woods, re-embarking
further down, and finally reaching in safety the
Missions on the banks of the lower river.

The full prosperity and definitive organisation
of these Missions properly date from the middle
of the seventeenth century, when the Order owned

thirty-three large establishments, or Reductions, of which eleven were situated in the territory now known as Paraguay, and which became the nucleus of that State ; the remaining twenty-two occupying the Mesopotamia formed by the Paraná and Uruguay, and extending on the left bank of the latter river into what is at present the Brazilian province of Rio Grande.   The Jesuits brought the whole of these vast tracts into cultivation, and parcelled them out in large *estancias* and plantations, on which they not only employed the native Guarani tribes in the most profitable branches of tropical husbandry, but trained them to every variety of manual labour.   In the large workshops attached to all their settlements, the indigenes were taught, besides the more ordinary trades and handicrafts, some of the higher industrial arts, such as watch-making and printing, and working in precious metals, and even painting and carving in wood and stone. Jealously guarded from all intercourse with the outer world, their establishments were, in fact, thoroughly self-supporting, and supplied all the requirements of the population.   In their schools, too, the Indians received a very fair amount of elementary education, certainly superior to what was current in those days in the rest of the Spanish dominions.   It would be tedious to enter into any detailed account of their laws and administration,

or of their agrarian system, which has given rise to
many controversies, and unquestionably had some
curious communistic traits : a certain proportion of
the lands belonging to each settlement being held
and cultivated in common by the inhabitants, as in
the Russian *mir*. Although much has been written
about this 'Christian Republic,' as it has been
called, hidden away in the heart of the continent, a
certain mystery will ever attach to its history and
institutions. But on one point the testimony of
even the most bitter adversaries and detractors of
the Order is unanimous—the flourishing condition,
namely, to which they brought the Indians under
their care. To the fame of their prosperity and
riches they, no doubt, in a great measure owed
their fall; but its immediate cause arose out of
the Treaty of Madrid of 1750 between Spain and
Portugal, by which a great portion of the territory
of Misiones was ceded by the former to the latter
Power. This cession was made in exchange for the
colony of San Sacramento, or Colonia as it is now
called, founded by the Portuguese in 1692, exactly
opposite the city of Buenos Ayres, and which had
become the centre of a gigantic system of contraband, extremely irksome to the authorities of the
strictly guarded Spanish territories on the southern
shore of the Plate. Although the existence of this
Portuguese outpost was as inconvenient as it was

galling to Spanish pride, the equivalent offered for its cession is characteristic of the absurdities of the Spanish fiscal policy, since, to stop the smuggling carried on by means of this one port, Spain surrendered a large portion of the productive territories at the back of it. The treaty, however, was likewise in a great measure directed against the Fathers. Under article 16 of the instrument, all the missionaries and their flocks—then reckoned at upwards of 30,000 families—were to be turned out and located elsewhere in the Spanish possessions.

The Jesuits resisted the treaty by force of arms. Their people had been trained to military exercises to defend themselves from the Mamelucos and their allies the fierce Tupi Indians, and this had indeed furnished one of the accusations made against the Order of meditating designs disloyal to the Crown of Spain. Under the leadership of the valiant cacique Sepe Tyarayu, the Guaranis made a stout resistance to the Portuguese charged to occupy their territory, and, although nominally subdued in 1756, took to the woods, whence they continued to harass the invaders, cutting off their convoys and smaller detachments of soldiers. This war is said to have cost the Portuguese twenty-six millions of cruzados, or upwards of six millions sterling. The treaty which led to it was annulled

in 1761 ; but meanwhile Pombal, exasperated by
the resistance of the Fathers, had expelled their
Order from Portugal in 1759. In Spain, too, the
storm, which had long been brewing, now burst
upon them with full force, a royal edict of April 2,
1767, banishing them from the whole of the Spanish dominions. The distrust and jealousy of the
colonial authorities, together with the hostility of
the regular monastic orders, no doubt hastened
this measure and overcame the sympathies of the
Court, which were rather in favour of the Jesuits.

The Marquis Bucarelli was sent out as Governor
to Buenos Ayres to carry out the decree, and did
so with unsparing rigour. The Indians appear to
have been driven to despair by the expulsion of
their rulers and teachers; Moussy prints a touching letter from the Cabildo (municipality) of San
Luis addressed to Bucarelli in February 1768,
imploring that the Fathers might be allowed to
return to them. They were, however, handed
over to the mercies of Spanish civil administrators,
who, to curb their independent instincts, resorted
to corporal punishments, carried their children
away to be educated or put out to service at
Buenos Ayres, allowed the colleges where they
had been instructed to fall into ruins, and applied
to them the treatment awarded to the Indians of
all the *encomiendas*. If the testimony of statistics

is to be relied on, the effect of these measures on the population soon showed itself in an appalling manner. The contest with Portugal, together with severe visitations of small-pox and measles, had reduced their numbers, at the date of the edict, from 140,000 to some 110,000 souls. Thirty years later, in 1796, they were reckoned by Azara— certainly no friend of the Jesuits—at barely 30,000. The War of Independence and the devastations of das Chagas and his Portuguese completed the ruin of the province of Misiones. Yapeyú, its former capital, which at the time of Azara's account still had 5,500 inhabitants, is said now to be buried in dense and almost impenetrable wood. Of the condition of Santo Tomé and La Cruz we had ourselves opportunities of judging.[2]

Not only here, but all over South America, the fruits of the edict, as regards the native races, were the same, the Jesuits having everywhere interposed themselves between the gentle, docile Indians and the brutalities of the civil power. In fact, next to the edicts of proscription against the Jews and Moors, this decree was perhaps the most unwise and disastrous in its consequences that ever issued from that strange Spanish council which, by an

---

[2] D'Orbigny, writing fifty years ago, estimates the entire population of Misiones at 8,000. It has no doubt increased to some extent in the last few years.

absolutely inscrutable design of Providence, was
for three centuries allowed to misgovern and
ransack the New World at its wrong-headed,
blundering will. In our own time the Paraguayan
war has afforded convincing proof of the genius
of organisation and administration of the Order.
The traditions of implicit obedience and devo-
tion implanted in the Indians of Paraguay by
the Jesuits, alone enabled the tyrant Lopez to
make a defence which can fairly be described as
heroic. Almost the entire male population perished
in the defence of the country. A census taken
three years after the close of the contest showed
that the number of inhabitants had dwindled from
upwards of 1,300,000 souls down to 220,000, of
whom not 30,000 were grown men.[3] History contains no ghastlier record of the results of war.

We lay for the night off Uruguayana. It was
our last evening on board, and rather a noisy one,
enlivened by songs and Christy Minstrel choruses,
during one of which even the most staid of our
officials were seen marching round and round the
saloon to the tune of the 'Mulligan Guards!'—much
to the discomfort of the whist-players. In the

---

[3] The figures, which I copy from the *Statesman's Year Book*, are
as follows: A Government enumeration made in 1857 showed a
population of 1,337,439 souls. An official return made at the beginning of 1873 puts the entire population at 221,079, comprising 28,746
men, 106,254 women over fifteen years of age, and 86,079 children.

morning we crossed over to Paso de los Libres—the Passage of the Free. 'What free?' I ask. To which the ever ready B—— at once replies: 'Los libres de derechos' (the free of duty), in allusion to the smuggling propensities of the place. With its high-sounding name it is but a mean, uninteresting spot, though graced by a monument to the eminent botanist Amédée Bonpland, the companion and fellow-worker of Humboldt, who, after a chequered existence, during some years of which he was forcibly detained in Paraguay by the Dictator Francia, withdrew to this place, where he married a *china*, and died in 1858: a sad and sombre ending to a life of brilliant scientific research. At Yatay, in the immediate neighbourhood of Paso de los Libres, or more correctly Restauracion, was fought one of the earliest and most sanguinary actions of the Paraguayan war, in which a small force of Paraguayans was defeated, after an obstinate struggle, by three times its numbers of Allied troops. Lopez's soldiers did no harm to the place, but at Uruguayana on the opposite shore they committed great ravages.

During our stay here we were again invaded by the natives, one of whom considerably disgusted us by doing the honours of the ship and coolly asking his companions whether they would not take some refreshment: 'Non tomará Vd. un

café?' just as if he had been in some public
eating-house instead of on board a private steamer.
As a set-off to this pestilent fellow, we had among
our visitors an extremely pretty, ladylike girl,
with auburn air and delicate features that curiously reminded me of a family which has furnished London society with some of its principal
beauties. As she stood afterwards on the shore
with her friends, watching our craft as it moved
off and got under way, one felt half sorry to leave
her behind with the boors of her dull Argentine
village. But in no country are the women of the
better classes so superior to the men in every way
as in this.

CHAPTER XVI.

SALTO ORIENTAL—THE GREAT RAPIDS—PAYSANDÚ—DOWN
STREAM TO BUENOS AYRES.

STEAMING against half a gale, which makes the river very rough and seriously impedes our downward progress, we pass, about three o'clock, an obelisk of stone, raised at the end of an island on our left, which marks the boundary between Brazil and Uruguay.   At half-past four we reach the creek at Ceibo, where we bid adieu to the ' Mensajero,' and, as yet an unbroken party, get into the special which is waiting for us.   We run through to Concordia without a break, drawing up at the station as the clock strikes half-past eight.   There is not much time to be lost if we would get to Salto, on the opposite bank, that night; so we part very reluctantly from Mr. S—— and B—— and two others of our party, and find our way, in the broad moonlight, to the landing-pier, where a good-sized cutter, kindly detailed for our service by the Captain of the Port, is waiting to take us across.

It is a longish pull of more than an hour against the stream, so that by the time we land and are walking up the steep and ruggedly paved streets of the town, it has got late, and certainly seems so to our supperless company. The streets are silent and empty and the house-fronts un-lighted. What life there is in these small South American towns, concentrates after dark in the *patios* at the back of the houses, whence issues now and then some hackneyed scrap of Verdi strummed on a jingly piano. At last we espy lights in a good-sized building on the left-hand side, which we rejoice to find is the inn we are in search of. Tired and hungry as we are, both food and beds seem to us perhaps exceptionally luxu-rious; but the fact is, that the Hôtel Oriental at Salto is so far superior to any establishment of the kind we are acquainted with in the River Plate, that it deserves more than a passing commendation. Its proprietor is a Gascon, who so thoroughly understands his business that we wonder he does not attempt a greater field of action than is afforded by a remote town of the Banda Oriental, by coming to teach Buenos Ayres what hotel-keeping ought to be.

Salto, seen by daylight, has a decidedly bright, cheerful look. It is a considerable provincial centre for this part of Uruguay, besides being the terminus

of the Alto Uruguay Railway (our opposition line),
and above all the seat of the prosperous ' Mensaje-
rias Fluviales' Steamship Company, who have their
dockyard and workshops here. Mr. W——, whose
residence it is, very kindly volunteered to do the
honours of the place. We strolled with him down
the main street, which has a few very well-built
houses with one-storied fronts—lavishly decorated
with marble—and inner *patios* bright with flowers,
giving evidence of considerable wealth. Our cicerone, who seemed to be on bowing or nodding
acquaintance with the entire population, amused us
by the distinguishing appellations he gave some of
these sumptuous dwellings. One was the house of
forty thousand *cuernos* (horns), and further on that
of thirty thousand—which, being interpreted, meant
that the young ladies whose homes they were had
the credit of being heiresses to that number of
cows. Of other houses he told us very different
and terrible things. A villa on the opposite shore,
overhanging the river, had a tradition attached to
it worthy of the ' Tour de Nesle.' Men were said
to have entered it alive and hale after dark, and
left it again—as did Marguerite de Bourgogne's
lovers — ' damp, uncomfortable bodies,' drifted
away by the stream ; so, at least, it was whispered
by the *mauvaises langues* of the place. But such
things should be forgotten—like the scandals of

King Arthur's court which some severe provincial dame blamed Mr. Tennyson for raking up.

The falls of the Uruguay are the great lion of Salto, and from them the place derives its name. The managers of the River Navigation Company most obligingly offered us a steam launch to take us up to them, so we proceeded thither about noon, in a broiling hot sun. Although I can hardly conscientiously recommend the excursion to others, it is not without interest. Of course the aspect of the falls must vary considerably with the volume of water in this singularly capricious river, but I am inclined to think that the title of Grand Leap (Salto Grande) given them is a piece of Castilian grandiloquence, and that they are never much more than rapids on a very great scale, though as such none the less obstructive to navigation. After steaming up the current for an hour and a half under a merciless sun, we left our launch at a point just below the falls where an *arroyo* disgorges itself into the river between two steep banks, under cover of one of which there lay a biggish schooner bound upwards, and arrested in its course by a sudden subsidence of the stream; it was partly unloaded, and may have been there for weeks, and have weeks to remain there yet. We ascended the opposite bank, and took a rough cut across fields covered with vivid patches of the scarlet and purple *verbena Tweediana*;[1] the river to our right was hidden from view by a wooded slope. A short half-hour's walk, over very uneven ground, brought us to the head of a kind of ravine, looking down which we had a complete prospect of what we had come to see.

A wilderness of shallow, troubled water was the general impression at once conveyed. The mighty river, vexed and hindered in its progress by a long succession of step-like reefs, had spread it- self out over an immense area, breaking its way in lines of foam through the narrow channels worn by its action, and eddying in the deeper places with a force that made the water appear to be seething upwards from concealed caldrons. The great slabs of dark, slimy rock which remained uncovered in the midst, or were simply trickled over by the surging flood, literally swarmed with water-fowl, drawn to the spot by the fish that lay temptingly in view in the shoal water all round. The entire long-billed tribe—cranes and herons and storks of every variety—stood there in serried files, watching their chance with a terrible earnestness—undis- tracted by the myriads of restless gulls which circled above them uttering their plaintive, wearisome cry. These professional fishers must have had a won-

[1] So called from a Scotch gardener of the name of Tweedie, who has the credit of having discovered the plant some fifty years ago.

derfully good time of it, for even from the height at
which we stood we could see their prey darting
about in the yellow current, while now and then
some big creature—probably a *dorado*[2]—would
leap out and flash for a second through the sunshine.

Our return down stream was made pleasant by
a southerly breeze, but the scenery was monotonous and lifeless in the extreme, the only object of
interest being a large eagle which followed in our
track for some time along the sparsely wooded bank.
We got back in time to take a drive with Mr.
W—— through and all round the town, which is
scattered up and down hill over a considerable extent of ground. As compared with Argentine places
of the same size, it is exceedingly trim and neat in
appearance, and has all the outward signs of prosperity. An unusually artistic fountain decorates
its central square, and is remarkable for its ornamentation of rough agates and cornelians. I had
already noticed a number of these stones in the
roads at Concordia ; they are exported in considerable quantities to Germany, where they are turned
into those thousand knicknacks in the shape of
bonbonnières, trays for cigar-ashes, &c., which make
up the cheap rubbish of the stalls at every German

---

[2] A kind of inferior salmon—poor eating, like most of the fish in
these rivers.

watering-place. Oberstein, on the railway from Forbach to Bingerbrück, is, I am told, the chief centre of this industry.

We got back from our drive at sunset, at the hour when the *niñas*, rich or not in cows, sally forth for their evening stroll in groups of three or four, or lounge gracefully in the doorways of their houses. Along the side walks resounds the sharp tread of the gallants who reconnoitre the fair ones as they pass, twirling a waxed moustache, and blowing clouds of doubtful fragrance from their cigarettes. A hum of female voices and subdued laughter fills the quiet streets and the pretty square, where the benches under the acacia trees are all tenanted—mostly by country folk, men in *ponchos* and *chiripas*, and sallow-faced *chinas*, with coils of coarse black hair twisted round their heads or hanging down their backs. The plashing of water from some fountain in an inner *patio* falls refreshingly on the ear, for the day has been unusually sultry, and an unpleasant steaminess still pervades the sun-scorched streets. Fortunately there are cooling drinks and a cool terrace at the Oriental, where we pass our last evening at Salto in pleasant talk over the condition of the country.

Things have again become somewhat critical in the Banda Oriental since the resignation of Colonel Latorre. It is barely six months since that officer

took the almost unexampled step of voluntarily
surrendering his dictatorial powers, with the quiet
remark that he found his countrymen ungovern-
able, and already the withdrawal of his firm hand
is showing its effects in a marked increase of crime
and lawlessness. His rule, whatever its faults, was
marked by unsparingly even-handed justice.   Mr.
W—— told us of an atrocious murder committed,
a short time back, on a wealthy landowner in this
department by some persons who were staying
with him as his guests. The assassins, seven in
number, were men of position—one of them a
colonel in the army. Latorre made short work of
them, and, after a summary inquiry establishing
the facts of the crime, had them all shot without further trial. This rough-and-ready style of
justice is unfortunately the best suited to a state of
society where personal influence and position, aided
by corruption, make a fair trial almost impossible,
and, in many cases, assure impunity to the offen-
der.   A still simpler mode, employed on occasion,
of making punishment certain consists in blowing
out the brains of the prisoner, and announcing in
the public prints the next day that he tried to escape and was shot in the attempt ' by sergeant so-
and-so.' There seems little doubt that towards the
end of Latorre's *régime* a security almost unknown
before reigned throughout the Banda Oriental.

We were sorry to leave Salto, but berths had been bespoken for us in the ' Jupiter,' and business besides made our return to Buenos Ayres imperative. Our start had to be made at ' the incense-breathing hour of cock-crow,' to borrow from the pet phraseology of a well-known Buenos Ayres paper. I don't know about the incense, but at that hour the courtyard of our hotel, with its beds of flowers, both smelt and looked delightfully fresh and sweet in the early sunlight. We left it, laden with orange blossoms and gardenias, three magnificent bushes of which latter plant, fully four feet high, grew in the centre, shedding their fragrance all round. On board the steamer we parted from Mr. W——, after obtaining from· him a promise of contributions from his clever pencil ; and a short run brought us abreast of Concordia where Mr. S—— came off to take leave of us with the Captain of the Port, Don Mariano C——, a very gentlemanlike man, whose brother is an officer of high rank in the Argentine navy. Mr. S—— gave us an interesting account of Don Mariano's wonderful escape from death, when quite a lad, in 1846. He was shut up, with other political prisoners belonging to families obnoxious to Rosas, in a room into which the *mashorqueros* [3] of the

---

[3] The *Mashorca* was a club, or secret society, of terrorists devoted to Rosas, who on occasion furnished the instruments of his private

tyrant were let loose one day with orders to spare no one.   The bloody work was done most effectually ; young C——, who alone was not mortally, though severely, wounded, swooning away and being left for dead with the rest.   On recovering consciousness he so wrought on the pity of one of the guards, that the man helped him to conceal himself till sufficiently recovered to effect his escape. We legitimately pride ourselves on affording an asylum to all political refugees indiscriminately ; but I confess it is to me a trying reflection that the author of an endless catalogue of atrocious crimes, of which the above was but a sample, should have lived and died in not unhonoured exile on our shores.[4]

There is little left to relate of our run down the river.   The 'Jupiter' was well stocked with passengers, mostly of an undesirable kind, one

revenge. The ruffians whom they employed were often recruited from among the butchers in the *saladeros*.

[4] The writer of an interesting book, recently published, on Italian emigration to these countries (A. Marazzi, *Emigrati : Studio e Racconto*) professes to give the exact number of the victims of Rosas during part of his rule, from 1829 to 1843. According to these tables of blood (*tavole di sangue*), as he calls them, 22,404 persons died a violent death during that period. From these must be subtracted 16,520 whom he puts down as having fallen in battle, the remaining five thousand eight hundred and odd having, by his account, had their throats cut (*sgozzati*), or been stabbed, or shot, in cold blood with, but more generally without, the mockery of a trial. These figures seem monstrous and are probably much exaggerated, but at no time, and in no country, was political assassination carried to greater lengths.

of whom had a peculiar way at meals of sticking his toothpick—a very formidable one—behind his ear, like a clerk's pen, during the intervals of using it. I have seen a good deal of this sort of thing in different countries, but this seemed new and original. The only place we stopped at for any length of time was Paysandú, of ox-tongue celebrity —a name which cannot but be familiar to travellers by the Metropolitan Railway, being placarded all over its carriages. The quays here have a lively look of bustle and activity; it is remarkable, too, for a church of considerable architectural pretensions, which obtrudes itself offensively on the sight. After staring, in spite of oneself, at this exceedingly ugly building, it was a relief to have one's attention drawn off by an inn hard by it, humorously dubbed by its proprietor 'Hotel Imparcial'— surely a charming name, suggestive of even-handed fleecing all round. Here, as well as at Concepcion, we took in numerous bales of wool, which were stacked high above the deck-cabins, in somewhat dangerous proximity to the funnel. When one had heard of the fate of some of the first boats started on these rivers, it was pardonable perhaps to feel a little nervous on the score of fire, and this was especially the case when, darkness having set in, one could see the sparks flying about all this combustible stuff. The night was very dark and

close, with a wonderful play of sheet-lightning on
the horizon, portending a heavy storm from the
south-west. For some time I sat reading in the
saloon, while the others played whist, till we were
all driven out by a sudden irruption of innumerable large white moths, which almost put out the
lights, and flapped about one's face and ears in the
most insupportable manner. The tables and cushions were completely littered with them in a few
minutes, and they fell in such quantities on the
deck outside as to make it quite greasy and slip-
pery. I have noticed the same curious phenomenon at Buenos Ayres, immediately before a thunderstorm, but never to such an extent as on this
occasion.

When we were called early in the morning, at
our journey's end, it was drizzling and blowing
hard—a regular *pampero sucio*. Seen through the
driving mist and rain the mole of Buenos Ayres
might have been the old pier at Hungerford Bridge,
and we felt far indeed from the verge of the tropics
we had trodden so lately. But we were home
again for one thing, and had letters and news from
the real home afar off to look forward to ; nor was
I personally disappointed, since, in the budget that
awaited me, I found assurance of no very prolonged
stay at this—to me in many respects the wrong
—end of the world.

CHAPTER XVII.

SUMMER IN BUENOS AYRES.

Soon after my return to my country abode the full summer heat set in. Nowhere, I think, have I suffered more from it than at Buenos Ayres. Not that the temperature rose as high as I have known it do elsewhere, though during the hot months of December, January, and February the thermometer frequently ranged between 80° and 90° in the shade, but that the atmosphere was so loaded with moisture, that even the night breezes seemed to have passed through steam before reaching me in my verandah, and to have lost all their freshness.

In the narrow, ill-ventilated streets of the city, one of course felt this damp heat much more, and the nights there were sometimes absolutely suffocating. As I had to go into town two or three times a week on business, I generally used my friend E——'s lodgings as a *pied-à-terre* there, especially on mail-days. E——, who is the soul of hospitality, had a couple of rooms at the disposal of visitors, and in one of these a *lit de sangle*, or trestle-bed, was put up for me whenever I wanted it. This primitive kind of bed, which used to be common enough in France, is known in native parlance as a *catre*, which a cheery Irish skipper ' in the Queen's navee,' who also much frequented these diggings, charmingly rendered into ' cataract.' I have the misfortune to be but a poor sleeper at the best of times, and although, next to a hammock, I could not have had a cooler crib, my cataract developed into a perfect Niagara, and I tossed through so many a restless night in it that I soon became painfully familiar with all the nocturnal and early morning sounds of the city. We generally dined late, in the open air, in the pretty *patio* of the Foreign Residents' Club, under the spreading branches of a large tree, with lovely purple and white blossoms, the name of which I tried in vain to discover ; and afterwards adjourned for our cigar to a public garden, a few doors from the house E——lived in, where there was a very fair orchestra, and occasionally a Spanish *zarzuela* company.

They kept late hours at this place, and long after I had left it and turned in, the strains of some waltz, with a rumbling accompaniment from the numerous trams and carriages that passed the door, followed me through the breathless night, and kept me awake well into the small hours. Towards morning, when it got perceptibly cooler, and I at

last managed to snatch a little rest, the reveille at
the barracks on the Retiro some distance off broke
through the stillness of the 'dark summer dawns'
and woke me again, not altogether unpleasantly.
First came a bugle call, quite by itself, and then
a sudden burst from the full band with a few bars
of a quaint old march which had evidently been
handed down from Spanish days; then the bugle
again, and all was still once more.   Presently, with
the first streaks of light, there appeared on the
scene my pet enemy, in the shape of a big brown
bird—the property of the old German landlady of
the lodging—whose cage was hung up against the
wall of the *patio* outside.   Ornithologically I believe
him to have belonged to the interesting family of
thrushes; although, unlike his congeners, he apparently had no gift of song of his own, or had lost
it in captivity.   On the other hand, in some evil
moment, he had been taught a fragment of a tune,
which he repeated with most damnable iteration
from earliest dawn till late at night; a curiously
aggravating little scrap that broke off with a dis-
sonance on a suspended note, as if the poor bird
got out of tune there, and, having once gone wrong,
could not pick up the rest of it.

I can hear it now, in Ċ natural: $d\ \breve{g}\ \bar{e}$; $\breve{c}\ d\ \breve{g}\ \bar{e}$;
$\breve{c}\ d\ \breve{g}\ \bar{e}$; $\breve{c}\ d\ d\ \bar{g}$?   The final g was a regular
note of interrogation, and seemed to say: 'Oh

bother! how does it go? Do please come and
help me!' It worked considerably on my nerves
at first, I confess, and rather made me feel like
wringing the bungling songster's neck, but after a
time I got not only used to it, but somehow per-
versely interested, and longed to help the poor
little captive out of his difficulties. If there be any
truth in fairy tales—and who that knows Grimm
and Andersen does not wish them true?—surely, I
thought, here might be the hero of one of them.
This wretched, dingy, iterative bird must be some
unfortunate enchanted prince—for local colour's
sake I would say an Indian cacique, were not those
chieftains so dreadfully unattractive—whose deliverance turns on his picking up the right note, and
singing out his little tune to the end. How hard
he seemed to try!—now and then varying it with
a touching little quirk or *fioritura*, but always
breaking down at that same fatal place. But alas!
there was no helping him ; for

> Fairies have broke their wands,
> And wishing has lost its power.

Our naval Paddy offered a good round sum for
him, but nothing would induce old Frau Bauer to
part with him ; and there, no doubt, he goes on
hopelessly singing to this day, up in his cage
against the blistering white wall, with the fierce
South American sun beating down upon him.

Hutchinson says somewhere in one of his books that the first noises which attract attention in South American cities are the sounding of bugles and ringing of bells, and this I found to be painfully true. Here, however, to the discordant jangle from many church towers must be added the shrill voices of a perfect plague of newspaper boys, who, long before any rational being can possibly get up any interest in the news of the day, are abroad all over the town crying out their wares still wet from the printing presses. 'El Nacional!' 'La Patria Argentina!' shout these horrid urchins, with a vigour that at first almost takes the stranger in, and makes him weakly believe there may be some portentous information in the sheets thus noisily hawked about.

The number of daily papers that appear here is quite out of proportion to the population, and is the more surprising that not one of them has anything like an extensive circulation. According to a foreign journalist of the place, there are at most two, out of some thirty of them, with a sale exceeding 3,000 copies. The same authority reckons the newspaper-reading public of Buenos Ayres at not more than 40,000, of whom nearly one half belongs to the fair sex and can therefore take but a small interest in the political controversies of the hour. Journalism, however, here,

as in the mother country, is a trade that carries
distinction with it and not unfrequently leads to
office and power, and the smart editor of to-day
may well hope to be the minister of to-morrow.
Some of the native papers, as the 'Nacional' for
instance, are no doubt very ably written; but
the purely local, or at any rate strictly American, topics they deal with, as a rule, make them
dry and uninteresting reading to the ordinary
stranger.

The foreign communities have of course news-
papers of their own. The Buenos Ayres 'Standard'
is too well known out of this country to need
mention, and it is sufficient to say that it is edited
with conspicuous talent and just a shade of
Hibernian eccentricity. Of the two principal
French papers, the 'Union Française' is in the
hands of editors of remarkable ability and literary
skill, and often contains valuable matter. The
unreasoning dislike it shows of England and all
that is English—and which is exaggerated by its
very inferior colleague the 'Courrier de la Plata'
—is on the other hand quite curious, and indeed
surprising on the part of such highly intelligent
and polished writers as those on its staff. The
foreign local press has so great a field and so
useful a mission before it in this country, that it
seems as if it should, above all, seek to direct and

enlighten public opinion and keep itself well above any petty prejudice or passion.

But to return to my friend E——'s lodging. Frau Bauer was quite a character in her way. She had originally gone out years before to Caracas, and had resided there for some time. Under a grim, almost forbidding, aspect the poor woman concealed a naturally sentimental disposition, which I suspect to have been crushed and soured in her younger days, and she was the kindest of souls. She had been driven from Venezuela by repeated revolutions, having had many people killed in her house there, and had come on—almost from the frying-pan into the fire—to this place, where she hired the upper story of a small house, and underlet it to lodgers. Besides E——, who occupied nearly the whole floor, and in whom she took the most motherly interest, her only other tenant was a quiet German music-master, who was out all day, but in the evening practised the piano steadily, and, so to speak, relieved the enchanted prince. Fortunately his room was at the back, looking over the inner yard, so that he did not trouble us much.

The waiting at this queer but delightful *phalanstère* was done by two juvenile Italians: a bonny little girl of fifteen of the name of Teresa, with lovely brown eyes and brilliant teeth and complexion—sadly untidy, I fear—who helped the Frau

in the house and kitchen, and was a very superior
kind of Marchioness; and a Genoese lad of about
the same age, who answered to the name of José, and
was E——'s body-servant—a capital, hardworking,
steady boy, but the most conceited, self-satisfied
young rascal I ever saw. The lad's naïve, solemn
ways so tickled E——'s sense of humour that my
friend had quite let him take him in hand, and
young Joseph did exactly as he liked with him. The
origin of his bumptiousness could be traced to the
time of the siege, when he had been put in charge
of a set of signalling flags which were run up on the
flat roof of the house for communication with the
men-of-war in the river ; and the boy, from working
them, had got to think that he was actually in
command, and had accordingly become full of self-
importance. He was suspected of hoisting the
signals occasionally on his own hook, and of even
having brought the captain—our Paddy friend—on
shore when he was not wanted. José's only weakness was the bowling-ground next door, whither
he adjourned whenever he had a chance. He was
especially great there on Sunday afternoons, when
I sometimes amused myself watching him from a
balcony that had a side view of the ground. It
was highly comical to see the impudent little rascal
looking on, with a critical air, at a game between
half a dozen great hulking compatriots of his, and

offering remarks on the play, which were apparently received with perfect respect and deference, such is the power of self-assertion. The only person who stood up to him, and treated him with the good-humoured disdain a girl generally has for a boy of her own age, was pretty little Teresita. Poor José was but a puny stripling and anything but muscular, and, in his unbounded self-confidence, sometimes tried his hand at carrying or lifting things that were much beyond his strength, when little Teresita, who was as strong as a horse and as straight as an arrow, would pounce upon him and contemptuously whisk away the burden he was struggling with in vain. Those must have been bitter moments for poor José!

Such pleasant breakfasts we had in the back dining-room opening on to the balcony that ran around the yard, as in ancient hostelries. It was quiet here, and comparatively cool, away from the clatter and glare of the street. The high dead wall opposite, that shaded the yard, was relieved by the green and pink of a few oleanders in big tubs; on the top of the flat roof a row of snow-white pigeons glittered like silver against the intense blue above; along the sunlit passage comely, bright-eyed Teresita came tripping with a dish of *pejereyes* or the *vaterländische Schnitzel*, which was solemnly received at the door by the important Joseph. Sud-

denly there was a white flash across the sky and a
whirr, as in the courtyard of Sultan Bayazid, and
the whole flock of pigeons alighted round the
platter, which was put out on the balcony, for their
daily meal. I think I then realised for the first
time how thoroughly unamiable these birds can be,
for all their soft cooing and tender ways. There
was amongst them one who always made for the
platter first, and when he had fed voraciously—
taking savage little runs in between at any other bird
that ventured near—would deliberately squat down
in the dish and spread himself well out so as to
prevent any one from getting at it. The rest of
the company for a time timidly watched him in a
circle at a respectful distance, till at last, after much
fluttering of wings and strutting to and fro, half a
dozen of them screwed up their courage to the
necessary pitch, and, making a simultaneous rush
at this gluttonous bird in the manger, expelled him
for good. There was a deal of negotiation, however, before it came to action, and considerable
arguing of the 'just you go forward and I will
follow' type, such as may be occasionally heard
when more important bipeds are getting up coalitions.

But I hasten to bring these intensely personal
recollections to a close, as otherwise the most
indulgent of readers might well turn upon me as

did the grumpy old Prussian general on the gushing young aide-de-camp who was riding out with him to the manœuvres at break of day. 'Look, *Herr General*,' exclaimed the enthusiastic youth, 'how lovely is the sunrise!' 'Sunrise!' growled back the old warrior; 'don't bother me with your private affairs!' (*Was, Sonnenaufgang! Lassen Sie mich mit Ihren Privatangelegenheiten in Ruh!*)

Of a summer evening the whole population turns out into the streets, and from sunset till nine or ten the centre of the town is as thronged with well-dressed foot-passengers as the Passage des Panoramas at Paris, or the Burlington Arcade on a wet day in the season. The great delight of the Porteño feminine world is to go shopping (*ir á las tiendas*) at that hour, the shopping being generally but a pretext for a display of the last pretty dresses and for seeing and being seen. After seven o'clock the streets are so full that even the uncompromising trams—themselves crammed with passengers— have to crawl along at a foot's pace like a London four-wheeler. Fashion, here as everywhere else, has set certain arbitrary bounds within which its votaries may alone indulge in this evening saunter, and these comprise at most a couple of hundred yards of the Florida and Calle San Martin, on either side of the point where those streets intersect the equally frequented Rivadavia and Victoria. This limited space, as any visitor to Buenos Ayres would remember, is the very heart or kernel of the city. The *niñas* (girls), as the young ladies are unceremoniously termed here, make up parties to go on these so-called shopping expeditions, and slowly promenade, in groups of five and six, up and down this narrow beat, till one wonders how their high-heeled shoes can carry them any longer. It is their only form of exercise, and they never seem to tire of it.

At this hour, as has been well observed, charming woman and an equally delightful free-and-easiness reign supreme in the streets. There is scarcely any bowing or lifting of hats; the merest acquaintances address each other quite naturally by their Christian names, as if they were near relations; and the smartest *niña* of them all thinks nothing of shaking hands with the gentleman who is attending to her behind the counter, or of bestowing a languid attention on the insipid compliments with which he interlards the bargain. The narrow foot-pavements are blocked up by a stream of young women with high-pitched voices, laughing and chattering and fanning themselves, and altogether as much at their ease as in their own drawing-rooms at home. As for the men, the right thing for the *gommeux* of the place is to lean up against the walls and in the doorways of the houses and shops, or line the outer edge of the pavement, the ladies filing past quite unconcernedly between this double row of not over-respectful admirers. It is not a very edifying custom, but so generally recognised and long established as to be practically harmless, though somewhat startling to a new-comer. A clever and observant French writer handles it sharply, and describes it as 'an insolent lane of lighted cigars, loose remarks, and at times unseemly greetings.'[1] This is severe language, though in some measure not uncalled for. The ladies are primarily to blame, of course, it resting with them to command and insure the outward respect which is their due, and which must always be forthcoming whenever they take pains to exact it.

No doubt, however, the Argentine youth of the period is a highly irrepressible creature ; and this owing mainly to unwise parental indulgence. He is too often emancipated at an age when, under European arrangements, he would still be strictly kept to his studies in the schoolroom at home, or in some public academy away from home. Boys of thirteen or fourteen are allowed here a liberty scarcely granted with us to lads several years their seniors, and, as a consequence, put on, when

---

[1] '*Deux haies insolentes de cigares allumés, de propos libres, et d'apostrophes quelquefois malséantes.*'

barely twenty, all the pretensions of full-grown men of the world. A natural physical precocity intensifies, of course, the evil. Society is thus over-run with immature youths of indifferent manners who are too often puffed up with ill-digested knowledge, or primed with the crudest theories, and have experienced neither the wholesome, subduing discipline of public school life, nor the more refining influences of sound home-teaching and example.[2] Parental, like all other, authority has not escaped the effects of democratic institutions, as understood and practised by these neo-Latin races. Parents and children associate on a footing of equality which almost degenerates into an easy *camaraderie*. In part this is due to a certain inequality of level, as regards education, between the older and the younger generation, for the extensive system of public instruction of which the Argentines are justly proud is of very modern growth, and nearly entirely the work of President Sarmiento. From young men thus brought up, and whose training has been almost purely that of the intellect, it would be idle to expect any old-fashioned regard for age or sex. The irreverential and sadly

[2] The Buenos-Ayrean collegian, like the *externe* in French Lycées, only attends school for a certain number of hours a day, and out of school is left to do very much as he pleases.

sceptical youth of the day is bent above all on securing his share of the goods and pleasures of this world, though wellnigh weary of them, as it were, before fruition.

A sombre, unattractive picture this, but for the most part drawn by far more competent hands than mine. Its uglier features will soon, it may be safely predicted, disappear. Greater maturity in the nation will generate more sterling qualities and produce a more equal level in the various classes of all ages composing it. The young generation, now pardonably intoxicated with a knowledge placed to its hand as it were yesterday, and which was in great measure denied to that which preceded it, will gradually make room for soberer, more thoroughly educated successors; the daily increasing contact with more perfectly trained European races will do the rest. As elsewhere, society will insist on what is due to it, and become its own policeman. But of the old-world customs and courtesies—may-be superstitions—so cherished and valued by us, little can be expected ever to take deep root in this soil.

Wandering as I am about the streets, it must be well understood that to the streets most of the above strictures are intended to apply. There exists here a remnant of thoroughly high-bred, old-world society, which, in self-defence, keeps very much to itself, and is by no means easy of access even to the stranger who comes out furnished with good introductions. It was my good fortune to become acquainted with some of the families composing it. One of the most charming of these owned an estate on the Western Line of Buenos Ayres, some twenty miles out of town, and of a hot Sunday afternoon it was pleasant to run down there for dinner.

A well-appointed wagonette, with a light roof to it and open at the sides, met visitors at the station, which takes its name from the owner of the property. The house—a spacious rambling villa, with numerous outbuildings—stands in the midst of well-kept shrubberies, and is approached by an avenue that leads up to a wide sweep of gravel in front of the main door, dividing the building from that very rare article out here—a large, though somewhat unkempt, lawn, encircled by lofty poplars and *paraisos*, dating back a good many years, whose tops rustle in a perennial breeze even on this stifling afternoon. The estate has been held by its present proprietors for upwards of a century, having come to them, I believe, through a match with one of the descendants of Don Juan de Garay, the real founder of Buenos Ayres,[3] on whom the

---

[3] Two anterior settlements made by Diego Garcia in 1530, and Pedro de Mendoza in 1535, were destroyed by the Querandi Indians.

Crown of Spain conferred vast possessions in this neighbourhood after a crushing victory over the Indians, which, from its sanguinary character, was called Matanzas (or ' the slaughter ' *par excellence*), a name that has extended to the entire department.

Passing from the crowded, dusty train into all this peaceful verdure, one experiences at once a sensation of real country freshness which has become quite unfamiliar. The great rough lawn, all starred with daisies and buttercups, naturally leads one's thoughts homewards to where ' the dewy meadowy morning breath of England ' is ' blown across her ghostly wall ; ' but the thick, rustling curtain that screens it carries me back in quite another direction, far away over the Andes, to the wonderful avenues of giant Lombardy poplars, meeting overhead like vast and dim cathedral aisles, that stretch across the sunburnt plains of Chile. The trees there, closely planted in double and treble rows, form a perfect wall of foliage, and under the cover of their impenetrable shade one may ride for miles in the hottest hours of the day, the scorching light filtering, as it were, through folds of green gauze, and tracing leafy patterns on the thick carpet of sand that deadens the horse's hoofs.

The same grateful sense of refuge from heat

and glare came over me on being shown across
the dazzling white colonnade into the cool twilight
of a lofty room that opened out of it. From a
corner of this spacious apartment two figures, clad
in soft white summer dresses, came forward through
the half-light to greet the arriving guests. Charming apparitions both of them: the one very dark
and the other as strikingly fair—the latter being
one of the married daughters of the house. It
was by no means my first visit here, but there is
a simple natural grace about these South American
ladies which would put the very shyest of Britons
at his ease and dispel all insular *mauvaise honte.*
As it is yet early in the afternoon, I almost suspect
our fair entertainers of having indulged in a slight
siesta in their cool, carefully darkened corner previous to our arrival; but all their native animation
has come back to them now, and they make me,
and the friend who has accompanied me, thoroughly
welcome in perfect French, with just a pretty tinge
of Southern accent. Presently other members of
the family drop in and join our circle, the men all
dressed in well-cut white clothes, and we while
away the time with music and conversation till the
heat has subsided enough for an adjournment to
the garden, where a few misguided members of the
party start a fantastic kind of croquet—an abominable game which, by the way, I am glad to see,

is exploded everywhere else. The two ladies who first received us are both very good musicians, especially the fair (doubly fair) one, who has been extremely well taught, and plays Chopin, among other things, remarkably well. The men meanwhile —a grave judge and a senator amongst them—stroll away to an immense tank in a secluded part of the grounds, into which they plunge one after another and disport themselves like so many light-hearted schoolboys out for a holiday. A couple of carriages are presently brought round, and in the crimson glow of a glorious sunset we are taken for a drive all about the place, and across the flat, here highly cultivated, plain that encompasses this verdant retreat : the ladies driving, and handling the reins with perfect ease, and a cavalcade of children of all ages escorting us on their ponies.

The effect produced from the very first by this large family-gathering—for there are three or four married sons and daughters—is that of perfect concord and of truly delightful domestic relations; and this becomes still more apparent when we all meet round the dinner-table, the venerable master and mistress of the house not appearing till then. The affectionate, but somewhat ceremonious, respect with which this charming old couple are treated by all reminds me rather of what may be seen in

French family circles of the best class than with us, and there is a kind of courtly, Faubourg-St.-Germain grace, combined with a patriarchal simplicity, about the whole thing, that leaves the most pleasing impression. Our host, who is a grandee in his way—one of the very few who could fairly pretend to such a title in this thoroughly new and carefully levelled society—is old enough to belong almost to colonial days. He still keeps open table, a custom which was universal in the olden time, but is now confined to the houses of a few of the greater *estancieros*. Leaving aside its hospitality, the habit contributes to maintain something of the ancient bond between patron and clients, and is almost the last and most commendable vestige of the social arrangements that obtained under Spanish rule.

The old-fashioned circle is in fact growing narrower day by day, and closing up more and more. Of families such as this, which, without making the least pretension to aristocracy, preserves and hands down the best aristocratic traditions, but few are left. Like its ancestral domain, it seems to be an oasis of freshness and health in the midst of the feverish wastes of speculation and pure money-seeking that surround it. One cannot but desire that such as it may continue, for yet awhile, to leaven and lighten the heavy dough of an almost exclusively mercantile, stock-jobbing community, which, not having grown up like ours among older forms, is too apt to live after canons of its own not altogether attractive or commendable.

CHAPTER XVIII.

SUMMER IN THE PAMPA—BEAUTY OF THE CLIMATE—WILDFOWL SHOOTING.

I HAD been asked several times by a friend and fellow-countryman to his *estancia*, some eighty miles south of Buenos Ayres—a model place in every way deserving a visit—and towards the middle of January, the heat continuing without abatement and trying me very much, I made up my mind to accept the invitation, and wrote to propose myself. 'Come at once, by all means,' was the cordial reply. 'I have a few of our mutual friends staying with me, and you will be doubly welcome. I hope, too, to show you better beef than our friend —— gives me credit for.' This, in allusion to a standing joke against the writer of the letter, who is one of the most careful and successful stock-breeders in the River Plate, and the owner of the famous Negrete breed of striped *merinos*; the fact certainly being that in a country raising cattle in myriads, and felling it in hecatombs, and among a population which gorges itself on meat,[1] the rarest thing possible is a tolerable beefsteak.

The assertion may well sound paradoxical, but all those who have resided for any length of time at Buenos Ayres would admit its truth. The beasts which are brought into town have too often been driven, with little mercy, over very long distances, and reach the market in a condition that makes them almost unfit for food. Stall-feeding, too, being hardly ever practised, even on the most expensively managed estates, prime meat, such as we are accustomed to in Europe, is quite the exception. No one was better aware of this than my good friend the *estanciero*, and he was, accordingly, rather sensitive on this point. He was, never-theless, as good as his word, and his beef was of a keeping with the rest of his arrangements—that is to say, excellent. There is no occasion, how-ever, for dwelling at length on his hospitality, which is well known far beyond the limits of the River Plate, and has been already done ample justice to by other pens than mine.

It takes about five hours to get over the seventy odd miles to V——, the station to which I was bound on the Great Southern. People are

---

[1] It has been reckoned that the consumption of meat of the in-habitants of Buenos Ayres (the town) is at the rate of 2 lbs. a day per head.

seldom in a violent hurry in this country, and take
their travelling easily like everything else, and it
seems to matter little to the general public whether
they reach their destination a couple of hours
sooner or later. For one thing, it is not so long
since they performed their journeys on horseback,
or over impossible roads in a slow-paced coach, and
locomotion at fifteen miles an hour may well seem
to them speedy enough for all practical purposes.
Most of the passengers, too, are connected in
some way or other with agricultural or pastoral
industry, which of its nature can only be pursued
leisurely, the seasons, in their immutable course,
marking out the work to be done with a routine
which admits of little hurry or impatience. There
are no manufacturing or industrial centres to take
men backwards and forwards in hot haste with
watch in hand; nor is there, of course, any travelling for mere pleasure's sake. Even the feminine
element is almost entirely wanting, and, with the
exception of now and then the wife or daughters
of some landowner going up to town for their
shopping, very few ladies are to be met travelling
by rail. The trains, with their mixed bucolic
freight of farmers and *peones*, smart *estancieros*,
Italian labourers in fustian, burly Basque shepherds and swarthy Gauchos in *ponchos* and broad-
brimmed straw hats, go dawdling along through

the changeless plains in the most approved *Bummelzug* fashion, pulling up every twenty minutes or so at some station without much apparent reason. It is hot, drowsy, and, above all, dusty work. The country never varies, and with the map in one's mind's eye one can almost imagine oneself being roused, after so many more hours of it, with 'Straits of Magellan!—Ten minutes for refreshment!—Passengers for Cape Horn embark here!'

A good-sized covered break, with four smart bays, was drawn up alongside the station, with mine host on the box, and away we merrily went over the level springy turf in an evening breeze which appeared singularly refreshing to me, coming as I did from the damp depressing heat of the town and its neighbourhood. The real beauty of the climate can only be thoroughly appreciated away from the turbid waters of the Plate and its moisture-laden atmosphere. The clear, dry air of the Pampa, even at this torrid season, always excepting the days when the abominable north wind comes sweeping down from the tropics, imparts a sense of health and vigour to each breath one draws in, and inclines one to credit the somewhat startling assertions which are gravely made respecting the longevity of its inhabitants.

According to a tabular statement, contained in

a semi-official publication which I have had occasion
to quote before, the general census of 1869 showed
the number of centenarians in the Republic to be
234, or one in 7,422 of the population, and, of
these, twenty-six were put down as having attained
the age of one hundred and twenty and upwards.
As if this were not enough, it was added that
of 468 old people, described as of unknown age,
one half at least might be assumed to have out-
lived a century. What would the late Sir George
Cornewall Lewis or Mr. Thoms have said to these
figures? Without impugning in any way the good
faith of the enumerators of the census, some
doubt may be fairly expressed as to the perfect
accuracy of the old colonial church registers on
which they relied. On the other hand, if to
breathe the most invigorating air and lead the most
monotonous and uneventful kind of existence can
contribute to prolong the span of human life,
there is no denying that the native of the Pampas
enjoys both in perfection. Certainly one gets an
occasional glimpse of some ancient crone, squatting
on the bare ground outside a sordid hovel, whose
wrinkled brown parchment skin may well have
been mummified by a hundred summers. There
died, too, a short time ago, at Buenos Ayres, an
old itinerant negro pieman—a well-known character—who was reputed to have served in the

Spanish ranks at the close of the last century, and passed for being at least a hundred and six when he sold his last pie and went 'where the good niggers go.' Be this as it may, by the end of the rapid, exhilarating drive of eight miles or so from the station to the house, I already feel a good deal younger and fresher; and a hearty welcome from my fellow-guests, followed by a pleasant dinner and evening, puts me altogether in better case than I have been in for weeks past.

We are up almost by daybreak the next morning, ladies and all—and ready for that most enjoyable of all things in hot weather in the Pampa, the early ride before breakfast. A confidential pony has been provided for me, and more showy, but equally reliable, mounts for two young ladies whom our host, a capital horseman, is perfecting in equitation. The mother of one of these, a charming person, is likewise of the party, so that we naturally resolve into two groups, the sedate and the more frolicsome one.

The girls, with their escort, gallop away ahead in open order, charging the small ditches with which the ground is furrowed here and there, and doing a little mild steeple-chasing. We follow at a more moderate pace, but even our staid animals eagerly sniff the morning breeze, and impatiently shake their bits as they trot or canter along. No wonder, for the going through the cool air, over this even, elastic soil, is simply perfect.

No words—certainly of mine—can convey an adequate idea of the beauty and freshness of the prairie at this early hour. The young sun, but just now risen like ourselves, floods the low and perfectly level horizon with a flush of pink and yellow light. At once you realise the full force of the well-known, hackneyed image which compares the boundless expanse of plain to an ocean solitude, for the effect is truly that of sunrise out upon the waste of waters. The fiery disc emerges from what seems a sea of verdure, all burned and brown though everything be in reality, and in its slanting rays the tip of each blade of green, the giant thistles with their rose-purple crowns, the graceful floss-like panicles of the Pampa grass (*paja corta-dera*), just touched by the breeze and all glittering with dew, undulate before the eye like the succes-sive sparkling lines that mark the lazy roll of the deep in the dawn of a tropical calm. The sky above, of a most lovely pale azure and of wonder-ful transparency, has not yet deepened into that almost painful hue of crude cobalt it acquires in the full blaze of the noontide. In the west the vapours of night have not entirely rolled away, while down in the dips and depressions of ground— *cañadas* as they call them here—and over the reed-

T

fenced *lagunas*, a thin blue mist still lingers, and .
mingles deliciously with the various subdued tints
of brown and green around. This tender tonality
lasts but a very short time, the sun shooting
upwards with a speed and force that at once
completely transform the picture ; the searching
agencies of light revealing it in its true parched
colours, and reducing it to a burning arch above
and a scorched and featureless flat below. The
fresh, rippling ocean turns into a weary wilderness staring up at a breathless, pitiless sky.

Hardly less striking than the waking up of the
great plain is the stir of bird and insect life that
accompanies it. The air is full of buzzing and
chirping, and of the flutter of wings. So thickly
is the Pampa peopled with birds, that it quite produces the effect of an open-air aviary. Brilliant
little creatures, with red or yellow breasts, *zorzals*
and cardinals, magpies and oven-birds, dart in and
out of the grass and bushes in every direction,
while, in the higher regions, numerous hawks and
kites hover ominously over these tempting preserves. All this feathered tribe are singularly fearless and unconcerned at one's approach, the only
exception being that well-known abomination of
the sportsman in the Pampa, the spur-winged
plover. This insufferable creature, who, as Mr.
Darwin somewhere says of him, appears to hate

mankind, swarms all over the prairie, and pursues one with a loud and discordant cry which is exactly rendered by his common name of *teru-tero*.   He is really a very handsome bird, with glossy black and lavender plumage tipped with green and purple, but, like much lovelier beings one has occasionally met with, his beauty is quite marred by his harsh, unmusical voice and froward ways.   He is both the spy and the scold of the Pampa.   Being too worthless in himself to stand in danger of being shot, his one idea seems to be to spoil sport.   As soon as he gets sight of you, he sets up his shrill, wearying note, and follows you pertinaciously about, of course warning all the game around of your approach.   Altogether an odious bird, who, to quote Mr. Darwin again, fully deserves to be hated.

Long before eight o'clock we are all back again at the house, where, after a refreshing bath and breakfast, we lounge and sit about through the hot hours of the day in the cool *patio*, with its colonnade, and well of icy water in the centre, surrounded by flowering shrubs; or in the shade of the charming garden and park-like grounds which our host and the preceding owner of the property have conjured up by degrees out of the primitively treeless waste.   The *monte* immediately round the place covers a large extent of ground, and is unusually thick and luxuriant, the Australian gum-tree, willows, acacias, and Scotch firs all thriving here to perfection, and forming walks and avenues such as I found nowhere else in this country. From a distance, the plantations have all the appearance of a great wooded hill, and are visible for miles round. The grass on the lawn and under the trees is singularly green and tempting, though, as I soon found to my cost, it will not do to yield to one's natural inclination and lie down on it. One very sultry afternoon I strolled out into the garden with a book and a cigar, and, selecting a cosy shady nook, flung myself down on the close velvety turf. For a short time it was delightful, and I was just on the pleasant borders between a day-dream and a *siesta*, when, of a sudden, a violent irritation about the calf of my left leg sent me into a sitting posture again, like a clown in a pantomime, and soon set me tearing my skin in the most indecorous fashion. I closely inspected the place, but could see no trace whatever of a bite, and, being at last driven nearly wild, went to consult my friend. 'Ah!' said he, 'I should have warned you of the *bicho colorado*, which has evidently been at you.' It is difficult to form any idea of the degree of irritation produced by these villainous little insects. They are a bright red, as their name implies, and no bigger than a pin's head, and are, I fancy, very much akin to the *jigger* of West Indian fame. I was kept awake, and in a perfect fever, for several nights by the bite, and even for months afterwards was liable to returns of insupportable itching in that one particular spot. With the exception of these plaguey little creatures and the annoying mosquitoes—less troublesome here than in town—the Pampa is singularly free from noxious vermin of all kinds. Only one deadly species of viper (the *víbora de la cruz*) is to be met there, as well as the venomous tarantula.

Our day generally ended in a long drive over the estate, which is upwards of six leagues square. We took our guns with us, and now and then as we passed one of the small *lagunas* that abound in the plain—mere saucers full of water, a foot or two deep, with a few reeds and tufts of Pampa grass round them—the shooters jumped out and let fly at a stray wild duck or so. Our host is, I think, the best and quickest duck-shot I ever met, and I have seen him bring down birds in this way at almost incredible distances. He was no less good at *batitú*, a kind of golden plover, which, when in season, as at this time, is the best eating possible. Before taking wing, these birds creep warily under cover a long way on the ground, from which it is difficult to distinguish them, and it requires a great knack of snap-shooting to hit them when they show across some open space, or rise where you least expect them. We used to go after them across country in a light gig which had a strong tendency to tilt over, and to shoot well from so unsteady a platform was anything but easy. It was capital sport in its way.

What, however, I believe to be simply unsurpassed, is the wild-fowl shooting in the *lagunas*, even at this time of the year, when the water in them is low and many of the birds have gone away further south. Some fifteen miles from the *estancia* house, there is a great shallow sheet of water, covering a good many acres, where I had an afternoon's sport that I shall never forget. We started soon after breakfast on our way thither—the whole party—on a charming day with fleecy clouds and a cool wind from the south-west. One of our young ladies now and then took a turn at the ribbons, and we trotted along gaily, our host sounding an occasional blast from a bugle, at the startling sound of which the herds of cattle browsing around pricked up their ears and came charging down to within a few yards of us. Presently, as we reached the crest of a slight rise in the ground, the big *laguna* lay stretched out before us, what water there was in it glittering in the sun in large patches, in between the tall rushes and sedge that half cover it. In the foreground there was a large open space, half mud

A LAGUNA WITH FLAMINGOS.

and half water, and there I at once saw the exact
living reproduction of one of the coloured plates
to Burmeister's Descriptive Physical Atlas of this
country—a column of flamingos gravely stalking
over the wet ground in double file, like a red-
coated. sergeant's guard marching up Pall Mall.
There were at least twenty of them together—a
sight to move the most *blasé* of sportsmen.

We jumped down, and, after taking out and
hobbling our team, leaving the ladies and non-
shooters to unpack the luncheon-baskets, my host
and I crept down the slope as fast as ever we could.
There was not a scrap of cover between us and the
birds, so that, long before we could get anywhere
within shot, the flock showed signs of disturbance
and began flapping their big wings, and then, with
a mighty whirr and a great trumpeting, rose from
the ground and were away like a fiery cloud.   We
gave them a parting salute, and then went well
over our knees into the marsh, and stood there for
a good two hours or more, crouching in the tall
reeds, and, I can honestly declare for myself, blazing away most of the time as fast as we could load.
It is no exaggeration to say that, at intervals ot
perhaps five minutes, flight upon flight passed over
my head, frequently well within range, and that
the barrels of my breechloader got so hot that I
had several times to stop and forego some excellent

shot. The birds rose out of the marsh like fire-works in every direction : strings of wild duck of half a dozen species ; clouds of sandpipers and teal ; bronze ibises—beautiful birds with glossy dark green and copper plumage—shooting past like arrow-heads, which they exactly resemble in their flight ; herons and cranes innumerable ; and then, flying in serried column and wheeling with great precision, came past again a squadron of the gorgeous flamingos, their scarlet wings all glowing in the sun.   Although by no means accustomed to this bewildering sort of shooting, I managed to knock over a certain number of birds of one kind and another, but lost most of them, as they generally fell among the rushes some way off, and we only had one dog with us, who remained with my companion at the other end of the marsh.

Meanwhile it was getting long past the hour appointed for lunch, so I reluctantly left my post to join my friend. We had just met, and were comparing notes about our bags, when another troop of great birds came over us with a pink flash, but so high up as to be quite out of range it seemed to me.   My friend, nevertheless, called out to me to shoot, so I let fly both barrels, and, to my great joy, a mass of pink feathers came down with a heavy thud and splash some twenty yards off—a splendid specimen of that rare and lovely bird the roseate spoonbill (*platalea ajaja*). This, with a couple of flamingos, was the principal item of our very mixed but satisfactory bag. With more guns and dogs, and a few Gauchos on horseback to drive the birds into the marsh again, we might have shot any number.

The only drawback to this wonderful shooting in the *lagunas* is the black ooze in which one has to stand motionless for so long, and which, when stirred up, is most offensive, being in fact full of decayed vegetable matter. There is an old prejudice in favour of these brackish *lagunas*, on account of the Indians having always sought out their neighbourhood for their encampments, whence it is argued that they are a sign of good land. The most competent authorities now assert this to be a fallacy, the lazy savages having simply kept to these natural reservoirs for their cattle and horses sooner than be put to the trouble of digging wells. Good water can be got everywhere in abundance by boring a few feet below the surface, and, on properly managed *estancias*, each *puesto* [2] into which the estate is divided has now its primitive biblical well, with a great leather *manga*—

---

[2] The *puesto*, or post, is the space allotted to so many hundred or thousand head of sheep or cattle, placed under the supervision of the *puestero*, whose hut, with its clump of peach trees and *paraisos*, is a kind of miniature *estancia* house.

sleeve or bag—attached to it, from which the precious liquid is poured into the watering-troughs.

It was getting towards dusk as we neared the house on our return. The queer little owls who do sentry duty over the *biscacha* holes were sitting out on their mounds, and, as we went by one of these, we got sight of the *biscacha* itself. One of the ladies expressing some curiosity about them, our host pulled up short, and was off the box in a second. He ran on a few yards, and then rolled over the quarry just as he was hopping into his den. A very large-sized one, bigger than the biggest hare, and with long grey whiskers and vicious-looking fangs—quite a different creature in appearance from what one expected so harmless a rodent to be like.

We had been somewhat disappointed in not finding any black-necked swans that day, so my friend promised to show me some before I went back to town. He accordingly drove me one afternoon down to the river Salado, which runs, as it were, in a trench it has cut for itself through the plain, between steep banks some thirty feet high. Within a few yards of the river we left our trap, and crept carefully through the low bush till we reached the verge of the bank and could see the stream beneath us, and, in a bend of it a little higher up, a flock of the splendid birds we were after. We now had to crawl some distance without any kind of cover, till we got within shot, when, just as we were in proper position, something startled the flock and they were on the move. Twice we were baulked in the same manner, but at last got a fair chance.

Bang, bang, from my friend: a bird falling to the first shot just as it was taking wing, and luckily dropping on our side of the river. Bang, bang, again from both of us: a second bird being badly winged when halfway across, but still managing to struggle on to the further bank. Just as he reached it a final shot from me, and he lay quivering in the reeds. My friend now let slip his pet retriever, who was trembling all over with excitement, and in a few bounds the plucky brute was down the bank and had plunged into the water. He swam straight across, and grappling the dying swan brought him over, quite forty yards through a strong current, and laid the noble bird—a full-grown male—at our feet. It was a gallant performance and deserved recounting. Each of the birds weighed fully twenty pounds, as we soon found out when we had to carry them back to our trap.

Between these shooting and other excursions in the neighbourhood—among others to a very fine native *estancia*, situated on the banks of the

Salado, with unusually well-kept gardens sloping down to the stream, where we were most sumptuously entertained and were shown some valuable stock lately imported from Europe—time passed so rapidly and pleasantly that the fortnight's holiday I had allowed myself came to an end all too soon. I can only wish all visitors to the River Plate as delightful an experience as I had of midsummer in the Pampas.

The dismal and decidedly repelling effect produced at first by the weary sameness of the prairies soon passes off, and makes room for a sense of their indefinable charm, somewhat saddening in its nature, and to my mind akin to that of music in a minor key, the soughing of the wind among forest tops, or the lulling cadence of the waves breaking on our northern shores. No doubt the clue to these impressions is to be sought in the fact that nowhere else perhaps, except in sight of the unchangeable but ever-varying ocean, or face to face with mountain solitudes, do you find yourself put so directly in contact with nature in her primitive and more solemn aspects.

Only a few miles off the beaten track and you are at once in the midst of scenes that have manifestly remained unaltered from the period when—according to the latest and most plausible theory put forward—the great diluvian bed of the Pampas was formed by the gradual denudation of the rocks of the Cordilleras. The huge plateau, raised inch by inch during the countless roll of centuries, contains in its subsoil unimpeachable evidence of its original features having rigidly endured throughout the process, in the remains of the extinct fauna of prehistoric ages that lie thickly imbedded in it at a certain depth, or have been found incrusted in the face of its river-banks—literally like the plums in a slice of cake, if so homely a comparison be permissible.[3] Across the same plains where now feed and wander remunerative herds and flocks—only at a much lower level—the megatherium, or that other monster sloth the mylodon, dragged its uncouth giant limbs, and the original Andalusian jennet, from which spring the now innumerable troops of native horses, was preceded ages before by the *hippidium*, or fossil horse—the genuine, hitherto accounted fabulous, unicorn. Dig, in fact, but a certain number of feet below the surface, and you come upon a crowded antediluvian world.

Nowhere in these solitudes has the human race left any trace of its passage. While those other analogous waste spaces of the Old World—the

---

[3] The museum at Buenos Ayres contains a remarkable—indeed, I believe unique—collection of these remains, admirably arranged by its distinguished director, M. Burmeister.

steppes of Eastern Europe and Central Asia—have witnessed the rise and fall of empires, or resounded with the tread of conquering hordes from Attila to Tamerlane, these wildernesses have not a single day of history to place on record.

This is especially striking to the traveller from the Eastern Hemisphere, accustomed everywhere to see that harmonious blending of landscape and human handiwork which makes up our ideal of scenery, and in which shattered monuments, and other countless works, point back to centuries of human genius and activity. In these mute, inglorious wastes man counts for nothing, and thus it is that the mixed races which, barely three hundred and fifty years ago, entered upon this vast estate, still seem to be new-comers and hardly as yet children of the soil. The tread of the Redskin is too light to have left any mark, and the wild prairie, stretching from sea to mountain, over some twenty thousand geographical miles, preserves the same aspect it must have worn when first the sun shone down upon its utter void and loneliness.

CHAPTER XIX.

SOUTH AMERICAN POLITICS—THE WAR ON THE WEST COAST—
CONFLICTING CLAIMS TO PATAGONIA AND THE STRAITS OF
MAGELLAN—PROSPECTS OF THE CHILEANS AND ARGENTINES.

CONSIDERABLE political excitement was caused
about this time at Buenos Ayres by the news that
came to hand from the Pacific coast. The contest
which had been going on there for upwards of
eighteen months, between Chile on the one side
and Peru and Bolivia on the other, was again
raging fiercely after a short lull—caused by various abortive attempts at mediation on the part
of neutral Powers. Late in January it became
known that the Chilean forces had totally defeated
the Peruvian army covering Lima, in a series of
most sanguinary engagements, and had triumphantly entered that capital.

The intelligence produced a feeling very much
resembling consternation, for the great majority
of the Argentine public had from the first sym-
pathised with the Peruvians, and, if the language
of the local press was to be trusted, the nation had

been restrained with difficulty from going to the assistance of Peru. So complete a victory not only made Chile undisputed mistress of the west coast, but, in Argentine eyes, greatly endangered the political equilibrium of South America. The success of Chile was, besides, all the more unwelcome and alarming to the Argentines, that, for some forty years past, they had themselves had a serious dispute of their own with their Transandine neighbours about the Straits of Magellan and the huge deserts of Patagonia, to which both countries laid claim; the Chileans, however, having already nine points of the law in their favour through their long-established settlement in the Straits at Punta Arenas, or Sandy Point. It had several times come very nearly to a breach between them respecting these highly unenviable possessions; but, fortunately, nothing but ink had thus far been spilt in the dispute—that, however, in sufficient quantities to float the navies of the two countries.

To prove their respective cases each claimant, in turn, had appealed to the vague and conflicting *cedulas*, or decrees, by which the Spanish Crown had, from time to time, portioned out its unwieldy territories between the various viceroyalties established in its South American dominions; and the archives of the mother-country, as well as every other. available source, had been ransacked in search of materials for the controversy. The erudition displayed on both sides in the matter was, in fact, overwhelming, and, one might almost say, typical of the extent and aridity of the regions contended for.

The two Governments fortunately showed great tact and moderation, and, throughout the discussion, professed themselves ready to submit their pretensions to arbitration before finally resorting to arms, as was, indeed, provided for by a treaty between them signed as far back as 1855. The press in both countries, on the other hand, took up the question very warmly, and did not a little to envenom it. So that now, here at Buenos Ayres, with the additional irritation produced by the Chilean successes, there was some risk of the popular excitement being raised to a dangerous pitch and forcing the hand of the ruling powers. As if to add fuel to the flame, a report was sedulously spread about that the Chileans had been guilty of a wholesale massacre of the Italians serving in the Peruvian ranks, whom they had made prisoners in the battles before Lima. The story had been officially declared by the Italian minister at Santiago to be a complete fabrication, but nevertheless a large open-air meeting was deliberately called to protest against these pretended

U

Chilean outrages. This ill-judged attempt to rouse the passions of the powerful Italian community, and through them to bring pressure to bear on the Government, luckily found but little echo, and fell as flat as it deserved. Equally imaginary atrocities have, nearer home, produced much greater and more enduring mischief.

Amidst all these passionate declamations, one voice—that of a true sage and patriot—was raised in warning tones, which, no doubt, appealed successfully to the reason and better feelings of his countrymen. 'The first duty of all,' wrote the ex-President Sarmiento in one of the leading Buenos Ayres papers, 'is to turn the people away from the abyss into which those who preach war to them would lead them ;' and he then went on, with trenchant irony, to propose that a prize should be instituted for the writer, either Chilean or Argentine, who should distinguish himself above all others as 'the most brutal instigator to war.'

In a letter which he addressed on his seventieth birthday to a distinguished Chilean statesman, and which was likewise made public,[1] the bitterness of his feelings and of his disenchantments was poured out yet more fully. Passing in review

---

[1] These letters appeared in the *Nacional* in February and March 1881.

the whole of Spanish South America, he said:
'Columbia and Venezuela afford no cause for
pride to Columbus and Venice whose names they
disfigure. Paraguay, Peru, and Bolivia have all in
turn been annihilated, and, no doubt, with good
reason. As for Uruguay, it is in a most rickety
condition; while Ecuador has organic defects that
deprive it of all vital force. There remain standing only Chile and the Argentine Republic, and
these two are possibly on the eve of a Pelopon-
nesian war.' He went on to argue that, rather than
let it come to such an extremity, Chile ought to have
the self-denial not to insist on the entrance she
claimed into the Atlantic, and, should waive her
rights in the Straits and in Patagonia.

He then proceeded with singular frankness
to express his views not only of his immediate
countrymen but of the whole Transatlantic Spanish
race. 'I do not,' he said, 'believe in Spanish
America as affording the proper stuff (*materia
idónea*) wherewith to constitute nations. There
exists, in my opinion, in this America of ours a
morbid principle that will always drive her to rend
herself to pieces. We are an apoplectic race; we
are suffocated by excess of blood. Nevertheless, a
well-organised Chile and a regenerate Argentine
State, with its population and riches and industry,
still leave a ray of hope.' 'But,' he added, 'so

unbounded is my belief in the public folly, and such the sad experience we have been accumulating, that I expect but little from our better judgment.'

I have ventured to quote at length these remarkable words of the illustrious Sarmiento, because they throw a curious light on the political condition of the Spanish American countries at that period; and because, although evidently written under the influence of an exaggerated pessimism, nothing so severe has ever yet been penned as to the, thus far, disappointing results achieved by the young nations of that new world which it was Canning's boast to have called into being to redress the balance of the old. The ex-President, in the purity of his patriotism, is, indeed, very unfair to the Spanish South American race, and especially hard on his immediate countrymen and their Chilean kinsmen. The weary controversy about the Patagonian deserts was shortly afterwards brought to an equitable settlement which left Chile in possession of the rights she had acquired, and, at the same time, preserved to the Argentines the eastern entrance to the Straits, and all the regions on that side, to which they were clearly entitled, if only on geographical grounds. The peace of South America has remained undisturbed, and there is every prospect of the two promising nations which occupy the most southern part of that immense continent peacefully developing into great wealth and prosperity.

It is, however, an undeniable fact that within a very recent period—owing in great part, no doubt, to greater facilities of communication and closer intercourse — the international aspect of South America has altered considerably, and the politics of the continent have entered into an entirely new phase. The several States built up on the ruins of the Spanish dominion, after leading for half a century separate and isolated existences, marked chiefly by internal troubles and dissensions, have come into direct contact on various questions, principally of a commercial or economical character—for of such was really the origin of the recent struggle on the Pacific coast, beginning in a dispute over a few beds of nitrate and developing into a struggle for empire—and have resolved themselves into artificial, and to some extent antagonistic, groups. Chile, engaged in a tremendous contest with her two nearest neighbours to the north, and viewed with no friendly eye by the yet more northern Colombians and Venezuelans, saw, for instance, in Brazil an eventual ally in case of need; while the colossal empire which, on its side, lives in constant distrust of the adjoining

Argentines, equally looked across the Andes for support.

As a result of this political transformation of the continent, discussions respecting the balance of power and the value of alliances have become as familiar to the politicians of Santiago and Buenos Ayres as they have too long been to us in Europe. M. Sarmiento, by the way, is very severe on the authors of these disquisitions, and cannot forgive all these children of Spain for so soon forgetting their common origin, and falling out among themselves and seeking to form coalitions like so many effete monarchies of the Old World. In the main he is right ; for if the heirs to these vast and scantily peopled territories, parted from each other by gigantic mountain ranges, trackless wildernesses, or mighty rivers, cannot live in peace and harmony, there is indeed an end to all dreams of a millennium upon earth.

But there is no reason to take so desponding a view of the future of the continent. Its two southernmost States—leaving the Brazilian monarchy outside—deserve in any case to be classed apart from the sister republics, for they contain in abundance the elements of vitality and rational progress. Chile, for her part, has triumphantly issued forth from an ordeal under which many a maturer and more powerful State might well have succumbed.

On the eve of the declaration of hostilities, the
Chilean military forces—wisely kept down to a
minimum by a governing class which above all
things dreaded militarism, with all its attendant
evils and dangerous temptations to those in power
—were barely composed of three or four thousand
men.   In less than two years they had grown into
disciplined armies numbering upwards of sixty thousand ; and after a series of brilliant victories, by sea
and land, the Republic had crushed both its adversaries and had for the second time dictated terms
of peace in the capital of the most formidable of
the two Powers leagued against it.   The question
of supremacy on the west coast, which, forty years
before, had already given rise to a war ending in
the occupation of Lima by the Chileans after the
victory of General Búlnes at Yungay, was, as far
as can be foreseen, settled for good.

Some digression may, perhaps, be permissible
here about this remarkable contest.   Thanks to the
remoteness of the scene of conflict and a general
indifference to South American affairs, the Chilean
successes passed relatively unheeded in Europe.
Yet few more remarkable warlike operations can
be cited, extending as they did along a coast-line
of such immense length, and ending in the capture
of the enemy's chief city, at a distance of some
thirteen hundred miles from the original base of

operations. It is true that from the moment Chile acquired complete command of the sea, after the collapse of the gallant naval defence made by the Peruvians, she everywhere carried her base with her ; but the efforts she made were none the less prodigious, considering the almost complete military unpreparedness of the country, and its scanty population. Her victories are greatly attributable to the energy and unity of purpose of a powerful class-government, or oligarchy, and can best be compared to those of Venice or Genoa in their most palmy days. A nation that could achieve such results, and, after achieving them, disarm and, following the great and noble example given by our own American kinsmen, turn its sword into a ploughshare and at once revert with all its energies to the arts of peace, has undeniable stuff in it, and a future that affords little anxiety. Let our stalwart offspring in the South Pacific look to it; for facing them, under the frowning shadow of the Andes, there lives a people of singular vigour and resource, with whom they may some day have to reckon.

The Argentines, distracted on the one hand by endless civil contentions—chiefly arising out of an unworkable federal system—or racked by the most intolerable of tyrannies, have been unquestionably outstripped by their neighbours in the task of forming a well-ordered commonwealth, where law and authority command universal respect, and the transmission of the supreme power takes place without cavil or question. Their start in the race of progress among South American nations has thus been very seriously retarded. Nor have they been braced up to it, as were the Chileans from the outset, through the labour entailed upon them by their limited soil and the neglect of their former Spanish masters. The very extent and abundant natural resources of the regions that fell to the Argentines—a striking contrast to the narrow strip of territory in which the Chileans are pent up between sea and mountain—from the first disinclined them to exertion. Like the indolent inheritor of vast and productive estates, they felt no call upon them to work at improving their patrimony. Unlike the Chileans, who, from growing barely enough wheat for their own consumption, were able in a few years to supply the wants of Californian and Australian gold-diggers, the native Gauchos kept to the primitive pastoral ways of their fathers, and, but for the impetus given them from abroad, would have been content to this day to remain a nation of herdsmen.

The Argentine, therefore, starts late, as has been said, but with such natural advantages that, now that he has realised the full magnitude of his prospects, his national destiny cannot but be bright. Rid of the Indian curse, and, it is to be earnestly hoped, of the still greater bane of recurring civil commotion, and daily strengthened by an infusion of fresh blood, he is now setting himself to make the most of his inheritance. Like the heedless, sluggish young giant he has hitherto been, he is stretching his limbs and testing his sinews, in view of the work before him. Without subscribing to the sanguine prognostications of those who assign to this country as commanding a position in the southern hemisphere as is held by the United States in the northern, a prosperous future may safely be predicted for it, and—as was somewhere cuttingly said of another country—having a future, it can well afford to wait.

But, in order to work out the destiny so clearly intended for them by Providence, and become a great agricultural and commercial community, in many points resembling and rivalling Australia, the Argentines require, above all, concord at home and peace abroad. Having fortunately escaped the dangers of a war with Chile, it is to be hoped that they will equally steer clear of any embroilment with Brazil about Uruguay. If they are able to maintain themselves both in external and internal peace for a series of years to come, their citizens will by that time have acquired such a degree of general well-being, as must insure lasting tranquillity to the republic, by making its preservation the common interest of all.

Already signs are not wanting of the leading men amongst them having realised the truth that there are more paying things than *pronunciamientos* and civil wars, even to those who come victors out of them. Something of the Yankee spirit of business is rapidly descending upon Argentine society, and directing the energies of its politicians to more lucrative occupations than party intrigue or barrack conspiracies. Power and office themselves are no longer aspired to so much for their emoluments and patronage, as for the opportunities they afford of participating, on remunerative terms, in the many undertakings which are needed for the development of a new country. Even the half-tamed, semi-chivalrous Gaucho is being inoculated with the utilitarian notions of the age, and is fast being converted into the 'cute citizen of an aspiring democracy.

CHAPTER XX.

THE CARNIVAL AT BUENOS AYRES — THE BATTLE OF THE 'POMITOS'—ROUND THE CHURCHES ON MAUNDY THURS-DAY.

WITH the last weeks of summer the town began to fill again. There were few signs, so far, of returning sociability, the Porteño gay world not having yet quite recovered its equanimity; but one was led to hope for better things. Not that I personally pined for social gaieties, being on the whole of the opinion, so pithily expressed by one of the sagest of our statesmen, that life would be quite endurable but for its pleasures. My native friends, however, were kindly desirous that I should see the Queen of the Plate at her best and merriest. 'Wait,' they said, 'for the Carnival, and we will then show you what we can do out here in that line.'

I must own to what—after the admission I have made above—may well seem an inconsistent weakness for Carnival; by which I mean the good old-fashioned celebration of it, so rapidly disappearing everywhere, but which, as it so happens, figures among my earliest recollections; and I was, therefore, not loth to renew acquaintance with its time-honoured, frolicsome features.   Carnival is indeed fast losing ground in all the countries of Latin race which through centuries faithfully acknowledged its sway and followed its rites.   In thoughtless, pleasure-seeking Paris, the King of Misrule has long been dethroned, and his worship and traditions may almost be said to be extinct. The ancient observance of the *jours gras*, with their shoals of maskers in the streets; above all, the tawdry, barbaric procession of the fatted ox, with its bodyguard of corpulent, ivy-crowned, ancient Gauls in flesh-coloured *tricots*, brandishing harmless clubs; its bedraggled squadron of mousquetaires, in cotton velvet, mounted on screws from the Cirque Franconi; and its car of fat Olympian goddesses, shivering under an icy February shower —all these are things of the past.   Gone, too, are the countless impudent *pierrots*, who thronged the pavement and swarmed round the endless string of carriages, crawling in double file up and down the muddy boulevards, with merry freights of dominos and *débardeurs*; the deafening *fanfares de chasse*; the great vans full of saucy, free-spoken *blanchisseuses*; the coarse, pungent wit and ribaldry which, after culminating at night in the mad frolic of a dozen masked balls, at as many theatres—from the stately old opera-house down to the *Délassements comiques*—ended in the dreary dawn of Ash Wednesday with the now legendary *descente de la Courtille.*

Those whose first juvenile reminiscences reach back to the days of the Citizen King cannot easily forget their carnival saturnalia. To say the truth, but little splendour or pageantry attended them, and as a show the whole institution had sunk to the commonplace level of the bourgeois reign. But the rollicking tumult and frenzy surging through the narrow streets of the dissolute old city—not as yet Haussmannised and cast into gilded imperial fetters —were astounding and thoroughly contagious; while the humours of the merry-makers were so frank and *insouciant* in their license, that even to the most censorious of spectators it could not but be a clear case of *honi soit qui mal y pense.*

In those sunny towns on the Riviera, where Carnival has since taken temporary refuge, like many another exiled potentate, his revels are of a much more subdued and exclusive character, suited to and presided over by the rich and idle who flock thither in quest of health or pleasure. Whatever rowdy or plebeian element there may be about them is swamped in the dainty crowds, armed with the fragrant spoil of a thousand gardens, who

promenade up and down the quays of Nice or
Cannes bandying nosegays and pretty speeches.

So, too, in the great Italian cities, where,
notwithstanding the essentially popular and democratic character of the rejoicings, the upper ranks
of society still take the lead in them, and side
by side with the humble *facchino* or *lazzarone*
in disguise, may be seen magnificent cars—great
fortresses on wheels—manned by masquerading
princes and marquises of the best blood of Italy.
It may, indeed, be doubted whether, but for this
patronage, the festival would not rapidly fall into
disuse.   Even in its birth-place—Rome—it has
already been shorn of its most striking features,
such as the *barberi* and *moccoletti*, and is mainly
kept alive by committees formed among the inhabitants to encourage its celebration for the good
of trade.   From a great national holiday of free
fun and license it has almost degenerated into an
advertising device for attracting foreign visitors—
to the chief benefit of innkeepers *et hoc genus
omne*.   Carnival with us in Europe having, in
fact, ceased to be popular with the masses, is fast
going the way of everything that is picturesque—
national dress and customs, great periodical fairs,
pilgrimages and Church processions, and all the
rest.

Here in the New World, on the contrary, the

institution is still held in great honour, though at Buenos Ayres it no doubt owes much of its vitality to the numerous French and Italian residents, who all take part in it with thorough zest and spirit. In some measure its traditions have been imported by these foreigners, and through them naturalised on Argentine soil. Nevertheless, when the festivities of which I had heard so much finally came round, I was, I confess, at first somewhat disappointed in them. The Corso of which they properly consist, seemed to me hardly equal to its reputation, though, as Corsos go, it certainly was a very big affair indeed. From an early hour on Shrove Tuesday, the tram-cars ceased running in the three or four principal streets, which were to be kept clear for the holiday-makers : a triumphal arch, erected overnight at the top of the Florida, marking the limits of the course at this end of the town. Crowds of pedestrians—only a sprinkling of them masked or in any way disguised—were astir along the line much before noon, but two o'clock had already struck when the first carriage or two with maskers passed the windows whence I was reduced to watch the sight—for, as ill luck would have it, I had hurt my foot and was unable to move about freely. This first modest instalment was soon followed by others, and in a short time the Corso was in full swing.

The *défilé*, as I viewed it from my coign of
vantage, outwardly reminded me a good deal of
the old Boulevard scenes, though it struck me as
very deficient in the Paris fun and *entrain*. The
double stream of vehicles was perfectly unbroken,
although it must have extended over three miles
or more. With the exception of a few private
carriages belonging to the irreconcilables of society,
every available conveyance in the town seemed to
have turned out for the occasion, from the diminutive mule-cart of the costermonger to the roomy
barouche full of showy dominos. At intervals, in
this interminable string, came the great cars of the
different *comparsas*, or carnival societies, which
take part every year in the festivities. There are
something like eighty of these, most of them offshoots of the local French and Italian political and
charitable associations. The appellations they give
themselves afford some clue to their composition
and tendencies. Mingled up with commonplace
'Stars of Italy,' or 'Rome,' and 'Daughters of
Peru '—or names clearly denoting harmless merriment, such as the 'Inhabitants of the Moon,' the
'Cheerful Lunatics' (*Locos Alegres*), or the 'En-
fants de Béranger '— came the 'Freethinkers,'
(*Libri Pensatori*), the 'Grandchildren (*nietos*) of
Garibaldi,' the 'Persecutors of Loyola,' and the
'Mysterious Ones' (*los Misteriosos*)—a terrible,

x

lugubrious company the last, in whose secret rites figure no doubt skulls and crossbones and all the gloomy paraphernalia of deadly conspiracies. Between two and three thousand persons are said to be enrolled in these carnival clubs ; a number which in itself gives some idea of the extent to which the celebration is carried.

Some of the huge cars, or rolling platforms, towering up to the level of first-floor windows, and drawn by as many as six horses, were most elaborate in their way, representing vessels with their crews, or forts duly garrisoned by mediæval warriors. Others affected an Arcadian simplicity, or were of a purely carnivalesque type—carrying shepherds and shepherdesses, grotesque pantomime figures, niggers innumerable, or groups of hideous masks recalling the infernal regions. The most characteristic feature in the procession was the marked predilection shown for ecclesiastical mummery, in derision of course of Holy Church and her clergy. Here the bitterly anti-clerical Italian element revealed itself strongly.

But though large sums of money must have been spent on all this display, there was little that was either picturesque or original about the show or the dresses, nor was there apparently much genuine gaiety or animation in the proceedings. At a moderate estimate, some hundred thousand people

were taking part in, or looking on at, this gigantic
Corso, but the immense, orderly concourse showed
hardly any signs of excitement, and, except for the
music of a few brass bands and the hum of the
mighty crowd, there was so little noise or racket
that the whole thing practically went off in dumb
show. This is partly due to the grosser 'barbari-
ties of the South American Carnival,' as Hutchinson
rightly calls them, being of late years strictly prohibited. In lieu of the bombardment with flour or
confetti which is customary in all Italian Corsos,
the popular amusement here formerly consisted in
drenching the passers-by with water thrown in
basins, or indeed in pailfuls, from the windows
and flat roofs of the houses, and this abominable
diversion having now been put a stop to, nothing
has, so far, replaced it.

Towards sunset, when the Corso terminates
officially, the ranks of the procession thinned considerably, most of the holiday-makers going home
to dine, and I was able to hobble down the street
to my own dinner at the club. The lull or truce
lasted for a couple of hours, after which the whole
festival burst out again in full force, and this time
fairly delighted me by its go and spirit. The
official carnival was over, and made way for a
reign of unbridled fun and merriment.

Almost all the carriages had now disappeared,

though, from time to time, a belated car came rattling by, all hung with coloured lanterns, or aflame with torches that threw a red glare over the house-fronts. It was now the turn of the pedestrians, and they entirely filled up the thoroughfares, brilliantly illuminated by the windows on the ground-floor of the houses, which were thrown wide open and disclosed rooms all lighted up *a giorno* with lamps and wax-candles, as for an evening party. Limping up the densely packed Florida to a friend's house to which I was asked, I passed through the best part of this striking scene. The crowds in the street—men, women, and children—were all armed with a supply of small elastic syringes, filled with perfumed water, with which they were vigorously assailing each other. It was, however, a strictly observed rule that only the men should attack the women, and *vice versâ*. Even under the roof to which I had fondly looked for shelter, I found myself so mercilessly dealt with by a dozen friendly dominos, that, with damaged shirt-front and utterly ruined collar, I became reckless, and soon plunged again into the fray outside.

In order to convey any idea of the originality, and indeed the beauty, of the scene, it should be explained that the *rez de chaussée* windows of the Buenos Ayres houses are fitted, as a rule, with iron bars, like prisons, and the floors of the lower apartments raised only a few feet above the level of the pavement. Each suite of rooms, brilliantly illuminated, as I have said, and full of masquerading folk—mostly pretty women and girls in fancy attire—thus formed a cage-like kind of little stage by itself, a sort of animated waxwork show on a platform, every incident on which was plainly visible to those outside. Some of the houses were being formally besieged by the people in the streets, who clung to the window-bars, and exchanged point-blank shots with the company inside. Little frightened shrieks and peals of female laughter resounded on all sides, the women throwing themselves with heart and soul into the medley, and the *brio* and gay confusion of the scene were beyond all description. For three or four hours the battle of the *pomitos*—as they call these small syringes—raged furiously everywhere; in and out of the houses, in courtyards and doorways, along the pavements and in the balconies; the combatants being utterly regardless of age or beauty, and young and old of all ranks equally joining in this universal game of romps. I myself saw the smartest of evening frocks and the loveliest of white, gleaming shoulders as ruthlessly drenched in this rough pastime as might have been in return the commonest of shooting-jackets and their owners.   The ladies, all dressed in light summer clothes, on this fortunately balmy summer night, must in fact have been wet to the skin.

To add to the movement and túmult, numerous companies of persons in disguise passed visiting from house to house, and brought fresh reinforcements to the fray. Some of the men had guitars with them, and paid for their footing by singing songs or declaiming impromptu verses, while both men and women went from group to group, chaffing and intriguing their acquaintance. Every door was thrown freely open to these unbidden guests, who came and went without question, after being hospitably entertained at the refreshment-tables which were laid out for all comers. In the drawing-room of one of the highest Government officials, a silent, masked figure, in a dark domino, quietly watching the proceedings from a corner, was pointed out to me as the President of the Republic.

It was long past midnight before the gigantic frolic came to an end, and the Porteños, high and low, recovered their sober senses and went to their beds, and, it is to be hoped, dry sheets. The perfect good-temper and frank gaiety with which this absurd *syringomachia*—to coin a name for it—was carried on, were above all praise, not a single unpleasant incident marring the diversions of the day. Of course the custom in itself seems very barbarous, and cannot be defended on any rational grounds, but, as practised at Buenos Ayres, it certainly gives rise to one of the prettiest and most thoroughly original popular *fêtes* it is possible to conceive. Some notion of the scale on which the favourite carnival amusement is indulged in may be formed from a calculation made that some 500,000 dozen, or six millions, of *pomitos* had been sold during carnival time, at twelve *reales*, or three francs, a dozen, the sum expended on them amounting to something like 60,000*l*.

Besides these public festivities, the Buenos Ayres carnival is celebrated for its great masked balls, the most fashionable of which take place in the fine rooms of the Club del Progreso. The Porteños pride themselves very much on these *fêtes*, and I should hardly be forgiven were I not to mention them. To my mind there is something oppressively dismal and gruesome, or, as the Germans would say, *unheimlich*, in a large masked crowd promenading up and down in a limited space, and the falsetto voices adopted for conceal-ment grate unpleasantly on my nerves. I will confine myself, therefore, to endorsing the local opinion of these entertainments, that they are the most brilliant of their kind given in South America.

Lent passed away—not over-rigidly kept by

the Porteños—and Holy Week came in its turn. Maundy Thursday is here the great day for visiting the churches, so I went the round of them like all the world. As in duty bound, I began with the Cathedral, where both the crowd and the heat were prodigious, as also the *va-et-vient* of the visitors, most of whom simply passed up one aisle and down the other, and so out again, without any attempt or pretence at performing their devotions.

The first thing that struck one on entering the church was an immense violet funeral veil, with a great crimson cross in the centre, drooping all over the high altar and suspended from the arch above. With the exception of one of the lateral chapels, which had been turned into a tall pyramid of blazing tapers, the vast building was very sparingly lighted. A few women were squatting on the carpets laid down along the side aisles, and through them the long string of spectators had to thread their way in the gloom. One of these aisles was almost blocked up by a large school of girls, in mazarine blue dresses with very broad collars, big straw hats, and blue ribbons to match, who were devoutly kneeling in double column, and reminded me of my Brazilian friends at Itaquí. By far the greater number of visitors were, of course, women ; many of them very smartly dressed

ladies, with what I would venture to term an un-
seasonable display of brilliant colours.

In this respect, however, the charming Porteñas
are simply following in the footsteps of their
mothers and grandmothers, only with greater
moderation. The fashion of making a great display of new dresses on this Thursday of Passion
Week is of very ancient standing. In a characteristic sketch of local manners and customs I find
that, down to five-and-twenty years ago, it was
still the right thing for the ladies to attend church
on that day in full evening dress, with low neck
and short sleeves, pearls or diamonds, white satin
shoes, and the Spanish mantilla—either black or
white—draped over one of those gigantic, beautifully carved tortoise-shell combs which may be
seen in old paintings. In this attire—the matrons
in ruby or violet velvet, and the unmarried ladies in
bright silks—the Porteñas of high degree repaired
to church, each household attended by a negro
page, of eight or ten years old, who carried the
family prayer carpets (*alfombras*) on his arm, and
was stuck into a showy livery with a big gold-laced
hat. The boy's business, on reaching the place of
worship, was to unroll the carpets on the bare
flagstones at a given signal, when all the family
fell on their knees, with the decked-out monkey
close behind them and praying with them. This

throwing down of carpets required some skill and was a ticklish affair, observes my petty chronicler; for if, by any mischance, the rugs impinged on those of the neighbouring household, the result was a slanging match between the rival imps, with much vituperation from their respective young ladies—to the great scandal of the faithful—the whole thing frequently ending in a bitter family feud. The little nigger-boys have long since disappeared, and so too has the mantilla—the more's the pity—although for a long time the clergy insisted on it as the only proper church-going head-gear, and pronounced bonnets and hats and feathers to be perfect abominations. The *manta*, which is simply a black shawl taking the place of the mantilla, and worn over the head like a hood, is now almost entirely confined to the lower orders. In Chile this *manta* was still *de rigueur* in church with all classes a few years ago, and, as coquettishly draped by the pretty Santiaguinas, was most becoming and effective.

Following the gaudy stream, as it poured out of the church into the great open square, I came past the arcade beneath the Cabildo, where I paused for a moment, my curiosity being roused by a small crowd that had gathered there. Two or three policemen seemed to be on duty at the spot. On drawing nearer I found that the attraction consisted of a colossal group of painted wooden figures, raised on a small stand decorated with plants and flowers, and composed of three personages. It aimed at telling that saddest and most human of divine stories, the bearing of the Cross. Of the painfully grotesque rendering of it, it is difficult to give any idea. The central figure—larger than life-size, and bending beneath the weight of the accursed tree—was clad in a flowing robe of threadbare violet velvet, tied round the waist by a heavy gilt girdle. On the long, coarse, matted hair was placed the crown of thorns, whence issued three great gilded rays, or more properly horns, in lieu of glory. Behind stood the sorrowing mother, in full regal costume, the lavishly spangled crimson cloak suspended from above the head in *manta* fashion, and the head itself crowned with a diadem, or *aureola*, of similar rays. In the background, the beloved disciple in a long garment of faded sky-blue. The effect of this group, when one came suddenly upon it in the broad daylight, was startling, to say the least, though there was a naïve realism about the poor staring faces, bedaubed with pink and vermilion and ghastly white, which was not without force.

I was unconsciously musing over the singular corruption of taste, let alone doctrine, which has brought the old Church to setting up these great tawdry dolls—for to the dignity of idols they scarcely rise—as objects of adoration for its children, when I was roughly roused by the voice of one of the *vigilantes*. 'Hats off!' called out this guardian of the peace, at the same time unceremoniously touching me on the shoulder. I obeyed, of course, and, as I moved on, noticed that at the foot of the group was hung up a wooden bowl, into which the passers-by, crossing themselves and kissing the golden girdle as they passed, threw their small offerings. Some one at least was to derive benefit from this exhibition, though whether it would be the sick and the poor was open to question.

I continued my rounds through the streets, which bore an unusually quiet aspect, hardly any carriages and but few tramcars being visible in them, and the latter being prohibited from ringing their bells or blowing their horns. The half-dozen churches I went into afforded very much the same sights. Of fervour or devotional feeling there was but little trace; all these well-clad people, who passed in and out in a continuous stream, having evidently come because it was the right thing, and, when they had shown themselves and made their genuflexions, hurrying away again to the next shrine further on. Somehow I was profanely reminded of the staircases at London re-

ceptions, in ascending which you meet your friends
' going on ' elsewhere.

San Ignacio, a dark little edifice in Calle Bolivar,
is the place of worship most affected by the fashionable world.   It was originally Jesuit property, and
was twice occupied by the Order, who were finally
expelled from it by Rosas, whose quarrel with them
is said to have arisen out of their refusal to let him
hang up his portrait in their sanctuary.   At the
Franciscan church there are still some cloisters,
tenanted by the last remnant of monks tolerated at
Buenos Ayres.   A waxen friar was seated at the
entrance, at the receipt of custom, so lifelike that
it was hardly possible to distinguish him from his
flesh-and-blood brother who was collecting alms at
another door of the building.

For the rest, the decorations and ecclesiastical
furniture of all these churches struck me as extremely meagre and shabby.   The Spaniards, in
fact, left no real art behind them.   In this domain,
as in all others, their rule over the continent was
barren and unprofitable.   In fairness, too, it must
be observed that from the first days of the conquest, the Church in South America, not unnatu-
rally, sought to adapt its outward forms and cere-
monies to the understanding of the simple, credulous races with which it had to deal.

Latterly it has fallen on evil days in all these

countries, and has lost not only power but, so to speak, caste. For some time after the end of the struggle for independence, in which a number of the national clergy had taken an active part, the Argentine Church preserved her prestige and influence; but the suppression of the monastic orders by Rivadavia, and a series of similar measures directed against the clerical immunities and privileges, soon sapped her authority, and reduced her to comparative impotence and penury. Much of her great power in the colonial days she had owed to the fact that her priesthood was largely recruited from among the better classes, scarcely any other career being at that time open to the young Creoles of respectable families. Thus it was that so many of the clergy, both regular and secular, ardently threw themselves into the movement against the mother country; and it is a remarkable circumstance that of the twenty-nine names appended to the Declaration of Independence, signed at Tucuman on July 9, 1816, twelve are those of ecclesiastics, of whom two were friars.

With the new era of freedom and equality, the young Argentines deserted the Church for other professions, and principally for the law. Nowadays the priesthood is chiefly taken from among the most ignorant classes, and is regarded with little reverence or affection. Whether the country has

benefited, as much as might be supposed, by this
wholesale exchange of the cowl or cassock for the
advocate's gown, may perhaps be fairly questioned.
The earlier Argentine history would be a blank and
harmless page but for the restlessness of briefless
barristers and disappointed military men.   A Presidential Decree of November 30, 1880, addressed
to the Department of Public Instruction, frankly expresses the view that training for the bar is already
amply provided for in the national universities, and
the law faculties of Santa Fé and Tucuman, 'without
its being necessary to grant greater facilities to that
profession, which already weighs, unequally and
disastrously, in the public education and public life
of the country.'

CHAPTER XXI.

VALEDICTORY—CHARMS AND AMENITIES OF SOUTH AMERICAN
LIFE—WHAT THE FOREIGN SETTLER HAS TO EXPECT.

THE period fixed for my departure from Buenos
Ayres now drew very near. I had foreseen for
some time past that my stay in the River Plate
would only be of short duration ; but when it came
to saying farewell to the friends I had made there,
and taking final leave of an interesting country
which there was but little likelihood of my ever
revisiting, I could not but feel unfeigned regret.

There is an unquestionable charm about South
American life, with all its imperfections. Many
of the artificial restrictions and social prejudices
which hamper and fence in every-day existence
under our old-world arrangements, are almost unknown here. What may be wanting in refinement
or external polish is made up for by a certain
largeness of views and a refreshing absence of con-
ventionality. In the modes of thought and the habits
of these new-born communities, there is something
of the contemptuous generosity of youth. It is as

though, having inexhaustible funds to draw upon, they could afford to treat as trifling many things to which, in our own condition of society, with its set and complicated forms, we are perhaps accustomed to give an undue importance. Life hence derives attraction from being so much more easy and unconstrained, and you experience, so to speak, a sense of greater elbow-room and of more ample breathing-space. Even those who are least enamoured of the hollow creed of absolute equality, which is the very essence of the so-called free institutions of most modern democracies, and in fact stands them in stead of substantial liberties but little understood or prized in themselves, must grant that the belief in it generates a healthy self-respect and corresponding habits of mutual consideration, thus imparting a certain simple dignity and frank cordiality to the relations between all classes. With fully as marked a disparity of lot and fortune as elsewhere, rich and poor, great and small, somehow seem to rub on more comfortably together.

But these are considerations on which it is in no way my purpose to dwell. I would rather record my tribute to the genuine, warm-hearted hospitality which distinguishes the Spanish Creole race, and of which I had, as it happened, special opportunities of judging. I can never, for instance,

Y

forget the kindly welcome and discriminating sympathy with which I met on my first arrival in Chile, under personal circumstances which, for a long time, rendered all social intercourse distasteful to me; the discreet attempts made to entice me out of my seclusion, the many thoughtful little acts betokening. both real friendly interest and thorough nice feeling. During my residence at Buenos Ayres, too, I received nothing but the greatest kindness from all those with whom I came in contact. The *banal* Spanish locution which invites you to consider your host's house as your own, is no empty form of speech with these genial South Americans. They are only too ready to provide in every way for the stranger who has the good fortune to secure their good-will, and their offers of service are sometimes almost embarrassing. As a trifling, but characteristic, trait of excessive open-handedness, I may mention that, during my residence at Santiago, I frequently found, on calling for my bill at the Union Club, that whatever I had ordered had already been paid for by some one of my kind friends. I remonstrated in vain against this distressing form of hospitality, which practically led to my not using that excellent and well-appointed establishment as much as I otherwise would have done.

Not the least of my regrets, in turning my

back for good on Argentinia, was not having had time to see more of the interior of the country, and especially having been unable to visit the so-called upper provinces. I had made every arrangement for an excursion to Cordova, whence I hoped to push on as far as Tucuman; but at the last moment my plans were upset, and I had to give up the journey. I therefore saw nothing of the venerable and picturesque old city which, for upwards of two centuries, was the main seat of learning throughout these regions, and is, to this day, honoured by the scientific labours of the National Observatory, placed under the direction of that distinguished astronomer Doctor Gould. Nor did I see the Garden of South America, as Tucuman has been called, with its wonderful woods of laurels clothing the first slopes of the lower cordillera, which from thence rises, stage upon stage, to the giant Andine range. Some of the trees there, according to De Moussy, measure over twenty feet in girth. It is only by visiting the upper provinces that one can acquire a complete notion of the vast and manifold resources of these magnificent regions; of their undeveloped riches in mines and timber and products of all kinds, which so far lay dormant, and are waiting, as it were, for the magic touch of capital to turn them into tangible wealth.

Nevertheless, I saw enough thoroughly to realise the great capabilities of the country, and to perceive what a tempting opening it offers to the European settler. And this brings me to a point which, in the closing pages of even such slight personal reminiscences as these, I cannot entirely leave untouched. Can these countries of the River Plate, and more especially the territories of the Argentine Republic, be altogether honestly recommended to English settlers?

The answer to this plain question is, I fear, by no means an easy one. If the statements of the local press, and more especially of certain of its foreign organs, were to be received with absolute faith, there could be little doubt as to the easy success and prosperity that await the foreign immigrant on the banks of the Great Silver River. It so happens, however, that there is at the present time a studied attempt to write up the country, with the laudable object of attracting to it more of the stream of European immigration than has yet flowed this way. It is not only mere hands that are wanted—however much these must be welcome, as in all new communities; the aim is principally to secure a better class of colonists, and with them some accession of national wealth. A feeling is growing up that there has been more than enough of the needy influx from Italy and the Basque Provinces, and that

what is now wanted is not so much the immigrant
as the settler; not the poor Southern labourer or
boatman, who has been driven from his home by
hard times and heavy taxation, and brings with
him little beyond his thews and sinews and his
capacity for heavy toil; but rather the small
farmer, or the younger son of respectable family
—if possible, from Northern European regions—
who, while seeking to improve his own fortunes,
will contribute some capital to the general store.
The object in contemplation is in every way legiti-
mate and praiseworthy, but the advocacy employed
to further it may perhaps be said to be to some
extent misleading. Only the brighter sides of the
picture are held up to view by those who, to use a
vulgar phrase, are cracking up the country, while
a veil is carefully thrown over its darker aspects.

To those in England who may be allured by
the prospects so temptingly displayed, I would say:
Come out by all means, but do so with your eyes
well open. Bear in mind that if there is much
that is good here, there is not a little that is evil.
No better field probably exists for patient self-
relying industry, backed by a moderate amount of
capital; but whoever comes here to settle and
try his hand at farming or stock-breeding in the
Pampas, must first of all be prepared for rude
contests with uncontrollable natural forces, in

the shape of destructive tempests and desolating droughts, plagues of locusts and wide-spreading murrain.   Nor should he forget that, however great may be the attractions of a life of active exercise, diversified by sport, on the great salubrious plains, most of the charms or refinements of civilised intercourse are utterly wanting to it.   In this respect the trial is a severe one, and it in a measure explains the painful failures of some of our countrymen to which I have alluded elsewhere.

Above all, the intending settler should be ready to face the relative insecurity of life and property in the more out-of-the-way districts in which he will have to seek his fortunes.   The spirit of order is no doubt acquiring greater strength, and the authority of the central government is establishing itself more firmly, day by day, throughout the country.   But in times of commotion—and it would be unwise to reckon on such never recurring again—lawlessness and organised pillage (as recently shown in Corrientes) are only too frequent, and unchecked, when not connived at, by the local authorities.   Even in ordinary times the efforts of the central government to punish outrages, and procure redress for the injured, are often rendered futile by the clumsy Federal arrangements under which a population of barely three millions is saddled with the burden of fourteen separate provincial governments, each composed of an executive, a legislature, a judicature, and all the other branches of a separate administration. The independence of these provincial authorities is still far from nominal, and to their tender mercies the stranger is practically left.

Nor can it be too well understood that, at the best of times, life, in the wilder and more remote parts of the country, is rendered peculiarly unsafe by the numerous dangerous characters who principally infest the borderlands till recently in Indian occupation, but are not unknown in districts which have been reclaimed for a much longer period. Many of these men are escaped convicts, or criminals flying from justice, or deserters who prefer outlawry to an enlistment which in many ways recalls the brutalities of the pressgang.

These malefactors, or rebels against social order, who have taken to the wild savanna—where, up to the other day, they found a refuge with the native tribes—are all classed under the expressive generic name of ' Gaucho malo,' and almost incredible stories are told of their ferocious instincts and depraved appetite for blood. A highly respectable chaplain, who was well acquainted with the Argentine prisons, gave me a terrible instance of this in the confession made to him by one of these men, who had been caught in the very act of murder and condemned to penal servitude. The fellow stated that, having lost his way one evening in a violent storm, he came across a miserable *rancho* where he resolved to ask for a night's lodging. The only occupant of it was a lonely old *china*, who charitably welcomed him and at once set about preparing for him such food as she could provide out of her wretched store. As she was kneeling on the ground at his feet, and stooping to light the fire, the sight of her poor old neck stretched out before him tempted him so irresistibly—this, mind, was the man's own deliberate statement—that, seizing hold of the hatchet she had been using to cut the wood, he deliberately chopped off her head, and then seating himself on the prostrate corpse completed the interrupted preparations for supper. There a patrol casually passing by, and also driven in by the weather, found him and seized him red-handed. What a scene of devilry! The assassin weltering in the blood of his victim, and drinking himself stupid, while the storm raged all round.

Shortly before I left Buenos Ayres two Scotch sheep-farmers were barbarously murdered at a place called Naranjitos, on the borders of Corrientes and Entre-Rios, by some Gauchos who had ridden up to the door of their hut and asked for shelter for the night. In this case, however, the crime was committed for plunder, and was of a common type well known all over the country, while it is a strange and sinister trait in these out-laws of the Pampa—as illustrated in the instance given above—that many of them are not robbers by profession, but desperate characters, at war with all mankind ; given to killing for killing's sake, and taking a positive pleasure in shedding blood. There exist probably no more murderous brutes on the face of the earth.[1]

When all this has been said, there remains the comforting reflection that the British settler is everywhere well able to take care of himself, and is not to be deterred either by tempests or ruffianism. What I would chiefly point out, then, is that those who hear of, and are tempted by, such large returns as fifteen per cent. and upwards on capital invested in cattle- or sheep-farming ventures, should not forget that so high a percentage denotes propor-tionate risks, let alone very serious discomforts. On the other hand, with the bright examples of success that could be quoted—even in the case of men who have exchanged our Australian colonies for these regions—it would be absurd to deny that the field open here to persevering energy, tempered

---

[1] 'Tous tuent,' says an intelligent foreign observer, ' souvent sans raison, sans mobile connu.'

z

by a reasonable amount of prudence, is in many ways admirable. Pure agriculture, too—as yet in an incipient stage—promises very well in the older and more civilised districts, and it has yet to be shown that it may not be made as remunerative as stock-breeding under far more tempting conditions.

To sum up. If the intending settler must not reckon too much on the fostering care of a strong Government, or the protection of laws impartially and firmly administered, he will, in return, be very little interfered with—except in times of political trouble—and will enjoy the complete independence so greatly prized by the Anglo-Saxon. He will thus be able quietly to shape his fortunes, and, in doing so, will have the satisfaction of materially contributing to the progress and consolidation of the country he has chosen for his abode. It is a land of infinite resource and promise, and, whatever may have been the past faults of its rulers, to ruin it would be, as has been happily said, a triumph of human perversity.

PRINTED BY
SPOTTISWOODE AND CO., NEW-STREET SQUARE
LONDON